I0723158

Demons & Ramen

Demons & Ramen

A.M. Loweecey

EPIC
PUBLISHING

ISBN (trade paperback): 978-1-7346486-8-3

ISBN (trade paperback): 978-1-7346486-8-3

Report of the Gendarmerie Corps of Vatican City State

(Translated from the original Italian)

19 July
To the Inspector General:

At eight o'clock this morning we were informed by the Cardinal Prefect of the Supreme Tribunal of an incident involving a Franciscan priest under trial.

When we arrived, Father Xavier Kaine was on the floor of his room with a shotgun fallen to his left side. Based on injuries, blood spray, bullet trajectory and fingerprints, Father Xavier Kaine committed suicide with said rifle.

The Cardinal Prefect informed us that, because the deceased was a member of the clergy, they would preside over the legalities of the incident. The Cardinal Prefect graciously gave permission for the local coroner to sign the death certificate, after which we returned to our office.

We note that Father Denis Kaine, the deceased's twin brother, became violent at the Tribunal's decisions regarding the incident. Father Kaine insisted a demon caused his brother to kill himself. The Cardinal Prefect rebuked Father Kaine—in our presence—and ordered his removal from the scene. He then took us aside and informed us that both brother priests were also exorcists. We acknowledged his explanation.

This report and the attached death certificate are the sole documents of this closed case.

Signed,
Aldo Moldani
Vice Inspector General

Chapter One

The sign's fat black letters proclaimed in Italian and English:

Danger
Keep Out
By Order of the Pontifical Commission for Sacred Archeology.

It was crowned with the official Vatican seal, too. Maybe their pompous crap worked on tourists.

I slung my leather messenger bag across my back and scaled the chain-link fence surrounding the excavation. My feet hit broken cobblestones on the other side with a puff of stone dust. I brushed at my black slacks and shirt. They were the wrong clothes for crashing a closed dig, but I hadn't confronted an entity yet who didn't at least pause at the sight of the Roman collar. Most of them pissed their ectoplasmic pants. We had... used to have... a reputation, Xavier and me.

There wasn't another living person in sight in this obscure

corner of Rome on this muggy August evening. Exactly what I wanted.

In the three weeks since Xav died, I'd scoured every ruined cemetery and archaeological dig in Vatican City for his murderer, the demon who forced Xav to eat a bullet. My rage and hate drew the scaly, red-assed bastards out like stray dogs scenting ripe meat. I slammed every one I could find back to Hell. So far none of them had claimed responsibility, but demons lie.

Any other entities wanting to play High Noon with the left-over Kaine got the same treatment.

Simply put, this was The Plan.

I clambered over broken stone which had once been the foundation of this ninth-century church. Tree roots had done more damage to it than a millennium's weather. Shame. I could see the remains of carvings on some of the smaller pieces of stone. Probably from the columns.

Beneath the sticky breeze I sensed a strong, hidden presence. Last night, I'd sensed it even through the fog of two bottles of grappa—I was pretty sure I'd finished off the second one; things got hazy around midnight. The presence hidden here had hit me like a two-by-four. Good thing the streets in Rome were narrow. I'd needed a wall to keep me vertical. Keep me heading back to the Friary, too. I had to be sober to challenge something with such strength. As sober as I got these days, anyway.

So. I set my messenger bag on a stable stone and unbuckled the straps. Never mess with a successful ritual. Ask any athlete. My ritual always began by fanning open the bag's three compartments. I'd arranged the contents to give me easy access to the essentials in case things went south.

Salt. Holy water. Silver-and-cedar flute.

I straightened, got my balance, and closed my eyes. Breathing in a slow, even rhythm, I shut out the world one piece at a time. The sound of the wind faded first. Then the rumble of distant traffic. The smells of gasoline and garbage. The light on my face from the setting sun.

When I didn't hear my heartbeat or feel my breathing, I reached inside myself. My hands cupped the power visible only to me, Xavier, and any otherworldly creatures in the vicinity. I gathered its pulsing energy which flowed through me like a second bloodstream and flung it outward like I was snapping a tablecloth over a banquet table.

I opened my eyes as a shimmering blanket of blue and white, the colors of shadows on snow, settled over the entire dig.

And I pinpointed it twenty yards northeast. Only one entity... ghost... demon... something. The magical wards on some kind of prison tomb were so strong they camouflaged whatever it was they imprisoned.

I scooped up the messenger bag and headed to the northeast end of the dig. A four-foot square pit butted up against the fence in the far corner. More dirt. Why the hell hadn't I worn jeans?

Holding the bag with one hand and steadying myself with the other, I skidded down a root-studded slope into shadows.

A mostly solid stone crypt door was hidden beneath the tips of the roots. I studied the layout of the ruin. If the pillars on the southern side had been the entrance, this crypt had been beneath the altar or sacristy. I wouldn't want to change into Mass vestments over a bunch of rotting corpses, but in those days rich folks seemed to think being buried under a church gave them a "Get Out of Purgatory Free" card.

Dirt obscured the writing carved into the seal across the crypt. I brushed most of it away and used my thumbnail on the rest. The one time I could've used a flashlight... I squinted and made out Old Latin and Cyrillic. Interesting. Why Cyrillic? The words across the seal informed me they kept the entity on the other side imprisoned in the name of the Blessed Trinity and His Holiness Pope—I scraped more—Nicholas III.

I whistled. Imprisoned more than seven hundred years and still powerful enough for me to sense it with my brain swimming in booze.

Couldn't banish it until I knew what it was. I took my flask of holy water in my left hand and palmed a vial of salt in my right. I pictured the shield of Michael the Archangel, my patron, the way Rubens painted it: golden flames on silver, burning with cold fire. My power rose with the image and a gold-silver-snow-shadow barrier bloomed in front of me.

When Xav and I discovered our power as kids, we'd grab the biggest sticks we could find and bash each other's shields until they shivered and dissolved back into our skin. Grand-mère caught us the third time and threw us into the pond. When we squelched out we explained, sort of. She marched us into the parlor, opened the glass-front bookcase, and took out a volume of French sermons nobody ever read. She opened it and showed us the diary hidden in a hole cut into the pages. In it her great-aunt drew the shield and glowing spheres she could create, and only on her deathbed told her great-niece about the diary.

We searched in France for her ancestry and found an ancestor who'd been exorcist to a Pope. But then the Inquisition happened and the grandson of said ancestor fled to Canada. Word of mouth in our family garbled over the centuries insisted we were blessed, not cursed, since we were all devout Catholics. Grandmère wasn't surprised we became priests.

A tickle of bluish green, the color of a deep river, explored my shield. So whatever was in the crypt sensed my presence. The first verse of "*Noel Nouvelet*," my mental shield, played in my head. And counterpoint to it I heard a whisper of a tune from whatever was in the crypt. Damned thing was reading me.

I followed the melody to its source and the riverlike incursion from it changed from a tickle to a stab.

Eh, screw it. Either I was stronger than it, or I wasn't. I didn't give a shit either way.

I picked up a piece of masonry, drew a cross on it with the holy water, and slammed it into the seal.

The doors shattered. I ducked wood shrapnel, covering my bag. Injuries to my back could be repaired easier than injuries to my tools.

The air behind the shrapnel didn't reek of the usual hate-evil-violence cocktail. Hate was there—nothing smelled more acrid, not even a wendigo after its latest meal. But this trapped air smelled more of rivers and snow and museums—a bizarre mix of vitality and decay.

The thing leaped into the sun and flung up its arm to shield its eyes. After seven hundred years, its body was nothing more than papery skin clinging to a withered skeleton. Its mushroom-white hair fell past its hips. Shreds of what used to be a dress hung on its—her—body.

I tried Italian first. "Who are you?"

She jerked around, breathing like she'd raced over the Seven Hills. I tried the same question in Latin.

Her emaciated claw—hand—shot forward and grabbed my shirt. "Who are you? Are you a holy man?"

She spoke in a jumble of Late Latin and what sounded like Russian. I caught the gist of it. Good thing I'd paid attention in specialized history classes.

"I am," I answered in Late Latin. "Do you want—"

With a shriek she clawed my face. I shoved her away and began a banishing spell I'd learned in New Orleans. Her shrieks turned into curses; some things had no language barrier. I flung salt in a cross pattern at her.

She leaped to the top of the crypt ruins like she was Spring-

Heeled Jack. Her gray rags fluttered in the wind before blending into the stone. She'd camouflaged herself to match them, or she was a super-powered shape-shifter.

"I'll be da—" My teeth clicked shut before I said something irreparable.

The sounds of evening traffic roared around me. The garbage in the nearby alley stunk up the place once more. The heat clung to my face. I touched my cheek.

"Aah—" My hand came away dripping blood. "You're welcome, you bitch!"

Sorry, Xavier. What about some help from On High, eh? The next crypt I open might be hiding a pissed-off mama bear demon protecting her spawn.

Great. It had only taken me three weeks from burying Xavier to begin talking to him like he was my Heavenly tech support.

I repacked my bag and headed to the Friary. This time of day, everyone would be teaching and I could repair the creature's damage without a lot of concerned-but-nosy questions.

As I walked back, a hand pressed to my cheek, I wondered: What exactly was the creature? Xavier'd always been quicker at research. He'd have nailed its nature down in an hour.

Shit, I was supposed to stop thinking about him. I was supposed to be kicking demon ass and shoving ghosts and haunts and other assorted spirits to meet their Judgment. Whether they wanted to or not. How the hell else was I going to deal with what happened to Xavier?

But I knew the answer.

I couldn't do this without Xav. It'd just taken me three weeks to admit it.

Well, then.

Chapter Two

One thing I liked about Rome: a priest could walk into a liquor store, buy two 750-milliliter bottles of whisky, and nobody would question him. At least I could complete one task tonight.

Because I wore my blacks, tourist after tourist in Vatican City acknowledged me as I walked the fifteen blocks to the Friary. In the dusk they couldn't see the claw marks on my face. I nodded and smiled and gave a blessing when asked. I knew my basic job requirements.

The modern Church had priest psychiatrists to diagnose the laundry list of mental issues which used to be lumped together under "demonic possession." But every so often a real, scaly, red-assed demon would come upstairs and slither into a human. Enter the exorcists. The modern Church likes us to keep quiet thanks to all those dramatic movies.

Regardless of the movies, the Kaine twins' name had been feared in Hell and respected on Earth for years. Without Xav it wasn't even respected by Vatican underlings.

Xavier was the Priest in Shining Armor. I was the embarrassment. He was the all-time champion demon slayer, period.

The Church got a bug up its bejeweled ass about its specially trained exorcist daring to expand his repertoire. So inconsiderate of me to spend time studying ways to destroy entities from Shinto and Hindu and Vodoun and every other tradition.

Xav would call me for backup on anything other than a bona-fide demon. I always told him he'd climb higher and faster if he diversified. He'd laugh and say we were the best team on both sides of the border of this world and the next.

And then I screwed the pooch.

Tonight's failure sealed it. Without Xav I was done fighting and done failing. I let myself in the back door of the six-hundred-year-old Friary. From the dish drainer I grabbed a plain glass, then slunk downstairs to its modern infirmary. The trusting, retired priest who ran it never locked anything up.

I climbed the stairs to my fourth-floor room with the glass and a bottle of sleeping pills tucked in the bag next to the whisky.

The Friary boasted gorgeous statues of St. Francis and his major players on the outside. Its weather-beaten dressed stone exterior carried over to the shabby but comfortable parlor, refectory, and basic nine-by-eight rooms for everybody but the four priests in charge.

I locked my bedroom door and set my plain wooden desk chair by the window. The Order had the money to fix the Friary's hundred-plus windows, but they never bothered. We got used to wind whistling through the warped frames and never-ending traffic noises. If anyone ever dared to mention it, we would've been told to offer it up like good Catholics, so we stuffed towels in the cracks and saved our money for extra blankets.

I should've felt sorry for the poor priest who'd find my body tomorrow morning. Couldn't bring myself to give a shit. At least my brains wouldn't be splattered across the wall the way Xavier's were. I'd just be prepickled.

I set the bottles on the windowsill for easy access. The first five sleeping pills washed down with two ounces of whisky had no effect. Apparently I'd increased my alcohol tolerance more than I thought in these last three weeks. I poured another drink, downed five more pills, then a third drink and another five pills. Finally the edges softened.

The streetlights and headlights below me bloomed like dandelions. I started to sip the fourth drink; the soft edges were getting to me. But this wasn't a relaxing drink to unwind from a stressful day. This was business. I slugged a handful of pills and the rest of the glassful in one swallow. Knew I was drinking too fast when it burned my throat. Good.

At seven fifteen, both bottles were half-empty. Not bad. Nobody liked overlong death scenes. At seven thirty, I'd all but finished both of them and the world's slow-motion switch flipped on.

All good priests were saying their required prayers or grading papers in their rooms at this hour. School night routine. Nobody would bother the visiting exorcist.

I touched the neck of the bottle to the rim of the glass when I poured another drink. My hands trembled when I tipped more pills into my palm.

Another two ounces. Good amount. Went down fast. Room started to spin. Poured another. Spilled a little. Thought about licking it off the floor. Tossed back five-eight-nine pills. Stomach not good. Didn't wanna puke this up. Hated puking. Poured another. Grabbed my right wrist with my left hand to get more lovely whisky to my lips.

Pounding. Not in my head.

I set down the glass. After three tries, I hooked my fingers on the windowsill. The room spun like a Tilt-a-Whirl. The door swelled and contracted every time I breathed.

Knocking. Someone knocking on the door.

"Yeah?" Sounded like a dying frog. I cleared my throat. "Yeah?" Better.

"Father Denis, there is a message from the Office of the Congregation for the Doctrine of the Faith."

I recognized the voice. Father Anthony's pet Novice. I dragged myself vertical... sort of.

"Yeah?"

"They wish you to report to the Office at your earliest convenience." The young man's voice cracked. Probably in fear. The Inquisition had changed its name, but nothing else.

"Yeah."

A pause. The room kept tilting. Then his footsteps receded.

Inquisition... bunch of old women. I'll be facing a real judge soon.

The full whisky bottle was on the floor for some reason. If I hung on to the windowsill, I should be able to plop down next to it without falling.

A gust of wind rattled the window and the image of a blue-green river washed through me.

I remembered the colors. The dig creature was back to shove my nose in my failure. I opened the window and stuck my head and shoulders out into the darkness.

The city cartwheeled. "Show yourself, you fuckin' bitch!"

Rivers and snow. A rush of cold invaded me, slamming against the oppressive heat in my room. Goose bumps. Shudders. My power reared up in defense and flung itself outward in an avalanche of shadowy snow at the creature.

The avalanche crashed into the whisky and pills in my gut. A phalanx of death-metal drummers invaded my head. Seven hundred milliliters of whisky and an entire bottle of sleeping pills heaved into my throat.

I stumbled across the room, clutching the desk and the bathroom doorframe. Crashed to my knees in front of the toilet.

It all came up. Nose, mouth, hell if puke could've come out of my ears it would have. I shook so hard the toilet rattled. My eyes tried to focus on the mess and saw trails of blood in it. The smell wrenched my gut tighter. I rolled onto the floor when the dry heaves stopped changing back into real heaves. I don't remember passing out.

I do remember dreaming about huge swathes of land covered with snow. And rivers.

Chapter Three

My alarm rang at five a.m. Took me a long time to crawl from the bathroom floor to the nightstand. The blasted thing pierced my head like the Doppler effect without the expected decrease. I slammed it against the wall.

Leaning against the nightstand, I listened to the silence. My clothes reeked. Hell, the room reeked. I needed to haul myself into the shower in time for Mass.

Logical idea, until I tried to stand. The bed caught me. Good bed. Wish it would muffle the jackhammer crews who'd moved into my skull overnight.

I opened one eye, waited for the room to settle, and opened the other. Tried for vertical again. First, sitting up. I checked the room over. The desk had been pushed out of position. An empty bottle of Crown Royal lay on the floor under the window. An unopened one stood next to it. An empty bottle of sleeping pills lay on its side against the wall. Warm air blew in through the open window.

I pressed my hands against my temples until I thought— hoped—my skull would cave in. The pain canceled out the jackhammers enough for me to think.

Right. I drank an entire bottle of whisky and took all those pills. I should be dead.

Why wasn't I? The door was—yes—still locked. No demon would help me survive a suicide attempt. They were licking their chops at the thought of me at their mercy.

I leaned on the nightstand and set my feet on the floor. So far, so good. Waited another minute and reached for the wall. I'd never been so glad the vow of poverty always meant living in small, narrow rooms.

Without the wall for support, I wouldn't have made it five steps. The doorframe saved me from keeling over at the sight of the toilet. I flushed it and said a brief prayer to keep it from overflowing.

I pretended the light switch didn't exist. The early sunshine through the small window above the toilet was torture enough.

The water heated up with its usual slowness. I leaned against the glass shower door for a long time before I stepped into the boxlike space fully clothed. With slow, careful movements, I soaped my clothes, then stripped and showered the rest of me. Then I sat on the tiled floor. I didn't move until the now-cold water had me shivering like it was already winter. I had to brace my right hand with my left one to turn the handles to "Off."

I made it to the sink. The third time I squeezed the toothpaste with no effect, I remembered I had to unscrew the cap first. When I looked in the mirror after brushing my teeth, two ragged rows of burst capillaries freckled my cheeks. I avoided looking into my own eyes.

Scrubbing the floor, wringing out my clothes, straightening the room. I broke tasks into small units. It took an eternity, but the longer I worked, the more my head cleared.

Last, I got dressed and turned my clock face-up. Ten thirty. Good God. At least everyone was long done with Mass and breakfast and off to work. I went down the back stairs to the kitchen.

I threw a cup of honey, a banana, milk, and plain yogurt into the blender. The noise was unbearable. I bore it. The horrifically sweet concoction made my eyes cross, but I swallowed it in measured intervals.

No hiding from what I'd tried to do last night. No weaseling.

I walked down the hall to the chapel, no longer using the wall for a prop. The original Friary had been built in the late 1400s. The bulk of it had burned once, been rebuilt, and modernized a few times, but the chapel was as close to original as any dig I'd explored. Its stone walls and wooden pews were meant for penance and reflection, not comfort. I sat in the first pew and stared at the replica of the San Damiano crucifix. The faithful witnesses accused me. I couldn't meet the eyes of the crucified Christ.

Nobody likes a whiner, so I didn't. I admitted my desire for self-murder. I asked forgiveness for almost committing it. And I outlined my plan for the future. No sugarcoating: I was lower than the dirt under St. Francis's sandals and I knew the path I needed to take.

I wasn't worthy to be a priest anymore. I'd go back to Washington DC but not to my teaching job at The Catholic University of America. I couldn't pretend to be who I used to be and teach Canon Law to seminarians. I needed to start as close to scratch as possible.

When I was sure my stomach would hold down the hangover cure, I put on vestments and said a last private Mass. The Host and sip of wine stayed down. I took it as a good sign.

No sense wasting time being maudlin. I didn't linger over the paten and chalice after I cleaned them or over the vestments as I hung them up. My life would be different now. I had two marketable skills. I'd find a job using my knowledge of books. I'd figure out a way to get exorcism work. Living would be my penance.

All but two of the jackhammer crew had packed up and left my head. When I logged on to the PC in the rec room, the screen didn't assault my eyes; it just slapped them around a little. I booked a one-way ticket to DC using the Vatican account. By eleven thirty tonight, I'd be on my new road.

My mail slot had one message: the Inquisition wanted to see me.

Right... the Novice talking through my door last night. Wonder if he smelled the whisky. If he did, the eager young man certainly reported it along with my Vatican summons. Father Anthony had no doubt considered me a bad priest before last night. Eh, now he'd be certain.

I'd already shipped Xavier's important possessions—Gretzky jersey and hockey stick, journal, Bibles and ancient books—back to my room on the Catholic U campus. My few clothes and books fit into one small suitcase, so I stuffed newspaper around the glass jars and vials in my messenger bag. The Vatican post office shipped it home for me for a price on the near side of obscene. No other choice; Alitalia cops would toss my scrawny ass in jail for centuries if they got a look at the powders, charms, and herbs in my supernatural kit.

Tourists thronged the public areas of the Vatican, sweating and waving travel brochures in front of their faces. I wondered again to what extent tour guides hated their jobs, dragging their sheep out in the full sun at one o'clock on an August afternoon.

Skirting the edges of five separate tour groups on the south side of St. Peter's, I slipped into the cold shade of the Palace of the Holy Office. The hall I followed was narrow by Vatican standards, but the ornate doors at its end made up for its deficiencies.

An undersecretary opened them at my knock and shut me in with a quiet thud. While I waited in a penitential wooden chair, I closed my eyes and attempted to look properly chastened. It wasn't an act. The light still wanted to claw out my retinas.

I contemplated which of my sins merited this chastisement from the Inquisition.

Someone could've seen me jump the fence at the dig yesterday. Hell, someone could've seen me in cemeteries or digs anytime in the past three weeks. I'd exorcised four minor demons and sent seventeen ghosts and poltergeists plus one bad-tempered marrabecca on their way.

Maybe one of the ghosts had been a Church official way above my pay grade. They're human enough to carry the baggage which makes the dead hang around. Every ghost we'd encountered had died clutching anger or hate or loss or the need to finish something. It was certainly possible I'd shoved a four-hundred-years'-dead Cardinal up to the Judgment Seat. Helluva lot of sins stuffed into some of those ancient red hats.

The flunky's—rather, the undersecretary's—phone rang. When he hung up, he ushered me toward the Imposing Closed Doors behind his desk. His supercilious face said it all: he figured I was quaking in my sensible black shoes. He didn't know I'd had years of intimate encounters with fear-inducing creatures. All the Inquisition could do was threaten to defrock me. Even then, they'd have to go through my Order.

Sunday-Sunday-Sunday! See the Big Boys square off in the Battle of the Bureaucrats! Thrills! Excitement! Veiled Threats! The Fate of one obscure exorcist Hangs in the Balance! The pews will fill up fast! Get your tickets today!

The imposing doors closed behind me with a muted echo. Gregorian chant played softly from hidden speakers. The slate-blue walls of the room complemented the classic paintings hung on them.

The Cardinal in charge of discipline left me standing in the middle of his polished wood floor and pretended to be engrossed in paperwork. He might play a good poker hand, but I knew better. Nobody occupied this room who didn't eat, sleep, and breathe chastisement.

Anal-retentive pricks.

Cardinal Tight-ass deigned to look at my unworthy self after four minutes and twenty seconds.

"Father Kaine, it has come to our attention you have been engaging in activities which shed an unfavorable light on the Holy Priesthood."

I kept my gaze on a reproduction of Carracci's *Quo Vadis?* painting on the wall behind His Douchiness's shoulder while he declaimed.

"In the past three weeks you have been seen in several archaeological digs without permission. You have frequented a wine bar designed for the laity eighteen nights out of the past twenty-one." His voice rose. "I do not have to remind you of your abhorrent language to several of our superiors in your threats of exposing the inner workings of the Supreme Tribunal just to have your brother interred in your Order's cemetery."

I analyzed Carracci's brushstrokes and use of color and decided I liked Monet's Giverny works a hell of a lot more.

His voice returned to normal. "Because His Holiness considers your... talents... of use to Holy Mother Church, I am authorized to censure you only."

I looked down. His expression, a combination of sucked lemons and infected teeth, invited laughter. Instead, I bit my cheek. I wasn't suicidal.

Anymore.

"When all you demon-obsessed types are eradicated, the

Church will finally become efficient and practical, like the business it should have been from the beginning."

I coiled to spring.

"Your brother's death was a boon for the Church. Yours will be a greater one, since you insist on—"

My right uppercut caught him in the sweet spot under his chin. He slid off his executive-style chair, which rolled backward to deposit him on the mat. The *thunk* of his head hitting the hard plastic was a beautiful sound.

I closed the doors behind me. His flunky didn't even look up as I left.

Chapter Four

I hauled ass back to the Friary before the various schools let out and left Father Anthony a brief thank-you letter. One encounter per day with Church authority was enough. Father Anthony was a good guy, if strict. He also wasn't banging his pet Novice, so I didn't have to use certain herbs and spells to etch runes around his bedroom doorframe, the way I did to Monsignor Anselm in Québec. The sanctimonious pedophile probably wondered until the day he died why he became ill every time he tried to bring a grade-schooler into the so-called hidden cubby behind the Confessional. 'Course, once he awakened in Hell, a demon or six would've told him about the runes I etched into the cubby's doorframe. I'd taken that burden onto my soul with a smile.

I grabbed my suitcase and left the Friary for good. For one last meal before my flight to the States, I went back to Paolo's Trattoria, the "wine bar designed for the laity." I had the place to myself for at least an hour. The regulars never arrived before four o'clock.

Paolo dropped the handful of forks he was drying when he saw me in the collar for the first time.

"Paolo, I'm leaving for America tonight," I said in Italian. "Can I get a ham sandwich and water with lemon?"

"*Sì, sì, padre. Un momento.*" He backed into the kitchen. "*Rosa! Un prosciutto panino for* Padre *Dionisio.*"

A feminine squawk followed by a great deal of muted conversation.

If I'd been thinking about anything but Xavier over the past three weeks, I would've realized how today's revelation of my priesthood would shock the good old guy. A silent, hard-drinking man at the same corner table every night was one thing. A silent, hard-drinking priest at the same corner table every night was something else.

I smiled at Rosa when she brought my food. She actually bobbed a curtsy. Poor girl was probably sweating her next Confession. How to explain the harmless flirtation she'd tried on the morose *Americano* who turned out to be a priest? It would've been pointless to tell her I was born a *Canadese*.

I made my voice as gentle as I could. "Rosa, you are a good girl."

Her eyes got even bigger. Her father stood in the kitchen doorway, pretending to inspect the paint.

"I have been *afflitto* since my brother died." I raised my voice so her father could hear me. "I needed to be *ignoto*, to be hidden, for reasons of the Church. This was not intended to deceive you. The fault is mine."

I hovered my hand above her curly brown hair. I murmured the words of absolution in Latin and made the sign of the Cross. She crossed herself when I did, bobbed another curtsy, and retreated to the kitchen.

Paolo hesitated before coming to my table and resting a hand on the seat opposite mine. I nodded and he sat.

"So, Dionisio... *scusi*, Padre Dionisio."

I chewed another bite of my sandwich. "So, Paolo. You

deserve an explanation." For flirting with his daughter under false pretenses, at least. I touched the collar. "I had a twin brother. He was also a priest."

His single eyebrow bent into a *V*. "I did not see the obituary."

"We were here in secret to help with an investigation for the Congregation for the Doctrine of the Faith."

He flinched at the mention of the Inquisition. "I am sorry your brother has passed on."

"Thank you. It has been difficult." I worked on the sandwich for a bit. "I have changes to make." I glanced at the water glass.

He made the universal Italian open-hand gesture. Acquiescence, forgiveness, we're-all-human.

"Your wine is most excellent and your food surpasses it. I will miss this place when I return to America."

He smiled at last. "My daughter would like to be able to add such a compliment from the Church to our menus."

I smiled back. "Unfortunately, I cannot speak for the Church. Although I see no impediment to the use of 'Father D.' with the letters of my Order and degrees." I took a pen from the zipper pocket of my suitcase and wrote my compliment on a napkin. The long list of initials added pomp to the words. When I passed the napkin to Paolo, he folded it with great care and slipped it into his shirt pocket.

"Father, this will cause much increase of patrons to my *ristorante*. You have finished? Allow me, please, to bring dessert and coffee."

He returned with espresso and my favorite indulgence from his menu: chocolate figs stuffed with amaretto cream.

I savored the first bite. "These are surely inspired by the angels."

The old man nodded. "My wife had the recipe from her grandmother."

I made the three fruits last as long as possible. My new budget wouldn't allow anything this decadent.

Paolo set out the chessboards. The pipe-smokers arrived at four on the dot. The bruschetta brothers ten minutes later, arguing politics. Paolo brought them their first plate: tomato, garlic, and basil. The world settled into place.

I paid for my meal but made sure not to overtip. I didn't want to offend the old man's generosity.

My flight landed in DC nine real-time hours after takeoff but twelve hours in body-clock time. I took a cab to Catholic U's campus seminary and walked across the quad to my room in the Friary. Two months of stale air choked me when I opened the door, so I yanked open the narrow window before falling onto my bed.

Seventeen hours later, my stomach woke me with threats of violence. After placating it with a cheap breakfast, I walked across campus. Nostalgia gripped me as I breathed the familiar air and passed well-known buildings.

I couldn't afford nostalgia. The path I needed to follow didn't include the low-key job of teaching Canon Law. My office held nothing I couldn't abandon, so I turned my back on the building and retrieved my accumulated mail from the campus post office. Carrying it all back to my room was a workout.

I spread it out on my desk and made quick work of campus announcements, Friary business, and junk mail. Then I made my first mistake: opening the box of Xavier's possessions. My second: reading his notebook. If my cover hadn't been brown and his blue, no one could've told them apart.

Pa used to say we'd make fine accountants. We liked things orderly. Made lists. Totaled accurate figures. Like these notebooks: Every ghost Xavier had moved on. Every supernatural creature banished. Every demon sent back to Hell. Every man, woman, and child he'd rescued. My total fell only three short of his. Overachieving weasel. Wonder why he hadn't rubbed my nose in his higher number?

Oh, yeah. Because he'd been summoned to Rome after his last exorcism and I'd been too busy fighting bureaucracy for us to talk. About anything. About why he got so desperate he blew his brains out instead of asking me for help. Especially about that.

Chapter Five

Sister Lisa met me at our favorite sports bar at eight o'clock that night.

I kissed her wrinkled cheek. "My phone call worked."

"You knew it would. Find us a table and order me a beer, please. I need to visit the Little Sisters' Room."

I snagged a table against a wall and with a full-on view of the Washington Commanders' preseason game. Her Blue Light and my Coke arrived when she did. We clinked bottle and glass and drank together.

"Welcome back." She checked the wall-mounted TV screen. "Go! Go! Go! No! Don't run out of bounds, you overpaid tackling dummy!" She looked back at me. "Good to see you smile, Golden Boy."

The muscles around my mouth slid back into their usual position.

Lisa wrinkled her nose at me. "I know the official story. Are you going to tell me what happened?"

The waiter arrived. Lisa waved a shushing hand at me and ordered burgers, fries, and refills for us. When he left, she gave me her attentive, birdlike look.

"You know how to wear me down," I said.

"I haven't survived forty-two years in the convent without becoming underhanded and ruthless." She drank more beer and muttered something uncomplimentary about a nose tackle on the TV.

She made it so easy to tell her everything.

Xav's last exorcism: a bitter, failed athlete with a weak heart and a lust for company in his misery. The panicked wife banging on the Friary door at two a.m. and Xav running to the rescue, like always. The insanely powerful demon using the athlete as its puppet. Xav didn't just kick its red ass back to Hell; he destroyed it. The athlete didn't survive either. The wife conveniently ignored her husband's damaged innards and sued the Church for wrongful death. Rome swooped in and everything collapsed. The Supreme Tribunal rushed the case to trial. It would've been a sensation if anything had leaked to the public. The Kaine twins would've been the stars of a headliner horror-fest movie. I'm a Canon lawyer. I used every argument I knew to convince them to let me represent Xav. I crashed and burned. But my complete failure was not seeing what a pit Xav had fallen into.

I shut up when our food arrived and ate too fast. Hadn't realized how many parts of me were empty. The little old nun—only the small gold crucifix around her neck gave away her status—ate in ladylike bites in between shouts, groans, and cheers at the game.

She pointed at me with her empty beer bottle when I got to the part about decking Cardinal Tight-ass. "Didn't your mother tell you not to stick your head in a wasps' nest? You got all the hotheaded genes and Xavier got all the sensible ones. I swear, you're going to drive me to an early grave."

"That train passed you several years back, old lady."

The bottle rapped my knuckles. "Respect, young man." She

finished her last fry. "You're going to get a letter of censure for your lack of restraint."

I shrugged. "What was I supposed to do? Explain to Cardinal Bonehead how Xav and I'd been able to see demons and spirits and ghosts since we were in grade school? How the Sight, as far as we can tell, is both genetic and a gift, like a Vocation? How if he bothered to check the secret Vatican archives, he'd see Pope Innocent the Twelfth named Jean-Baptiste Kaine, our umpteen-times great-grandfather, the official Papal Exorcist? How every generation of Kaines produced at least one exorcist? And how Xav and I were the Wonder Twins of the Kaines, without false modesty? If he can't see it and touch it, it doesn't exist, so fuck him and all deliberately blind bureaucrats."

"Don't pretend you don't care. I know how you two think."

My glass hit the table hard enough to splash Coke onto my hand. "Don't talk about Xav like he's still alive."

She put her hand over mine. "I know. What do you expect me to do? Go all pious on you? Tell you he's looking down on us from Heaven?"

"Of course not. I'd check you for a fever." I covered her hand with my free one. "I have to do the work of both Kaine brothers now. Gotta get stronger so we never lose another one. Xav's guy was the first one we lost. Lost to life, I mean."

She signaled the waiter. "One cherry pie, one blueberry pie, and two coffees please."

I grinned at her. "It's a good thing I don't have issues with strong women."

"Your grandmother trained you well." The bar erupted with cheering. Lisa's head snapped up. "Yes! Run! Run!" she shouted at the TV. "Yeah! Six points. About time we drafted someone who could get the ball over the goal line. Ah, sugar and caffeine."

The waiter set out dessert. Lisa plucked two creamers from the bowl on the table.

"Do you know how many chemicals are in those things?" I sipped my acrid black coffee.

"Only someone in regular contact with evil can drink this sludge without help. I'm too pure."

I spluttered.

She stabbed her fork into her cherry pie topped with fake whipped cream. "Eat your dessert."

"Yes, Sister."

"Another smile from you. I have skills." She sipped her doctored coffee. "Here is my professional opinion regarding your new situation, having had time to consider things between your phone call and dessert. My grad students Jude and Edward can teach Canon Law to the seminarians. I can find assistants for my Latin and Hebrew classes. You need a complete break for your new start. Get out of DC."

The raucous diners around us became so much white noise. "Stop reading my mind."

She scooped pie and cream into her mouth with an audible smack. "You boys can see the supernatural but I've always been able to see into your heads."

"You're telling me to leave you hanging with a flock of baby priests in classes for Canon Law and Greek New Testament linguistics?"

"Please. I can't walk thirty feet on campus without tripping over a Bible scholar. Sorry to bruise your ego, but at school you're replaceable."

The waiter hovered with the coffeepot.

I shook my head. "Check, please."

"Where you're not replaceable," Lisa continued, "is out there kicking demon butt."

"For someone without the Sight, you're awfully complacent about what we—I—do."

"And you call yourself a Catholic. Seriously, Denis, how could I teach the hidden side of Church history to hotshot exorcists for thirty years without believing?"

"A certain Cardinal didn't."

"He has bruises from you as a reward."

The check arrived. I slapped cash onto the table. Lisa pulled her plain black wallet from her plain black purse and added the tip.

"Text me once in a while." She looked at the TV screen and winced. "Dear God, why didn't we draft a kicker this year?"

Chapter Six

"**B**lackhawks 3, Capitals 1. You lose, old lady."

I sent the text and turned off the radio. The team's post-game dissection was known for enthusiasm rather than analysis. This is where I missed my TV.

If I'd settled in New Orleans instead of Chicago, my Vodoun teacher Madame Gagnon would be cleansing every apartment in this old house with sage. Mikkel in Saskatchewan would blame Mercury Retrograde for my run of bad luck. I blamed the amateur demon who checked me into the boards like a pro two weeks ago. Sure, the "boards" were a granite mausoleum and he used a tombstone instead of a hockey stick, but the result was the same.

First, a bone bruise on my lower arm; then the TV died, followed by my MacBook. The TV'd been a Goodwill special; it had lasted seven months, a minor miracle. The death of my refurbished Mac hurt worse, but I could still get email on my phone.

I flexed my wrist. Only a twinge from the bruised radius. About time after two weeks in a sling. Couldn't button my coat properly, couldn't tie my shoes, couldn't reach the top shelves in the bookstore where I worked part-time.

Couldn't confront even a lovelorn cemetery ghost, let alone a demon lusting for battle with a Kaine.

That was The Plan, after all. I'd spent the eight months since I'd moved from DC to Chicago honing it. Drown my guilt and hate in the supernatural blood of every demon I could find. Continue the Kaine twins' work—carry it on my shoulders, no matter how inadequate they were alone. Like now, when my whole body itched with the need to kick otherworldly ass. I had only myself to blame for the bone bruise, too. Grandpère would've laughed if he knew.

Red-assed little fucker was responsible for my empty refrigerator, too. My part-time bookstore salary couldn't both keep me fed and pay the rent, and I depended on my exorcism and banishing income more than I liked. I might need the Diocese's health insurance, but I'd go back to the local soup kitchen before I'd beg for anything else.

Three thirty. In an hour I'd banish a poltergeist and end my income drought. I crossed the twenty feet from the living room into the bedroom and brought out my working clothes from the bottom dresser drawer. In less than five minutes Father Denis Kaine, OFM, ME in Latin, Hebrew, and Greek, ThD, JCD, stared back at me from the mirror on the closet door. Good thing the bone bruise wasn't visible. People liked their doctors and exorcists looking healthy.

Someone knocked at the door.

On a Sunday afternoon? If it was a Girl Scout, she'd be disappointed. My liquid income consisted of the twelve dollars and three quarters in my wallet. I pulled off the Roman collar so she wouldn't get a bad impression of priests in general and unbolted the door.

It crashed open with a blue-green-flowery gust of wind. I

spun around and slammed it shut. My messenger bag was within arm's reach on the kitchen table. All I had to do—

"It is ridiculously cold outside. Where is your fireplace?" This tall, black-haired female intruder strode into my living room. "Are you a herder of reindeer that you can stomach this cold without a fire? I require heat, coffee, and food."

Her flowered dress looked more suited to August than early April. Her windblown hair reached below her waist, the overhead light striking midnight-blue highlights from it. The colors of her energy reminded me of something I couldn't place.

"Look, whoever you are, I didn't invite you here." I opened the door, which put me even nearer to my messenger bag. "Out."

She laughed.

I flipped open the front of the messenger bag and snatched the squeeze bottle I kept holy water in, then popped the nozzle and squirted the perpendicular strokes of a cross at her.

"*Merda.*" She shivered and vanished.

I closed the door and cast a net through the house the way I did in cemeteries searching for otherworldly beings to banish. Nothing. Whatever she was, she moved faster than most entities. As I repacked the holy water, it hit me: she'd said "shit" in Italian not like she was angry. More like she was annoyed because I'd gotten her dress wet.

She hadn't given off a human vibe, but she certainly was female.

My nine-year-old Impala took me to my next job. She was a good old lady, this car. Rattled when I turned off the ignition, but we got along.

Out my passenger window, the classic brick mansion in the

Lakewood Balmoral district spread its skirts like a dowager princess. Fronted by an impeccable lawn and surrounded by heirloom roses, its three stories of smartly trimmed eaves and carved pillars invited homage. If only the neighbors knew.

The cold mauled my ears as soon as I left the car. My knit Blackhawks cap didn't go with the look and I refused to wear an *Exorcist* fedora. I walked as fast as I could up the cobbled driveway without imperiling my dignified image.

The prosperous bank CEO and father of three opened the door before my hand touched the gargoyle-head knocker. He looked like five miles of bad road.

"Father Kaine. Thank God. It's been a nightmare since we got back from Mass. Come in, please."

His stick-thin wife hovered in the foyer behind him. The dark circles under her eyes would make her plastic surgeon rip out his hair. I didn't see any of the kids. A maid appeared at my side and took my coat. I smiled, but she kept her face impassive. Poor woman might be illegal and under this idiot's thumb as much as his wife was.

"Tell me about today, Mr. Eaton." I followed him into the parlor. He and his wife perched on the edges of two teak chairs. I sat in a third and rested my hands on the arms of the chair so both of them could see how steady I was.

"Oh, Father," his wife said, "I took off my hat after church and set it on the hall table. Eleanore needed help with her shoes, but a moment later, when I turned around again, my hat had vanished."

She shuddered, and not only from the unheated air in this seldom-used room.

"Has your hat returned?" I asked in my smooth, professional voice.

"I found it, Father," her husband said. His sunken eyes enlarged until I could see the whites around his hazel irises.

"Three minutes later, at the top of the tallboy in the spare bedroom."

"You might dismiss it," she broke in, "but on top of everything else—the dead flies, the bloody words in the upstairs hall, and Eleanore's doll..."

I leaned forward, using a wisp of power to create a bubble of calm around them. "I never belittle the supernatural, Mrs. Eaton. What else has happened?"

They stumbled over each other describing it all. A voice whispering threats in the pantry. Holes resembling eyes and a mouth ripped in the oldest daughter's lace bed-curtains. An ashy handprint appearing on their son's throat long after the maid had cleaned the fireplaces.

I nodded, increasing the power in my bubble. They couldn't see what I was doing but gradually his hands stopped picking at his clothes and she stopped fussing with her severe hairdo. Their facial tics decreased.

"I'm going to go through the house," I said. "I'll go room by room and herd this entity before me until I've trapped it exactly where I want it. I have your permission to enter everyone's bedroom, do I not?"

"Oh, yes, Father, of course. Whatever it takes to free our family from this awful creature." Mrs. Eaton's lower lip trembled.

"Mommy?" Four-year-old Eleanore stood in the doorway, clutching her new doll. The other one's eyes had been gouged out and left on the hearth for the maid to find last Friday morning.

Mrs. Eaton stood. "Come on, sweetie. Let's read some Berenstain Bears."

Eleanore jumped up and down. "*Papa's Pizza! Papa's Pizza!*"

Both parents smiled.

"All right, *Papa's Pizza*," her mother said. "Should we make pizza for supper?"

"Ew. Daddy puts stinky fish on pizza."

Mr. Eaton followed them out. "I promise to keep the stinky fish only on my part of the pizza."

Their voices faded on the way to the library at the back of the house. I took three myrrh candles from my bag plus a salt stick impregnated with sage. The bag stayed with me as I climbed to the attic for silence and privacy.

I settled myself on the floor so I wouldn't keel over if something powerful distracted me. A few minutes later, in a now-silent world, I cast a gigantic net through the attic, down to the third-floor sewing, storage, and bedrooms, to the second-floor bedrooms and playroom, the first-floor parlor, laundry, dining, and family rooms, kitchen, and library, and, finally, the multiple storage rooms in the basement.

All set. Initial diagnosis of one pissant poltergeist confirmed. I dissolved my net.

I returned to the hall. On the top of the doorframe I drew the angular-S rune sowilo with the salt for wholeness and cleansing. It glowed sage green for an instant before sinking into the wood. The third-floor rooms received the same treatment. I added the rune jera—two *V*s nesting into each other—to the maid's room to give her an extra dose of peace.

The oldest daughter, Elise, sat outside on the second-floor balcony texting with an air of boredom.

Eliot, the middle child, probably thought he was Kid Ninja. Since he was about as stealthy as a Scooby-Doo villain, I'd known he was shadowing me since I'd marked the sewing room.

My ninja shadow bumped into a narrow hall table once as I worked through the third and second floors. I'd seen his DVD library, including the G-rated movie cases whose labels didn't match the R-rated horror discs inside. Eleven years old was too young, in my opinion, to watch so many pseudo-occult and overblown Satanism movies. But the Devil tended to be more powerful than the men of God in those movies, so I would make a bit of a show of the power of Good when I got rid of the poltergeist.

Mr. and Mrs. Eaton were doing voices for all the bears in Eleanore's book. I knew they saw me enter the kitchen when the beary voices faltered. Fifteen minutes later—forty-five minutes since I entered the house—I drew a salt circle on the foyer's parquet floor and placed my candles in a triangle with me in the center.

"Mr. Eaton," I called, "could you bring everyone into the front hall?"

His wife's head poked out of the library. "Even Eleanore?"

"Perhaps she can help with dinner preparation."

Mrs. Eaton sagged. "Yes. Yes. We don't want—Ines?"

The maid appeared in the kitchen doorway.

"Please take Eleanore." To her daughter: "Sweetie, will you help Ines find good things to put on the pizzas?"

"Olives and cheese, yum!" Eleanore, still clutching the doll, ran into the kitchen.

Ines glanced at me, pulled a crucifix from under her collar, and kissed it. Then she spun on her heel and returned to the kitchen.

Mr. Eaton went to the bottom step of the central staircase. "Eliot! Elise! Please come downstairs."

Clattering footsteps screeched to a halt when the kids saw me. Elise, fourteen and trying to look grown up. Eliot, gangly and clumsy at eleven and a half, thrilled to be able to watch me without sneaking around. Eliot thought exorcists were cool, so I got to see the secret "devil's tattoo" on his butt when I visited the house last week. Stupid kid. Lucky he hadn't gotten blood poisoning from his friend's needle and homemade ink.

If the work of art was two inches higher it'd be a tramp stamp. Eliot and friend got hold of a pirated video of *The Devil Rides Out*—Satan and naked women: a preteen boy's wet dream—and tried to copy Baphomet from the Hammer film's opening credits image.

Some things can't be unseen. Like a middle-schooler's attempt at the man-goat. Schools should never cut art classes from the budget.

I lit the three candles and centered myself. Elise whispered something and her mother shushed her. Eleanore chattered in the kitchen.

The girls' silver-white auras shone clear. Their parents' were shot through with red fear and muddy greed, but those colors were nothing I hadn't seen before. Eliot's was mustard yellow and gray. The kid would need years of therapy if he could see the entity clinging to the ink on his butt cheek.

My eyes rolled back in my head. One of my smaller useful skills.

Mrs. Eaton's nails scraped the banister.

Eliot muttered, "Cool!" and his father cuffed him.

A splash of true evil clung to Eliot. He hated their new house, was bullied at school; his soul was curdled with jealousy over his little sister. The kid had nursed it all in true "Poison Tree" fashion and scoured the Net until he made himself into a fine little pseudopoltergeist.

I began the standard exorcism in a mix of Early Latin and Hebrew in case either of the adults had a classical education. At the same time, I reached out with my power to the kid's tattoo and got the smoky scrap of demon in a death grip. It fizzled with a smell like a rotting opossum before I finished the second verse of Psalm 67.

A small part of my brain registered the gasps and gagging from the stairs. Good. I opened my hands and the stink dissipated. Then I drew a cross in the air and recited the appropriate prayer in regular Latin, so Mom and Dad Eaton might be able to understand it.

More gasps. I let my eyes slide back into position in time to see the blue-white image fade. I smelled sage and myrrh and winter air on mountains.

Eliot had puked all over himself. I pretended not to see it and met Mr. Eaton's terrified eyes with a reassuring smile.

Mrs. Eaton clutched the kids to her, Eliot's puke-stained shirt messing up her designer dress. Mr. Eaton sat on the bottom step. His wife and daughter started to cry. Eliot tried to rub his tattoo without his mother noticing, his face scrunched in pain.

"Ew!" Eleanore's voice broke up the tableau. "Who made poopy gas?"

Her father laughed.

"Eliot, go upstairs and change," his mother said.

Elise scooped up Eleanore and danced down the hall with her. I waited until they got into the kitchen before I drew the pointy-ankh rune othala in the circle to keep the house and family whole.

Mrs. Eaton stage-whispered to her husband, "It glowed! Did you see?"

I snuffed the candles and wiped the slates clean.

"Mr. Eaton, please burn one of these candles during family prayers first thing in the morning. Burn each one until it's a small puddle of wax, and then burn the wax in each fireplace. Living room tomorrow, library Tuesday, master bedroom Wednesday."

He took the still-warm candles from me, a touch of fear and respect in his eyes. I gave them my standard advice: Find a good family counselor who believes in the supernatural. Here is the contact information for three in the Chicagoland area. This experience requires professional help to work through. Only a few sessions, but you'll be stronger for it.

Counseling should bring Eliot's issues to a head, and the professional could take it from there.

They thanked me a ridiculous number of times. By now, I just wanted out. My conscience pricked me. It didn't care how subterfuge and demon-clobbering had probably kept a kid out of juvie and a family from splintering.

Mr. Eaton took his checkbook out of his suit jacket. When I took my coat from Ines, she nodded. I wondered if she knew the kid had been behind it all. Her aura's warm colors and scent of sun on the water gave me a strong indication Sight ran in her family.

Mr. Eaton handed me the check. I put it in my pocket without looking—a bigger test of my self-control than he knew.

"Daddy! Come make your pizza!" both daughters called from the kitchen.

Ines closed the door behind me. In case anyone was watching me from behind the curtains, I drove all the way to the bank before I looked at the amount on the check.

A thousand dollars. It would've been less if they hadn't seen the Cross and rune glow. And if I had told them the truth about darling Eliot when I suggested counseling? It would've been a 70-30 chance of no payment at all. Lesson learned the hard way.

Rent was due in three days. This would keep a roof over my head and the internet working.

What I wanted to do was dissect today's demon banishing with Xavier over beer and burgers.

Instead, I'd go home and put on his Wayne Gretzky jersey and add this family to my book. My new normal sucked.

Chapter Seven

My apartment door opened before I got the key into the lock.

"You will not tell me such a runt of a demon caused those troubles."

The black-haired female from earlier stood with one hand on the doorknob and the other on her hip. In my kitchen. Her spiritual signature enveloped her like a corona—the blue green of a deep river in winter. Where else had I seen it?

"Well?" Her contralto voice made even her sharp question pleasant.

I shook myself. I must have been more tired than I knew. "Get out."

"Do not throw water on me again. I am finally warm."

"How—" I stepped around the table to see into the living room. "You lit a fire?"

She started to answer, but I drowned her out. "*Exsurgat Deus et dissipentur inimici ejus: et fugiant qui—*"

She put a hand over my lips. At her touch a blast of her colors blew through me, like a memory overlapping the present moment.

She dropped her hand and stared. "What is the meaning of the colors I see when we touch? Where do you know the white snow with blue shadows like Mt. Elbrus?"

She could see the colors of my power when we touched the way I saw hers? Something this powerful and uncontrolled had to be exorcised. I started again. "*Exsurgat Deus et dissipentur—*"

She stamped her foot. "Stop. I am no hell-spawn for such words to banish me. You know this."

True. The deep-water color should've clued me in. Demons were all red and black and rotting brown like dead flowers.

"Fine." I set my bag on the kitchen table and unbuckled the straps. "Whatever you are, get out. You're not welcome in my apartment."

She made an exasperated noise. "They did not exaggerate. You have the manners of a goat."

"And you're trespassing. I win. Out."

"First, you will tell me the reason for the circus you performed in the fancy house." She pulled a chair away from the table and sat.

I hung up my coat and scrolled through my notebook and Xav's for what had invaded my kitchen. "The boy tried to be evil, but he's weak and ignorant. He pretended to be a poltergeist and a feeble demon-fart attached itself to him."

She laughed. I caught myself admiring her voice again and cut her off.

"Those people didn't want to know their darling boy caused all the trouble. So I gave them what I call the full treatment."

"*Tch.* One-tenth was perhaps necessary."

"One-hundredth." I kept scrolling. Not a banshee, not a selkie, not a nalusa falaya.

"You are vain."

"I'm skilled. An expert knows how to gauge the strength necessary for the job. Don't touch my bag. I'll be right back."

In the bathroom, I popped two aspirin and listened. No rattling from my bag. Crap. I hoped she'd sneak into it and touch some element which would zap her into another dimension. All right, then. When all else failed, salt. With a few Vodoun touches thrown in.

When I came back to the kitchen she was leaning against the counter finishing off my last spinach knish.

"This is quite good. Why is your refrigerator so empty?"

"You ate my supper. Do you have any concept of privacy?" My stomach growled at the sight of the tiny piece of filled pastry still in her hand.

"I was hungry. Why do you not plan better for yourself? You are a priest, you do not have a wife to do your shopping." She ate the last morsel.

"Because exorcism doesn't pay worth a shit and will you please stay the hell out of my stuff." I flung open the leather flap on my bag and felt for the powdered juniper to banish her, since it was obvious to me she was injurious to my good health.

The exasperated look came to her face again. She opened the cupboards, frowned, and walked out the door, grabbing my coat on the way.

Juniper powder still ready to fire in my hand, I slammed and locked the door behind her. Now I'd have to buy another coat. It didn't matter the weather forecast claimed spring was going to arrive with flags flying by noon tomorrow. Chicago weather: wait five minutes and it'll change.

———

Twenty minutes later someone knocked at the door. It had to be her. She might be stubborn, but she had nothing on a bull-headed Kaine. I grabbed more powdered juniper and poised to cover her with it as I opened the door.

She shouldered past me. "Move aside. I cannot walk through you." A plastic bag hung from her left wrist. She cradled a brown paper grocery bag in her right arm.

Too many months on my own had me forgetting society's tricks for keeping out unwanted guests. She set the bags on the table and took out a loaf of bread.

"There is no wine. They would not sell me alcohol because I could not prove I am more than twenty-one years of age." She chuckled.

"You took my coat but you had money for food?" I replaced the juniper. I didn't need to waste expensive herbs on her. She'd let her guard down while playing house. In my house.

"You are not serious." She took out a bag of apples.

"You stole all this? Good God, you glamoured old man Russo? You must have. He'd have shot you otherwise. He keeps a twelve-gauge under the counter."

She shrugged, a package of sliced turkey in her left hand. "He would not want to confront me."

I wanted to shake her. "You walked right back here, didn't you? Of course you aren't a demon. No demon is stupid enough to leave a trail. Any one of Russo's kids could've followed you. Well, lady, no cop's going to arrest me as an accessory."

I snatched the cold-cut package out of her hand. She spluttered. I stuffed the turkey, bread, and apples back in the bag.

"How many times do I have to tell you"—I shoved both bags into her arms—"to get out and stay out." I pushed her through the door and slammed it. The dead bolt slid home with a satisfying *chunk*.

I could head to the store and get ham and cheese, since I no longer had to depend only on the twelve bucks in my wallet. Seeing the package of cold cuts in her hand made my mouth water.

Better face Mr. Russo and get it over with. I reached for my coat before I remembered the creature still had it.

Chapter Eight

A seaweed-colored tentacle snaked through my keyhole. It felt around and up, more of it slithering through a hole too tiny for its girth, until it touched the dead bolt. The tip wrapped around the thumb turn and it snapped open. The bolt slid out of the doorframe.

The tentacle retracted, compressing itself to the dimensions of the hundred-year-old door's keyhole.

The door opened on my insistent houseguest, whose arms appeared human again. "You squashed the bread."

I needed to study her. I couldn't do a proper banishing until I knew what had invaded my apartment.

"Are we going to stop this foolishness? I wish to eat supper and I am cold again."

"Truce." I stepped aside.

She huffed. "It is about time. Take this bag, please."

I closed the door for the fourth time and took the brown bag from her. She followed me to the table, immediately taking out the apples as she stared into the bag's depths.

"This is your fault." Her left hand held up a dented loaf of pumpernickel.

If she expected me to apologize, she'd have a long wait. Instead, I tried a question to suss out what type of creature she was. "How did you unlock my door?"

She turned on my oven. "I have been doing much reading. There is a writer named Lovecraft. He makes amusing stories of creatures whose names I cannot pronounce. I thought I would create one of his creatures with its useful tentacles."

She opened my refrigerator and brought out mustard for the roast beef and provolone cheese. My stomach growled loud enough to rattle the chairs.

"I will make fat sandwiches and baked apples and you will make strong tea for both of us."

The walls closed in. She might be trying to get to me through my empty stomach. I slammed my hands on the table. "No."

She jumped.

Yet another knock at the door. What the hell was this? Freaks Descend on Denis Day? I yanked it open, ready for practically any creature I'd ever heard of.

The grad students from the apartment across the hall stood where the welcome mat would be if I ever thought of welcoming anyone.

The one with the buzz cut said, "Dude, we missed the game. Research project. Tell us you DVR'd it."

"No. Sorry."

"Shoot. Don't tell us the score. We'll see if we can find a replay on cable."

The one with the chin-strap beard saw my pushy houseguest.

"Whoa. Sorry, dude. Didn't mean to interrupt." He waved at her. "I'm Paul and this is Gaetano. Nice to meet you."

She gave them a charming smile. "It is a pleasure."

"We'll turn up the volume on the game to give you some

privacy," Gaetano said, his head all goose bumped from the cold air in the hall.

Her laughter filled the room. The guys retreated from my scowl. I locked the door, breathing slow and deep. I had to focus.

As though she knew the places I kept everything, she'd found a baking dish and was pouring cinnamon and sugar into two cored apples.

"Why did you attack the table in anger? If I were baking a cake—which I do well, since I enjoy cake—you would cause it not to rise, and I would be annoyed."

"Are you serious? You barge into my apartment, you steal my clothes, you steal food from the grocery store, you—"

"Hah. You are annoyed because you could not exorcise me. You are also hungry. You will not be so miserable after you eat my baked apples. I learned how to make them many years ago."

"Why are you here?"

She held up one finger, knifed butter into both apples, and slid them into the oven. When dessert was off her mind, she cocked her head at me.

"You do not remember? I wonder how you gained your reputation." She shook her head. "Eight months ago, in Rome, you freed me."

I must have looked blank. Her flowered dress changed into gray rags.

"Christ on a bike."

"You remember now? I think I called you an unpleasant name."

I touched my cheek. Rome. The seven-hundred-year-old tomb with Cyrillic on the seal. It—she—had cursed and clawed me and vanished.

She smiled and the rags became her flowered dress again. "Good. I have ignited your memory. I have also not answered your question. I came to thank you."

Those were the last words I expected. "Most prefer to curse me."

She laughed. "With your manners, I am not surprised."

"Like you did, if you remember."

She gave me the same Italian gesture Paolo had used my last day in Rome. "You may place blame upon your predecessor."

For a second, I thought she meant Xavier. Only years of maintaining a poker face while fighting demons concealed my thoughts. "Who?"

Her hand gesture expressed profanity better than several words might have. "A certain Pope. He possessed a small mind and rotting teeth. I spent much of my imprisonment devising suitable torments for him. When you said you were a holy man, you received the brunt of my hatred."

"You shot the messenger."

"You startled me. Also, we have traveled from the subject at hand."

"Good point. Are you telling me you traveled from Rome to Chicago to thank me for letting you out of those ruins?"

"I possess manners, unlike a certain priest." She took tomatoes and lettuce from the bag.

"Bullshit. Tell me why you're playing the perfect Italian housewife in my kitchen when you're neither Italian nor a housewife."

She opened drawers until she found knives and forks. "The reason is as I said. I am here to thank you for setting me free. It seems I have not sloughed away every oddity which humans possess."

She looked up at me from her task of opening the bread. Her expression dared me to battle her in wits and power.

The tingle along my neck reminded me of high school with Xav. We were always daring each other with reckless stunts. Skate on the pond where the ice was thinnest. Steal Grandpère's autographed photo of Syd Howe. Let the cranky old ghost in the church basement possess Xav so I could bind it and nudge him on. The funniest part of the possession was when the ghost begged me for a cigarette and I gave him one. Xav coughed so hard he practically expelled the ghost on his own. He called him a pansy-ass in Xav's voice before he floated out of him and through the ceiling on a cloud of Marlboro Filtered. I laughed until I couldn't breathe. Xav put his head under the bathroom faucet and swallowed about six liters of water. Then he plugged the drain and shoved my head in the same ice-cold water.

"I prefer you when you smile. You no longer look like an irate mountain lion."

The aroma of apples and cinnamon filled the kitchen. The table was set with sandwiches, pickle spears, and coffee mugs with tea bags in the bottom. She turned off the gas under one of my pots and poured boiling water into both mugs.

"I don't drink tea."

"This fact is obvious from your lack of a teapot. All good homes require a teapot. Come. Eat."

She sat opposite me and dunked her tea bag.

I kept my hands on the back of my chair. "Not without setting some rules."

"A sensible suggestion. First: you will stop trying to exorcise or bind or banish me."

"What? Look, lady—woman—what is your name?"

"Emma Koroleva. We will codify the rest of the rules while we eat. I will be offended if you let this supper go to waste." She took a bite of her sandwich.

The smell of the meat and spices mingled with her deep-water essence and took me someplace cold and ancient and wild. Then my stomach pulled off a bloodless coup and I sat.

She wasn't the only entity in the room with manners. I ate

my sandwich like a well-bred human. She caught on and matched me bite for bite.

"These pickles are not crisp enough. We will select a jar with a different name for our next purchase."

"Next time?" I sipped my tea and tried not to gag.

"Yes, yes, we must set more rules. You are—how do they say it?—tied too securely."

I snorted into the mug. "Wound too tight, you mean?"

She considered the expression. "It is poor grammar, but yes, you have understood my meaning."

I pushed away from the table and got a glass of water. She checked the apples and set them on the stove.

"I prefer the term 'methodical.' I run a business. I have records to maintain."

"A prosperous business would not cause you to starve yourself."

"Who asked you?" I stared at my empty plate. "Sorry. I didn't mean to be rude. Thank you for making supper. I'll give you the money to slip into Russo's cash drawer tomorrow."

"Now you are giving me orders?" She picked up her tea.

"You're not turning me into an accessory after the fact."

She looked puzzled. I explained the phrase.

"Your conscience is inconsistent. You will take a great deal of money for exorcising the weakest of spirit, but you insist we will repay the shopkeeper for less than forty dollars of food and drink."

"Russo lives hand to mouth. A corner grocery store will never make anyone rich. The Eatons were under spiritual attack. Just because I played up the cleansing doesn't make it a fake." I might have jumped down her throat too hard because my conscience was pricking me. "Since you were playing Invisible Girl, you must have seen me use the runes and my power to protect the house and everyone in it."

"Of course. It was well done."

I tried to keep the sarcasm out of my voice. "Thank you."

She gave me an arch look. "You are able to use manners when it suits you. Hand me your dish. The apples will now be cool enough to eat."

Chapter Nine

After we put the dishes away, she placed herself in the center of my living room and turned in a full circle. "You do not have a television? Everyone has a television."

"You don't like it? Go to a hotel." I rearranged the logs in the fireplace.

"I want to watch American television programs. I have seen mostly Italian programs, but sometimes they would show older American ones. There was one with an airplane in space and people with pointed ears. I wish to see more of the pointed ears."

"My TV broke right before my Mac broke." I chose my well-worn Greek apocrypha and waved a hand at my bookshelf. "Read a book."

"You should have harnessed a boccánach to fix such things." She scanned the bookshelf.

"A boccánach as a pet? Are you insane?"

"Not at all. They can be quite useful with the proper training."

"I don't deal well with humans and nonhumans piss me off. It's mutual."

"This does not surprise me." She pulled something from the top shelf. "This will do. A poet I am not familiar with." She blew dust from the top edges. "Your housecleaning skills are not equal to your exorcism skills. It is a good thing I am adaptable."

I hadn't read a word of the page I'd opened to. "Lady, claustrophobia isn't one of my bugaboos, but you're making my apartment close in on me."

She stopped turning pages. "Bugaboo? This is not English. Speak in a language I understand, please."

"Why should I? You're a helluva lot older than me. You must've come across colloquialisms before." The back of my head flinched. I swear it felt exactly like Grandmère had whacked me for rudeness. I wouldn't put it past her to convince Heaven's gatekeepers to let her out to administer her brand of correction.

My visitor had replaced the book and knelt next to my music shelf. "This stringed instrument resembles a gusli, but I have not seen it before. Play it."

Any thought of apology evaporated. "Stop ordering me around."

"Cease looking like the angry mountain lion. All men like to parade their accomplishments, no? Be a peacock."

The ludicrous side of all this hit me finally. I laughed. She beamed, her black hair shining in the firelight, her gray eyes softening with comfortable crinkles around them.

"What?" I said when my laughter had eased.

"I enjoy making you laugh. You are a challenge." She held out my mandolin.

"I'm not your fixer-upper." I took the instrument, blew dust from it, and plucked the strings. "Ouch." I hummed a G and turned the first tuning peg. Xav had always been jealous of my perfect pitch. I'd always been jealous of his ability to dance. Typical musician. I tuned all four strings and played a chord progression in F. "Greensleeves" came first to my fingers. At the end of the second verse, she held up her hands. I was glad she didn't touch me again.

"Your song is well played, but sad. I wish to hear something bright."

"You're a real Saturday night audience, aren't you?"

She furrowed her dark eyebrows. I explained the theater metaphor. Lisa had once sung comic operettas and told a lot of stories about audiences. Friday night crowds were tired from the work week and ready to enjoy themselves. Saturday night crowds had a day to recover from work stress and projected "We expect to be entertained. Prove your talent."

Emma's expression shifted to a scowl. "You do not understand at all what I meant."

Instead of answering, I played a traditional bourrée meant to make people dance at weddings. She clapped time and by the second verse she was dancing in the space between my coffee table and the sagging armchair.

"This song is like a Komi dance. Play more of it. I wish to dance longer."

I'd learned this bourrée in grade school, so I put my hands on autopilot to study her. When she was happy, she became water glittering in the sun, simultaneously in the moment and incredibly ancient. The "Komi" remark coupled with the Cyrillic seal on her Roman prison confirmed that she'd lived in Russia when she was alive. More information to tuck away for the moment I finally banished her.

I played the last, extended chord and she flopped into the chair, panting. Yet she wasn't sweating or truly out of breath. More like she remembered how dancing made people tired and was reenacting a memory.

"You will play again for me, but not now. Now I wish for a warm bed and a long sleep."

Proving the dance hadn't tired her, she sprang from the chair and walked into my bedroom.

"This bed is too small for both of us. Why is your sleeping plan insufficient?"

I set the mandolin on its shelf—carefully, it was more than one hundred years old—and stomped into my bedroom.

"This is my place. My bedroom. Not yours."

She made a dismissive gesture. "Of course, you are a priest. You are not supposed to sleep with anyone. Bah. The rules were different long ago."

"The rule in my house is: I sleep in my bed. Period."

"Fine. I will not trespass on your territory. Instead I will sleep by the fire. You will bring me blankets and pillows."

She turned her back on me and headed for the fireplace. I wanted to grab her and yell at her. I wanted to recite the standard exorcism, and if it didn't work—and I doubted it would—I wanted to start with a Vodoun spell and then a Shinto ritual and on through every part of my arsenal until she vanished screaming in a puff of smoke or snow or mist.

"You yourself are giving off enough heat to light this wood," she said as she broke up the glowing heart of the fire. "But do not step closer. I enjoy you more when you are smiling."

"You sound like you're quoting from bad porn."

"I do not know the meaning of the last word, but I think you are talking of things a priest is not supposed to know. *Tch.*"

I heard the smile in her voice. "Dam—" I stopped myself. My expletives should not have eternal consequences.

"Blankets, please. I expect better manners of a representative of the Church."

Son of a—How was she getting the better of me? I could handle dullahans, hellhounds, ghosts, even demons with less trouble than this woman. I took a blanket and the spare sheets from the all-purpose closet next to the bathroom. I considered telling her to use a couch cushion for a pillow, but my cushions were pretty beat-up. With reluctance, I took one of the two pillows from the bed and shook it free of the pillowcase.

"Here. This is all I've got."

"Then I will be content. Sleep well."

"Uh—you too."

She tried to hide an expression somewhere between triumph and coquettishness. I couldn't think of anything to say that wouldn't start another fight, so I retreated to my bedroom.

Retreated.

This had to change.

Chapter Ten

I woke to the aroma of coffee. She was still here.

My alarm went off. I slapped it and climbed out of bed. I had no robe, so the ancient female would have to live with the sight of me in rumpled track pants and T-shirt.

It was my place.

She turned on me as soon as I crossed the threshold.

"You are a poor housekeeper. Why is there no way to steam the milk? I wish to make lattes for us and I must stand over the stove with a whisk. You do not even possess electric beaters." She flounced in place at the stove and returned her attention to the small pot on the burner. "At least you have a proper gas stove."

I yanked open the fridge door. "Do you do anything besides complain?"

"I am making breakfast."

She paused long enough to let me know to prepare myself for a verbal jab.

"Decent men shower before breakfast, but I will make an exception because you are a priest and not used to living with a woman. Bring two mugs which are proper for lattes, please."

I slammed the fridge shut and banged open the cupboard above the sink. When the door sprang back and nearly gashed open my scalp, I admitted to myself that I was acting less than mature.

Emma kept whisking the milk. I chose to ignore her smile. Instead, I took out two soup mugs and set them next to the coffeepot.

"Good. Now please butter the toast. The eggs are keeping warm in the covered pan."

On cue, four slices of pumpernickel popped out of the toaster. My stomach growled next, and this time she laughed.

"What have you been eating all these months for your stomach to make such a sound? Plain meat on dry bread?"

"Ramen, mostly. I'm on a budget." I buttered a slice of toast.

She poured coffee into the first cup and added the frothed milk in a slow stream. "Is it the hard block of noodles with the salty packet of spices to which you refer? I was forced to consume it once." She made a disgusted noise in her throat.

"I do what I have to do to pay the rent and eat."

"But why? The Church has always been richer than ten kings. You should use their money."

The knife clanked on the glass butter dish before I controlled my reaction. "Mind your own business."

Another pause. "There are two eggs for each of us. I chose blackberry jam yesterday. If you do not like blackberries it is too bad." She filled the second cup halfway and poured in the milk. "If you tell me you add sugar to your coffee I will lose all respect for you."

I smiled. "What would you have said if I told you I only drink decaf?"

She set the cups on the table a little too hard. "Such words would never come out of your mouth!"

I gave her the look which always made Lisa insult me in ancient Hebrew. After a beat I said, "True."

"A priest who deceives? Shameful. And look, you caused me to spill the coffee."

I mopped it up with a napkin. "A good deed covers a multitude of sins."

"Do not misquote holy books to me." She held out her plate. "I cannot eat my eggs if they are still in the pan on the stove."

"You're high maintenance." I stood and brought the pan to the table. The sunny-side-up yolks were a little firm for my taste, but I knew better than to criticize a cook's food while I was eating it.

During the silent meal, I catalogued what I knew about her so far. The big: age, power, adaptability. The little: sweet tooth, lack of conscience, major attitude. I drank the excellent coffee. The last one wasn't so little. Might be smart to keep watch on it. Might be the right weak point to wriggle my way behind her shields and give her the boot.

Her fork clinked on her plate. "Well?"

"Well, what?" I folded the second slice of toast in half and took a bite.

A theatrical sigh. "Must you be taught everything? I have cooked you food. You have eaten the food." She gestured with her left hand as though expecting something to be set into her palm.

"Oh. Yeah. This was good." I swallowed something intangible and finished with, "Thanks."

"*Madonna mia*, it is like blood from a stone." She picked up her dishes. "Do not strain yourself."

"What? I said thank you." I shoved the rest of the toast in my mouth and washed it down with the last of the coffee. "I'm going to shower and head to work. I don't care if you leave the dishes, as long as you're out of here when I get back."

She muttered something that sounded like a hybrid Russian-Italian insult. I stifled laughter. She was dangerous. Not only because her powers were all over the map—shape-shifting, vanishing, plus more if those were any indication—but because she was getting through previously unknown cracks in my rhinoceros hide.

Ten minutes later, dressed in jeans and a Henley—the weather might have decided to stick with spring—I entered an empty kitchen. The pile of dirty dishes in the sink didn't bother me at all.

———

"Denis! Thank God."

Martin Conover, the owner of Dog-Eared, the used bookstore where I worked, shoved an index card in my hand as soon as the door closed behind me.

The wind chimes tinkled their high-pitched cacophony above us. Someday I would replace them with a Hallowe'en sound gizmo making the Wicked Witch of the West's cackle every time the door opened. If I didn't, I'd end up dragging the chimes off the door and stomping them into metal pancakes.

"Stop glaring at the chimes and read this. Coco, leave Denis alone."

I squatted to pet the mostly white collie while I read. Martin had hired me in desperation because no employee lasted more than two weeks. I located and dispersed the seriously ticked-off gjenganger hiding in the bathroom walls on my first day. Since then, Martin pimped my services under the table. I earned enough extra to pay my rent and he didn't have to raise my part-timer's salary. He claimed the stories I brought back were his payment. He was a good guy and I knew how to spin a yarn.

The card he'd handed me had an address on North Cleveland in Old Town. A Japanese surname. A bit of gibberish.

"Martin, what does the scribble at the end mean?"

"Sorry. I got this thirdhand. Evelyn's sister-in-law's grandmother told her daughter who told Evelyn, and Evelyn couldn't make heads or tails of what word she kept saying. Something about a vision of bones in the basement and the grandmother thinking something's choking her."

Martin's other dog, Scout, padded over for his share of attention. We both switched to rubbing the fluff under their ears.

I looked up from the dog's half-lidded eyes. "You're going to tell me organizing the fifteen boxes of romances in the back can wait."

"Of course I am." His light brown hair flopped over his eyes as he nuzzled Scout's nose. "You'll get the new inventory done on schedule, no matter what."

"Boss-man, you are taking advantage of my conscientious nature."

"On the contrary, I am demonstrating confidence in my hiring acumen." He gave the collie a final pat. "If it's an easy one, I'll see you after lunch. Otherwise, the romances will be waiting for you tomorrow."

I held the blasted chimes with one hand when I opened the door. Behind me, Martin laughed.

Chapter Eleven

Twelve minutes to drive home and change. Forty-five minutes to the site. Not bad for prime rush hour. Early bird tourists on those Old Town walking tours wandered the sidewalks, water bottles or coffee in one hand, maps in the other.

I parked two blocks away—again, pretty good for a Monday morning. I rolled up the window and got out, messenger bag hanging from my shoulder. One of the many advantages of owning an old, boring car: I could lock it and walk away without the worry of thieves distracting me from the job at hand.

Some of the tourists glanced at me in my blacks and I nodded. I kept my eyes focused about ten feet in front of me so I wouldn't be distracted by the glut of spirits and entities in this neighborhood. The angry ghost of a teenage suicide lurked on the second floor of a mansion now split into apartments. Blobby, drooling greed-imps infested the antique jewelry store, the gems coated with their invisible spittle. Three lavellans glared at me through the storm grates, their ratlike fangs dripping poison the way some spiders do. I'm not exactly a fan of cranky wet rats.

Then I turned the corner and got a snootful of rotting bone marrow.

I never got paid enough for this.

At least the reek narrowed things down. Wendigo, onomoraki, rakshasa. Wendigos and I were old adversaries. In the remnants of their brains, a human whose clothes looked too big meant I was starving, which meant I was another human on his way to becoming one of the cannibal brotherhood. As in, competition. So they went all HULK SMASH directly onto the hidden phosphorus tube I prepared. Eight times out of eight so far. The resulting fireworks stunk like the third circle of Hell, but customers didn't argue about paying me. Wendigos never stopped to think of another reason I might be too skinny for my clothes, like guilt, poverty, and insomnia. Wendigos didn't think about anything beyond food. Eh. Worked to my advantage.

Onomoraki I'd defeated once. A rakshasa, never. Maybe the gibberish on the index card was Japanese for a plain old wendigo. A compartment in my bag had tubes filled with phosphorus plus the extra ingredients I added to the immolation mix to give it my own special zing.

Five houses down the block, I reached the restored brick mansion with the thing in the basement. A beautiful place. I scanned the front windows from cellar to attic.

For the love of—A ghost lurked in the attic. She had the air of a nursemaid or a governess. We stared at each other, the distance between us negated by her energy and my Sight. I held her gaze and created a narrow path to her to allow her to cross to the next place. It shimmered like a waterslide on a hot summer day.

She knew sign language. I wasn't an expert, but I kept in practice. This had been her family's land for centuries, she signed. This house was her home. Children lived here again. She wanted to stay and look after them. Her fear of the creature below was greater than her fear of me, the angry holy man, but not much. She stopped just short of begging me not to cast her out.

Christ on a bike. She thought I'd force her through as though she was my enemy. My energy must have a label reading "one hundred percent unmitigated bastard."

I dissolved the path and told her in slower signs that I wasn't there to make her do anything she didn't want to do. I was here to cleanse the cellar, I signed, and walked out of her sight up the path to the brick mansion's front door.

A dog's ass might smell better than this house. I breathed through my mouth as I rang the doorbell, but it didn't help. I tried holding my breath. Counted to ten. Unclenched my nostrils. A teenage girl opened the door and rotting-corpse stench engulfed me.

I gripped my messenger bag tighter and puked all over their azaleas.

Over the noise I heard her calling someone. I held up my free hand and stayed on my feet. Never thought to pack a travel-sized mouthwash. I spat the last of breakfast onto the glossy leaves and faced the sudden crowd of people on the top step.

A middle-aged Japanese woman, the older version of the teenager, glared at me. Two younger boys made theatrical gagging noises, their faces filled with grossed-out delight. The older woman opened disapproving lips at the same moment a tiny old lady in a worn kimono darted between mother and daughter.

"See! See! The priest smells the gashadokuro!" She clutched my arm and hauled me inside. "My daughter thinks I am a senile old woman." The two exchanged glares. "Her eyes cannot see the legends. The ability leaped over her generation."

"Mother, it is ridiculous to assume—"

"Silence."

The mother's teeth shut with a click. Muddy red spiked into

her bright yellow aura. At the same time, soft blue washed over the old woman's metallic silver one.

"The ability has not revealed itself in my grandchildren yet, but at least they keep open minds. They read manga."

The teenager giggled until her mother transferred the glare to her.

None of this was distracting me from the overwhelming stench. "*Obaasan,*" I said, "you must show me the cellar before my stomach humiliates me again."

The old lady slapped me on the back. "There is no shame in your actions. A gashadokuro makes even the strongest man toss his cookies."

She winked at me. Her granddaughter giggled again. Her daughter clucked her tongue.

"Mother, you will teach Miya poor language habits."

The old lady slipped her arm through mine without replying. "It is this way."

She didn't ask for my credentials. She didn't ask if I knew what a gashadokuro was or if I knew how to defeat it. Her confidence radiated from her like warmth from the sun.

Which was good, since I'd only read about these gigantic skeleton creatures, never seen one. But it didn't matter. All hungry bone-boys had the same weakness: fire.

She opened the cellar door. The reek tried to knock me down.

The old lady peered up at me, her eyes bright as a blue jay's. "It only smells like garbage in the summer to me."

"Be grateful, *obaasan.*" I sized her up: midseventies, tough but frail, made a mean wasabi paste, shared her grandchildren's love of manga. "I would like you to stay up here during this."

"I will not get in your way, *shinpu-sama.* But I am an old woman and my life is tame as a caged bird's."

I didn't want to waste the energy arguing. I knew I could protect her.

"Very well, but I will exact the payment afterward of a taste of your wasabi."

Her eyes and mouth turned into three surprised ovals. She bowed without letting go of my arm. "At least my daughter knew enough to bring a true holy man here. I feared she would try to deceive me with a false psychic meant for tourists. Come show me to a seat which will not be in your way."

The stairs were well-lit but steep. The old lady leaned as heavily on the railing as she did on my arm. The odor of dank cement floor fought with the gashadokuro stench. My empty stomach flipped again.

The old lady gestured to the left. "The part with the cement floor was once the laundry room. The rest of the cellar"—she waved at the dim space to our right—"has a floor of packed earth."

I blinked watering eyes. After today, I would never again complain about late trash pickups in summer.

We walked onto the dirt floor. Bare bulbs hung from the low ceiling every twenty feet or so, pushing back small circles of gloom. Boxes stacked on pallets lined part of one wall. A model train table took up the center space under the only frosted glass ceiling light. At the far end of the cellar, next to a locked coal chute, sickly green phosphorescence outlined a wooden door's six wide planks.

I pointed. "Does the wooden door lead to a fruit cellar?"

"Yes. I am teaching my granddaughter to make preserves and ripen cheeses and meats."

"Old woman, are you hanging provolone in there?"

"Yes, but—"

"And curing ham?"

"Yes."

I looked down at her. "You have a hungry ghost in this cellar smelling your meat and cheese."

She clapped her wrinkled hands over her mouth. "Did we draw it here?"

"Not at all. It takes decades for one of these creatures to assemble itself."

I left her next to the train table and walked toward the wooden door. The rot-green glow didn't get any brighter as I got closer. But the door was only six feet high. If the lore was trust-worthy, gashadokuros were huge. Fifteen to twenty feet huge. It couldn't fit in a fruit cellar.

Five feet away from the nonlight, the stench got too strong even for my empty stomach. I didn't get a corresponding sense of evil or hate, though. Only hunger.

First piece of business: get the old woman safely off the floor. Most of the wooden pallets were solid enough to protect her. I slipped my bag's leather strap across my chest—it didn't leave me until I opened it to start ritual prep—before heaving several pallets into a kind of throne. When I had a high base, back, and sides, I picked up the old woman and set her on the base.

"Can you sit cross-legged?" I asked her.

In response, she tucked her legs under her kimono and her hands into its sleeves. "There. I look like a tea cozy."

I smiled. "My grandmother knitted tea cozies for every house in our small Québec town. Never a kimono-shaped one, though." I fenced her in with one of the sturdiest pallets. "Now, *obaasan*, you must obey me. Do not make a noise. Do not move this wooden barrier. You may watch through the slats and tell your grandchildren about it afterward."

The old woman nodded, her white bun bouncing on the nape of her neck. "It shall be as you say."

"Good." I took a mix of powdered mistletoe and chicory

from my bag. "Close your eyes and hold your breath." When she complied, I blew the powder over the pallet. It sank into the grain and through the slats onto her skin and clothes, only a stray glimmer of white light revealing its presence. "I have hidden you from the creature. Now I work."

The train table's two-by-four legs became a sturdy working surface. After my setup ritual I lit two white candles, dripped hot wax onto the nubbled "grass" surface, and stuck down the short wax pillars. I didn't need to open myself to the house. The gashadokuro announced its presence like rotted kimchi.

This creature's stink indicated its size and proportionate appetite. Since gashadokuros liked to rip their victims' heads off, thank God the old woman's daughter had humored her mother's fears before her family members became CNN's latest sensational murder mystery.

"*Obaasan*, one question," I said as I assembled a Kaine Special Roman Candle. "Was the fruit cellar door in good repair when you moved into the house?"

"No." Her bright voice was hushed. "The wood was so rotten it crumbled when my son-in-law touched it. Half of the boards were missing as well."

"Your words are what I expected to hear." I worked more mullein into the cardboard tube.

The lights dimmed but the candles burned clear and steady. I reminded Michael the Archangel that he was supposed to have my back. I fixed my gaze on a spot between the candle flames and let my eyes unfocus.

A faint ringing in my ears broke my concentration. I shook it off and re-unfocused my eyes.

The stench in this cellar would make a dead skunk move to another part of town. My ears started ringing again. It couldn't be the seesawing weather—

I shoved one end of the tube into the flame. White fire shot out of it as I spun around and jammed the Roman Candle into the rib cage of a towering skeleton.

It screeched and clamped its hands over my ears. Fucker's hands were as big as my whole head. I twisted the pipe deeper as the flames consumed the cardboard, shoving it down to where its stomach should be. Its hands squeezed and twisted my head. My eyes bulged. My temples compressed. Pain lanced through my skull.

"I'm—not a—beer bottle—"

It wrenched my head way too far left. My neck popped. I traced the rune sowilo—cleansing flame—across its chest. The angled S burned with my personal blue-white fire.

Whump. Flames engulfed the creature's yard-wide rib cage and poured down its arms.

It bellowed as flames shot up its neck and out every opening in its enormous skull. The light over the train table shattered. It released me to clutch its skull. I ducked down and back right before my hair would've crisped.

Now I could see all of it. It crawled toward me. The ceiling wasn't high enough for it to stand. I backed toward the fruit cellar, away from the old lady. The flaming skeleton plunged forward, a final rumbling scream pouring out with the fire from its jaws.

One tibia crumbled into ash. Then the ribs. Half its skull caved in. Less than a minute later, I stomped all along the narrow mounds of smoldering ash to extinguish any lingering flames. I saved the skull for last, because from the spot it crumbled my left hand was close enough to reach into my open bag. My fingers knew where to find the correct flask and vial for the final step.

I walked around the piles of ash, sprinkling holy water and powdered ginseng, then scooped it all into a clotted mound. It scorched my fingers as I kneaded it into a paste. Nothing a little aloe wouldn't take care of.

When the paste had the consistency of Play-Doh, I rolled it into two long tubes. Next, I scraped away a square of dirt and formed a foot-high rune nauthiz for constraint and breaking of power. I pressed and molded the ash dough until the "*t* with an angled crossbar" rune became seamless. When its shape satisfied me, I spread the dirt back over it and patted the floor smooth.

The candles burned clear and steady now. The still-intact ceiling lights had stopped flickering. I'd been concentrating too much on other things to notice when. I snuffed the flames with my fingertips and sent out a quick thank-you to the archangel. He's one dependable warrior.

No sound came from behind the warded pallet. If the old woman had had a heart attack—I pulled the pallet away, ready to administer either CPR or Last Rites. She sat in the same place, hands in her lap, her eyes fixed on the spot in the floor where I'd covered the rune.

"*Obaasan*, are you well?"

A beat. A long, shaky breath. Her eyes moved from the floor to my face.

"*Shinpu-sama*... you are... we should have..." Another long inhale. "We are in your debt." She raised her arms. "Help me up, please."

I set her on the floor. Her legs tried to give out. I kept my hands under her arms until she could stand on her own again.

"If you are ready, we will tell your daughter the house is safe."

I escorted her to the stairs. Her grandsons clung to the exposed beams on the right-hand side of the staircase. The size of their eyes made them look like chibi manga characters.

I scowled at them. "You weren't invited down here."

They blinked, but their chibi eyes didn't change.

"Awesome!"

"You're like Godzilla!"

I kept my face stern.

"You know," the one on the lower step said. "First you torched it with your heat ray, then you stomped it flat. Can you make the Godzilla roar?"

His brother slugged him. "Shut up, jerk. He's a priest."

Their grandmother's voice cut them off. "Haru, Ryuu, go."

The boys bowed and ran upstairs, their voices tripping over each other.

"Mom! Mom! You should've seen it!"

"It was totally cool!"

"Grandma's skeleton monster was like fifty feet tall!"

"Didja hear it scream?"

The old lady and I followed, the boys' voices drowning out their mother's. When we appeared, their mother tapped their heads hard enough to shut them up.

"Father—" she said to me, and hesitated. "I'm sorry, my friend never told me your name."

"Kaine."

The old woman released my arm. "This priest saved my granddaughter's life."

"Don't forget your life, old woman," I said, mostly as cover while I funneled strength into my body. Damned skeleton had drained me more than expected.

The boy on the left cut in. "He did, Mom, and ours and yours and Dad's too!"

His brother took the cue. "It tried to rip his head off! Its hands were, like—"

"Snow shovels! If it had grabbed me or Ryuu or any of us we'd have been—"

"Dead," they said in unison, with too much relish.

Their grandmother told the story, interrupted by colorful additions from the boys. Their sister gasped and clutched her mother, staring at her brothers, her grandmother, me, and then back around the circle. Her mother's perfectly made-up face didn't grow pale and no wrinkles marred her smooth forehead, but her eyes fixed on me and didn't budge.

When the old woman finished, her daughter clamped a hand on each twin's head. "Is all this the truth?"

"Mom, didn't you hear it? Didn't you smell it?"

"We had a gashadokuro from the old country in our cellar."

"Wait'll we tell the guys at school!" Ryuu broke away from his mother's grip and came to me, hand out, his face serious. "If all priests were like you, we'd go to church."

I shook his hand with solemnity. His brother popped up next to him and we also shook hands.

The old lady said, "I will be back with your wasabi. Daughter, pay this man for saving our family."

The teenager was texting so fast her thumbs blurred. The twins ran down the hall and a door slammed a second later. Their mother appeared at a loss; then she walked to a narrow hall table and pulled out a checkbook.

I spelled my name for her, first and last. She hesitated over the little "amount" rectangle but filled it in with a firm hand.

The teenage daughter kept texting while I waited by the front door. I needed out of this house. The stink of gashadokuro coated my sinuses. My neck needed a chiropractor, which couldn't happen until tomorrow at the earliest. The gashadokuro's dying screech pinged around the inside of my skull and I couldn't ask these people for aspirin. Bad enough I'd puked on their landscaping as an introduction.

The old woman returned bearing a jar of pale green paste.

"This is part of the first batch we made in this house."

It weighed my hand down and said "guacamole" to my

empty stomach. I should stop into the grocery store for avocados and tortilla chips.

"Many thanks, *obaasan*."

"Our thanks to you, *shinpu-sama*."

We bowed to each other. The teenager's phone clicked. Great. Archbishop Raymond's flunky would be on the phone to me as soon as the picture showed up on social media.

Her mother handed me the check. I pocketed it without looking, like always.

"Ask the older neighbors about the history of the land," I said to the old woman on my way out. "A motherly spirit resides in the attic. She would love to help with the kids. If you need my help inviting her downstairs, I will be happy to do so."

If only to prove to the ghost I wasn't a one hundred percent unmitigated bastard.

Chapter Twelve

Hours later, the bookstore's three kitschy clocks barked, chirped, and sang in Mickey Mouse's voice the hour of eight p.m.

I stretched my back. Of the fifteen boxes of romance novels, twelve lay flattened against the wall. My nose smelled only dust and acid-free paper. I heard nothing but street traffic and pedestrians on the sidewalk. Alphabetizing hundreds of titles and authors had crowded out most other thoughts.

My apartment had been blissfully empty when I went back to change clothes after depositing the check. Three hundred dollars. I suppose raising three kids and supporting one's mother stretched even two incomes pretty thin.

Martin worked wonders on my neck in exchange for the story of the gashadokuro, thus saving me a chiropractor bill.

At noon the dogs and I played shake the rag to the amusement of the lunch-hour customers. Happy book browsers bought more books. Martin had been skeptical until I showed him the spreadsheets from my customer-related experiments. No music and no dogs—Martin's default before he hired me—

was my control. Hidden speakers broadcasting ocean waves or birdsongs also kept sales flat. The same speakers playing light rock or classical increased sales an average of three percent. When I added happy dogs to the rock or classical, a four and a half percent increase.

Pa would've approved the spreadsheet. Martin bowed to my analytics and brought in Scout and Coco every day. It was a toss-up as to who liked the arrangement more: the dogs basking in all the attention or Martin as he balanced the cash register at closing.

I'd never been so glad a restored eighteenth-century building was haunted only by a gjenganger. When I had wandered the streets eight months ago looking for work, every bookstore in a four-square-mile radius boasted unseen squatters. The chain store had a still-angry suicide ghost hanging around its coffee bar, plus it wanted too many references. The pretentious one with a poltergeist who liked to trip senior citizens required its employees to wear a suit and tie every day. I let the suicide pour out its grievances to me before I moved it on. I banished the dead little snot from the pretentious joint with a swift kick in its butt.

Martin's place bathed me in warm orange and the scent of fresh bread. I told him about it after I evicted his undead squatter. He said there was no bakery nearby. I explained how houses with intense owners absorbed their nature, and his was warmth and comfort. He bought a bread-making book from his shelves and I became his carb taster.

Food. The screaming-fighting-kill-Denis creatures sucked all my stamina. I'd devoured an entire chicken finger sub before eleven and three fish tacos sometime in the afternoon. Unpacking and cataloguing the books had been exactly the detox I needed, but now my body demanded about a gallon of Gatorade and still more food. I shut down the inventory program and locked up before Mickey Mouse giggled the half hour at me.

Twenty minutes later, with a container of Pad Thai in one hand making my mouth water, I closed the apartment house entrance behind me.

Deep water and snow plus something else—spaghetti— washed over me the instant I touched my doorknob. I counted to ten before I let myself in.

"You keep ridiculous hours," a certain female called from my living room. "It is your fault the linguine is no longer *al dente*."

The Pad Thai, still fragrant in my waiting hand, clashed with the aroma of tomato sauce on the stove. She'd poured red wine as well as made salads and bought real Italian bread.

"Why the hell—" I stopped shouting across half my apartment and walked into the living room.

The open windows let in the early spring breeze. I'd bought furniture designed to create a welcoming atmosphere in the small room, and here she was, looking completely at home in *my* home.

She hunched over the coffee table, typing slowly on a new MacBook. "First I will send this message and then we will eat."

"What the hell are you doing?"

She hit "Send" and closed the laptop. "My actions should be obvious."

All my neck muscles cramped up again. "I meant, why are you still here?"

She gave me the same look Lisa used when I was being more dense than usual.

"You ask many stupid questions for an intelligent man. I will lay the blame on hunger, which dulls the senses."

She stood, and I got a good look at her clothes.

"Good Christ, when did you turn into an emo teenager?"

She ran her hands along her skin-tight black shirt.

"Stop preening like a cockatoo smoothing its feathers." I clenched my fists to contain myself. "You would drive the Dalai Lama himself to a three-day drinking binge."

She laughed. "The morose young women in the computer store called this style 'goth.' It is a much better term which evokes an era of literature." She eyed my bookshelf, whose ratio of nonfiction to fiction was approximately ten to one. "You need to enjoy yourself more. I shall find a bookstore and purchase some appropriate books."

"I work in a bookstore. Leave my reading preferences alone. You still haven't answered my question."

"Which question? Ah: Why am I dressed in this manner? I enjoy the challenge of extreme styles. Do I not allure you in these tight black clothes? Are you not captivated by my dramatic eyes and ghostly face?" She struck a modeling pose. "This is a different type of ghost than you are used to seeing."

Saints and angels, prevent me from tossing her ancient ass into the street.

Or not.

"Your midlife crisis is late. Where did you get the Mac? Yesterday you were broke."

She brushed past me, her black-painted lips pouting. "It is time to eat."

I grabbed her black-clad arm. "Did you steal the Mac and those clothes?"

She huffed. "You are not pleasing me."

"I don't give a shit. Answer me."

Her river-and-snow scent deepened behind my eyes to storm-swollen water overflowing its banks. A moment later it receded and I saw her face again. A normal man would be intimidated. We glared at each other.

"Fine." She twisted her arm. I didn't ease off. "You have seen those horserace gambling houses? I won the money there."

Muddy tendrils spiked into her aura.

"Stop lying." I shook her arm, making sure I didn't injure her. I kicked evil supernatural ass only. She wasn't evil. Probably.

"It is not a lie. Well, not all of it."

She tried a coquettish look, which the goth makeup sabotaged. When I didn't succumb to her charms, she reverted to her usual self.

"Gamblers are fools. I am no fool. I altered myself to blend with the furnishings until I entered the secret room where the winners are revealed. You are aware the television broadcast for horse racing is delayed, yes?"

"No. I never gamble."

Those gray eyes stared through me. "Not with money, no. As for me, I moved between the secret room and the large room where bets are placed. Everyone was intent on the television screens or on the money they were risking. I turned the fourteen dollars with which I arrived in Chicago into two thousand eight hundred and forty dollars."

My jaw dropped. I clamped it closed.

"You would have enjoyed the ways I altered my appearance so they did not become suspicious of me. They rely on hidden cameras. *Pah.*" She snapped her fingers.

"You're a cheat and a thief."

She looked out the window with a sigh. "You weary me. Release my arm."

After a beat, I did. I was too tired, too drained, too hungry. I had Xav and The Plan to think of, not this woman's escapades. She didn't matter. "Do what you want. I don't care."

I returned to the kitchen and opened the Pad Thai. The

sauce on the stove smelled better than my takeout. It reminded me of Paolo's wine bar in Rome.

She snatched the container out from under my plastic fork. "You will not eat out of a cardboard box when I have cooked food for us." She hurled it into the sink, splattering noodles, tofu, and shrimp.

I flung her toward the door. "Get the hell out of my life!"

She planted herself in front of me. "You have a head like brick. If it were not for me you would not be having this life."

Her last words penetrated. "What?"

She gave me the "men are all alike" look again. "Brick. One makes buildings of it."

I waved her sarcasm away. "What do you mean, I wouldn't have this life?"

"It is no wonder you cannot remember. I refer to the night you chose to poison yourself with pills and alcohol." She waited.

My mind closed off the kitchen, the house, the city, the present. The last time I drank any liquor... Rome. The bottles of whisky. The bottle of sleeping pills. Snow and deep rivers and me shouting profanity out the window...

When I saw my kitchen again she glowed with satisfaction.

"Good. You have remembered how I forced my power into your body to eject the poison you were killing yourself with. You may now thank me, and we will be even." She scooped the wineglasses off the table. "Here."

When I didn't take one, she huffed and touched a glass to my lips. "A toast must be drunk, not scowled at."

I backhanded the glass out of her hand. It shattered against the overhead cupboard, splashing wine and glass fragments into the mess of Pad Thai.

"I don't drink alcohol. Any alcohol. Get it through your head." Images of the whisky-and-pill binge poured into me, a nightmare in shaky-cam.

I'm sorry, Xav. Sorry for everything.

Her voice sharpened. "You are going to weep?"

I shoved the nightmare film into my brain's locked room to deal with later. "It's none of your business what I do."

"You are the rudest, most obnoxious man I have spoken with in seven hundred years." She set her glass on the table. "I chose to make you angry enough to expel the poison from your body. You did not deserve it."

Our combined auras were blinding me. Red and black fog pulsed between us, mixed with snow and rivers and the bitter cold of the Canadian mountaintops. "Nobody asked you to screw up my life."

"You have screwed it up well enough on your own." She made a spitting noise again. "Priests. You think the world revolves around you."

"You seem to think so too, the way you're hanging around me like a leech." The reds dominated the blacks now. A headache throbbed at my temples. Her gray eyes glowed silver through the haze. She was beautiful.

"You arrogant *mudak.*"

"My parentage is well-documented." Why the hell was I thinking about her looks?

She gasped.

I glared. "Of course I understand Russian. I know how to use my brain. I know—" I grabbed her shoulders and kissed her black-painted lips.

She fought me. I kissed her harder. God, it felt good. She clutched my hair and yanked me closer, crushing my lips in return.

A moment later, she wrenched herself away. We stared at each other. A smear of black lipstick marred her white cheek. My pulse drummed in my head. Her chest rose and fell like she'd been sprinting.

She touched her lips. Moved her fingers until they reached the smear. I wiped my hand across my mouth. It came away with traces of black lipstick on it. If either of us moved closer…

We stepped back.

"I will"—she inhaled sharply—"drain the linguine. You will clean the sink first, please."

"Yeah."

Chapter Thirteen

We ate in silence. I complimented her cooking. She roused herself for a flash of attitude.

Where the hell had a kiss come from? I didn't like this woman—female—creature. I'd been celibate since Xav and I entered the seminary. Ridiculously celibate: I hadn't kissed a woman other than Mom and Grandmère since then either. If I admired a "type" of woman, it sure wouldn't be anything like this arrogant, capricious creature, despite her hair like the night sky and her—

I stuffed a forkful of salad into my mouth so I'd have something else to concentrate on.

She studied her red wine. "Why do you not drink?"

"I used to. Xavier and I used to help our parents make wine. Our family would watch every Oilers game with a spread of homemade food and drink, especially when Xav and I could get back home." Those had been good times. Xav in his Gretzky jersey and autographed stick I'd bought him for Ordination facing off with me after the games on our frozen pond against Grandpère and his cronies. Once we got so drunk Grandpère's team actually won a game.

"Oilers?" she said.

"Professional hockey." I sat straighter. The last thing I needed was a trip to maudlin-ville. "Anyway. After the drunken night in Rome I haven't touched liquor."

She opened her mouth and closed it again. My face must have looked more intimidating than usual to shut her up. I mopped up the last of my sauce with a piece of garlic bread.

"I will show you what I have been doing on the computer, but you must help me clean the dishes first." She stood, her makeup incompatible with her imperious facial expression.

"You can stop repeating yourself. I always pull my weight."

We washed and dried in more silence. She returned to the laptop while I put away the pots.

She called from the living room, "Everything is ready."

I joined her on the couch. "I swear, your voice sounds like you're snapping your fingers to get me to move faster."

She smiled. "I have retained my skills. Now, pay attention. This is the website I have designed."

The splash screen read "Auxiliumgroup.net." Plain black letters on a plain white screen, with an "Enter" button below the words. She clicked the button and the screen dissolved into another plain page with sparse copy and a "Contact" link and my phone number. Which I hadn't given her. She'd probably opened my phone when I was asleep the other day.

The screen read: "The unseen world is as real as the world that is seen and touched every day.

"Many supernatural entities desire only to fulfill their needs in peace.

"But not all. Poltergeists, ghosts, and creatures thought to exist only in folklore often attach to an object, a house, or even a person. Their sole desire is to harm or even kill humans.

"If an entity is attacking you or your family, Auxiliumgroup.net is able to help. "Click the contact link or call the number above and describe your situation."

A single page. No other tabs. No pictures. No art.

She grinned at me. "You are impressed, are you not?"

"I'm confused. What's the soft sell supposed to mean?" I had an inkling, and it wasn't a good one.

She flopped against the cushions like a European soccer player. "More brick. How do you raise your head from your pillow each morning? At least tell me you understand the Latin I chose."

"Of course I do. It's basic Latin for help. It's the 'group' I don't get. I work alone." I grasped at the only crack in her trap. "Are you setting yourself up as a demon hunter? Your makeup alone will scare the minor ones away."

"*Blyat,*" she said without rancor. "Is it not obvious? I have created a partnership between us."

I jumped up and crossed the room in a hurry. The curtains ballooned in the breeze. I stuck my head out the window and leaned my forehead against the cool cast-iron bars, but all I did was escalate the trapped feeling.

When I brought myself inside, she was testing background colors for the website as though I hadn't moved from the couch.

"Red or yellow is more eye-catching, but they give the appearance of children playing with a paint box. A serious design is required to attract the right clients."

I planted myself across the coffee table from her. "What. Exactly. Are. You. Talking. About?"

"I am speaking correct English. Is it that you do not wish to partner with a woman? You must overcome these priest issues."

"I do not have priest issues."

"Your aura does not agree. It is radiating muddy streets in winter instead of mountains and snow. You are not amusing when the dark appears."

Heat inched up my neck. "I'm not your court jester."

Her head snapped up, eyes narrowed. "What is your meaning, please?"

"You're one to talk about muddy auras." Hers shifted to red spiked with black. If she'd been a Choctaw thunderbird, a melatha, I wouldn't have been surprised to see lightning flash in her eyes. "I meant exactly what I said. Despite your desire to be amused, I don't exist to provide you entertainment."

The storm subsided with a merry laugh. "If it pleases you to think so, I will not contest your denial. You will not deny, however, the abominable state of your finances."

"What business is it of yours?"

"I have chosen to make it my business. You are what I see in housing advertisements described as a 'fixer-upper.' I enjoy a challenge. Now listen to me: the rich become complacent in the guarded houses which their wealth buys them. The complacent are ripe to be sheared like sheep. I will haunt their houses. They will contact you through the website, which I will make certain they see. You will pretend to banish me and they will pay you much money."

Too many responses crowded my tongue. Who did she think—How did she dare—I closed my eyes and counted to ten in Latin. Then in Greek.

When I opened my eyes, she looked exactly like the next-door grad students' black cat. All she needed to look more satisfied was a few feathers at her feet.

I pushed my hair away from my face. "I'm honest."

"Honesty is for victims. The beardless boy at the computer store claimed he was a 'genius.' I agree with his estimation of himself when it refers to his internet knowledge, but he is an amateur when he attempts to resist a woman's smile."

"You charmed a kid at the Apple store into setting up the

Mac and the website." How did she pay for the domain name and hosting? No way was I going to ask.

"Ghosts are simple," she continued as though I hadn't said a word. "The stupidest of shape-shifters can create a ghost. I am not stupid. Poltergeists are even more simple. I will throw a vase across a room. I will make an earring disappear from a dressing table and reappear in the flour bin. I will make a cross fly from the wall when the family is at prayer. They will be desperate to give you their money to banish me."

I had to escape before her trap closed and locked around me. I grabbed my apartment keys from the kitchen counter and hit the street.

Chapter Fourteen

It was a good thing I didn't drink anymore, because the rest of the night would've been a repeat of those three weeks in Paolo's wine bar.

First, I walked. Five miles, at least. Found myself at Oak Woods Cemetery. I'd been keeping to the smaller, semineglected graveyards for The Plan. They offered fewer chances of scaring the hell out of a visiting relative.

Wasn't going to waste an opportunity, though. I walked the long sidewalk looking for an opening in the wrought-iron fence. There wasn't one, so I jumped it. At least I didn't ruin my jeans.

The dead battered at me as soon as my feet touched the grass. I created a barrier before any of them got a sense of who I was. This gave me space to catalogue them.

"Big" didn't begin to describe this place. I remembered reading a news story about Civil War reenactments being staged here. I'd bet a month's rent a handful of still pissed-off ghosts joined the cosplayers.

Illumination from the streetlights reached a few dozen yards through the trees. Gravestones crowded this part of Oak Woods like crazy dominoes. I opened myself up.

So many ghosts. Of course: people had been interred here since 1860. Angry women. Jilted men. Murder victims. Two kids as well. They'd be my first priority. A few unusual residents added spice to the mix. At least one qarinah, and something which tasted like chindi. Also... I reached farther... Something unusual. And big. Excellent. I'd return on Friday after work to enact The Plan here.

When I'd put two blocks between them and me on my way home, I dissolved the barrier and walked back to Hyde Park. On a warm night like this it was full of tourists. Live, human tourists who ignored me. They packed my favorite coffee shop since the early movies had let out and the later shows wouldn't start for another twenty minutes.

I found a single seat at the counter and ordered the house brew: no sugar, double cream. This place used real cream.

Why had she chosen me as her fixer-upper? Her "I came here to thank you" story had to be a cover.

I sipped from my cup. "Still the best coffee in town, Gene."

The owner gave me a thumbs-up.

I savored the next mouthful and considered the ancient shape-shifter in my apartment without anger for a moment. She might have spoken the truth when she said she traveled here to thank me. If I'd been locked in a dungeon for seven centuries I'd be grateful to whoever broke the locks. Ridiculously grateful.

Had I cracked the riddle? Was she filling my apartment with pheromones because she thought I wanted to be paid with sex?

No. She looked as startled as me when I kissed her. Problem was, I wanted to touch her again. Wanted her mouth on mine. Wanted to feel the heat between us.

Sex was one more complication I didn't need.

My phone buzzed against my hip. I pulled it out but stopped my finger before it hit the green button. Instead, I waited until voicemail kicked in. A minute later I picked up a message from Archbishop Raymond's flunky.

"Father Kaine, His Excellency wishes to speak to you about your latest appearance on social media. On a teenage girl's page, no less. You must think of the Church's reputation and use discretion when indulging in your otherworldly activities. You may be sanctioned by His Holiness, but you do not have permission to flaunt yourself. We expect you at His Excellency's residence at nine tomorrow morning."

His Excellency liked to forget about my day job. He'll be even more pissed when one of his secretaries calls me to ask where I am and gets voicemail again. So sorry, Archbishop, but this worker bee can't jeopardize his rent money to obey your summons.

The TV nearest the counter started the eleven o'clock news. I paid my bill and headed home. If God was kind, the shapeshifter would be asleep in front of the fireplace. It was too much to hope she'd be gone.

Chapter Fifteen

By ten o'clock Tuesday morning the last boxes of romance novels succumbed to my organizational prowess. Way too many of their covers featured heroines who resembled my apartment-squatter.

Martin gave me a lot of space. Even someone with the sensibilities of a bag of hammers would've picked up on my snarled state. Martin had no Sight, but he wasn't dense. Even the dogs didn't play lunch-hour games with their usual enthusiasm.

We were relieved when the insufferable clocks announced five p.m. Even better, I came home to an empty apartment. I sent power through the entire apartment building—no sign of her.

The Mac still crouched on my coffee table, but I didn't see her flowered dress or her emo gear.

Wednesday morning, it poured. The door chimes at noon signaled only the eighth customer so far.

"Good day. I am here to take Denis to lunch."

Damn.

I came forward from the nonfiction section. Martin practically stood at attention.

Today the woman was playing "high-powered executive." From what I knew about clothes she hadn't bought her suit at a cut-rate department store.

She looked the part like she'd been born to order people around. Dark blue suit and matching high-heeled shoes, blouse the color of red wine, her cascade of dark hair pulled into a bun. She had makeup on, too. Not too much and she looked good.

Stop.

I stalked to the checkout counter. "What the hell is this?"

Martin's jaw dropped like he was a cartoon character. The woman held out her hand to him.

"I am Emma Koroleva, Denis's business partner."

"Martin Conover." He shook her hand. "Business partner?"

She opened a small black handbag and handed him a plain white business card. He read it, looked at me, looked at her, read it again.

I held out my hand. She put a card in it. In the center it had "Auxiliumgroup.net" in basic Times New Roman. Nothing else.

"It means 'help' in Latin," she said to Martin.

He brightened. "Denis, it's perfect! Much better than 1-900-Exorcist like I would've suggested. Ms. Koroleva, may I have some of these? You'd be amazed at the stories I hear through friends. Now I'll have something to show them. Not everyone trusts word of mouth."

She shot a smug look at me as Martin typed the website address on his keyboard.

"Nice job, you two. Understated is definitely the way to go." He clicked, and his eyes scanned the other page. "What about testimonials?"

Emma shook her head. "We do not wish to resemble a midnight television commercial."

Martin laughed. "Good point. You can't sell exorcisms like they're nonstick frying pans."

My teeth clenched so hard one of my molars gave a sharp twinge.

"Come," Emma said to me. "I have made reservations for twelve fifteen. It is a shame you are not dressed to my expectations, but I will overlook it since I did not give you my schedule today."

Martin grinned like he did when I cursed at the door chimes. "Ms. Koroleva, you are exactly what he needs. Denis, take as long as you need for lunch."

I grabbed my backpack, smiled at Martin, and opened Emma's umbrella over us as we left. Of course she had an umbrella. God only knew what else she'd brought into my apartment.

"You're railroading me."

"Explain, please." Her heels created tiny geysers on the sidewalk.

I refused to look up at her. Those heels made her at least five inches taller than me. She was dying to use the height to her advantage; I knew she was.

"You know exactly what you're doing and why I'm pissed off."

We dodged a wave of filthy water from a passing car. She pointed to a narrow building on the next corner.

"Our destination is located beneath the bright pink-and-yellow sign."

"Fine."

She looked down at me, but I hadn't spent eleven years bullshitting demons to blow it now. If she expected to see a vein throbbing in my forehead, she was doomed to disappointment.

The downpour hadn't affected the restaurant's business. The hostess dressed like a Calabrese maiden straight from the old country seated us in the center aisle at a table meant for four. Eight waiters navigated tables crowded way too close together.

A perky waiter appeared at my elbow after I had the shield configured to my satisfaction.

"One glass of valpolicella," Emma said.

I ordered my usual water with lemon.

"So," she said when the waiter left, "you see how your employer approves of the good website I designed. He will give the cards, which I also designed, to people who are being haunted and they will call you. Soon you will have enough business to keep food in your refrigerator and purchase a television."

"Legitimate business."

She quirked an eyebrow. "You attach to an idea like a selkie to its skin."

"It's called perseverance, and it's how we gained our reputation."

"We?"

Our drinks arrived. This waiter's perfect timing earned him a bigger tip. "Our specials are *aglio e olio*, spaghetti Bolognese, and *polenta primavera*." He poised his pencil over his order pad.

"I will have ravioli with sausage," Emma said.

The waiter bounced when he turned to me. The man was too perky to live.

"Spaghetti Bolognese, please." When did I start thinking of this woman as "Emma?"

My phone buzzed. I answered it without looking. "Yeah?"

"Father Kaine, this is the archbishop's office. You had an appointment with His Excellency this morning at nine."

"Yeah?" Serves me right for not letting voicemail take it.

The female on the other end drank vinegar instead of coffee, if her voice was any way to judge. "We have called you twice. Please hold for Monsignor Powell."

Emma looked at me like I was a specimen under a microscope. "Who is the caller with power to change your aura from sunshine to a thundercloud?"

I stopped my hand before it pulled a strand of my hair around to confirm it hadn't turned from blond to gray since I answered the phone. "The archbishop."

Her lip curled. "Priests."

"I am a priest."

She waved a dismissive hand.

I leaned across the table. "What the hell is the hand wave supposed to mean?"

A click from the phone cut this conversation off. "Father Kaine, this is Monsignor Powell. The archbishop is not pleased with your behavior."

"Yeah?"

Powell's high-pitched voice ratcheted up a notch. "Think of the way your cheap attempts at self-aggrandizement reflect on the Church. Think of how you will affect the reputation of your Order."

Dickweed. "Look. I have a job. A job means I can't ditch my responsibilities every time the archbishop snaps his fingers."

Pencil-dick spluttered.

I interrupted the noise. "If the archbishop wants to piss in my cornflakes, he can do it on the weekend when I'm not earning a living. Tell him to leave me a message." I hung up. The one trouble with cell phones was the inability to slam them down onto the receiver.

Across the table, Emma held her napkin over her mouth to unsuccessfully hide her laughter.

"You will not respond to messages from this priest. Does he know this?"

"He pretends not to. Pencil-dick takes all the grief."

"Does the priest with the insufficient *khui* deserve it?"

We both leaned away from the table so the waiter could set down our dishes.

"The grief or the undersized dick?"

Perky-boy almost dropped a plate of spaghetti in my lap.

"Both." Emma smiled at the waiter, whose face had turned a rich shade of plum.

"He's a useless toady who would pimp out his grandmother for the chance to kiss ass in Rome."

"So he kisses the ass of his current superior as practice? I have known many men and women who do such." She speared a ravioli. "Is this why your anger is turning the air around us as red as my wine?"

"Blame yourself, too."

She choked on her ravioli and swallowed a mouthful of wine. "You are"—a last cough—"endlessly amusing when you are not making me angry enough to break crockery."

"How nice for you." I twirled a forkful of spaghetti and ate it. "So, Ms. Business Partner, I don't recall asking for either a website or business cards."

"You see why I am necessary for you. Since you will not take the reins of this animal, I have done so for you."

The spaghetti soured in my mouth, but not even this woman's machinations could ruin food this good.

"I've been managing fine, thank you."

"I disagree." She chomped down on a thick slice of sausage. "Your life does not have the signs of those who properly manage a business." Her wineglass halted at her lips. "In civilized countries, the shape your lips are making would not be considered a true smile."

"How interesting." I concentrated on giving my lunch the attention it deserved.

The waiter, his face now a neutral mask, took our plates and asked about dessert.

"Two espressos and two white chocolate gelati, please," Emma said before I could ask for the check.

He clicked his heels and vanished.

"Emma." When I had her attention, I hefted my backpack. "This is my traveling messenger bag. Do you understand what I mean? I carry this when I want to be inconspicuous. If you ever again want to see whatever freezing water in Russia you dragged yourself out of, you will back the fuck off. Or I will banish you to the eighth circle of Hell before Perky-boy brings my espresso."

I'd pitched my voice so only she could hear it. My ancient shape-shifter—no, not mine, get your head out of your ass, Kaine—sat still across from me.

"You would not."

"Try me."

Cue Perky-boy. Dregs of my anger still floated around us as evidenced by the espresso cups rattling on their saucers as he set them down and scuttled away.

A ghost's hand appeared on my shoulder. I skewed my eyes sideways. A translucent Italian grandmother stood at my elbow: black dress, flowered apron, hair in a net, the complete package.

"*Mangia, mangia,*" the ghost said, indicating the dessert.

Easy as pie. I mouthed a neat little spell I learned last year in Bergerac. The ghost lost half of her translucency by the fifth word. Her eyes dilated in fear.

Emma put her hand on mine. "Stop."

My concentration fractured. The ghost took a step toward Emma but stopped in the middle of the movement and stood still, trapped between us. This blasted female's power was almost as potent as mine.

Emma gave the ghost a warmer smile than she'd ever favored me with. The ghost returned the smile, regaining most of her original color as she did so. The two women locked gazes and Emma nodded.

"Tell her you like the food," Emma hissed at me.

I glared at her.

"Say it," she hissed again.

"*Il cibo è molto buono.*"

My voice was less than gracious, but the ghost beamed and patted my cheek. The next moment, she glided to the table behind Emma. Those couples remained oblivious, but they ate their spaghetti slower, relishing each bite more than before.

I downed my espresso in one gulp.

Emma sipped hers. "What is it that causes you to banish anything not living? It is closed-minded of you."

If I said what I was thinking, I'd get tossed out of the restaurant. I definitely wanted to come back for more of this spaghetti, so I ate my melting gelato without replying.

The waiter brought the check. I didn't have enough money to cover it, but my "business partner" did. What a shock. She set thirty dollars on the tray as cool as you please.

The rain had thinned over the last forty-five minutes. We returned to the bookstore in silence. She left me at the door. The only small mercy of the day came as I entered the store: a gaggle of Catholic high school girls clustered in the back of the middle aisle, rhapsodizing over the romances I'd shelved earlier. They stayed for an hour. By the time they left, loaded with a dozen each, the rain had stopped and more customers took their place. I filled the gaps the girls had created with their buying frenzy. Martin didn't have a chance to ask me about my "business partner."

My phone buzzed as we closed for the day. Visions of Monsignor Powell danced in my head. I let voicemail take it.

I'd been sitting in the car for five minutes with my hand on the ignition when I realized I didn't want to go home.

"Damn her to Hell."

The words I'd said hit me. I drew a reversal charm in front of my mouth. The pattern glinted on my windshield an instant, then faded. Lisa's repeated instruction rang in my mind: Your words have power. Be careful what you say.

She was right. Lisa was hardly ever wrong.

When I finally sent Emma the ancient shape-shifter to the next world, it'd be from a rational place, not a knee-jerk reaction to one of her many irritating maneuvers.

As a last procrastination before heading to my apartment battleground, I checked messages. A male voice—not Monsignor Dickweed's—shouted in my ear.

"Is this Auxilium group? We need help now! What the hell kind of emergency business doesn't answer the phone?"

The sound of a woman screaming cut him off.

So now I was the 911 for exorcisms.

The computerized voicemail recording said, "Next message," with the date and time. The same man who left the previous message continued, "Look, word is you're the best and I can afford the best. Get your holy ass over here now!" He gave an address out on Shore Acres.

Nothing I owned, including myself, was classy enough to set foot in such a neighborhood. Hadn't the address he'd given me been in the news not so long ago? I Googled it.

Oh. Him.

Chapter Sixteen

I rang the historic mansion's doorbell an hour later. Not even the Pope ignored a summons from organized crime. This renegade exorcist sure didn't.

Emma hadn't been in the apartment. I used the unexpected silence to slough off the chaotic day and bring all my powers into focus.

Everything favored me: rush-hour traffic was backed up going the opposite direction. I rode a wave of green lights across town straight to my destination's driveway.

The lingering cloud cover brought premature darkness to the early April evening. Thunder in the distance, though. Crap. Lightning messed with me in subtle ways. Static electricity made my shield glitch and made my blue candles spark when I didn't need them to. Hold off, storm. If I screwed up this banishing, I could sign the apartment over to Emma tonight because tomorrow I'd be six feet under.

Lou "The Knife" Pascale opened the door.

"Father. Thank God. Come in. Sorry I lost my temper on the phone. Fuckin' thing—excuse me—haunting us locked my wife in her closet." He threw the dead bolt. "You're a helluva lot younger than I expected. You sure you got the chops for this?"

My answering smile radiated professional confidence. "Mr. Pascale, why don't you show me what's been happening and you can judge my skills for yourself."

The black armpit-stink of fear surrounding him didn't increase. A good start.

"Right. Come into the kitchen. You wanna beer?"

"Thank you, sir, but you called me here to rid your house of a malevolent presence. I'd prefer to get to work."

I projected a bubble of calm and confidence around him when we sat at the kitchen table.

He licked dry lips. "Here's the thing, Father. Anita's my second wife. My first, the cheating bitch—sorry, Father—fell down the stairs in my old house and broke her neck last Thanksgiving."

I kept my mouth shut.

"I married Anita last St. Joseph Day. You'll like her, Father. She's a good Catholic girl who was raised the proper way." He shifted in the wooden chair. "I moved her into the bitch's rooms and everything was great for about a month. Then the noises started. Stuff disappearing. Creepy laughter. Whispers. Bruises on her face. Those made everyone point the finger at me, you know? But I never hit her. Never."

I heard the sincerity in his last statement. "What did you do next?"

"My sister brought over this woman to cleanse the house or some hippie crapola. Weird old bat said a jealous spirit was haunting the place. Nothing had ever happened in the house until the bitch died—sorry, Father—and I remarried. So I said to Anita, it's only a house. We'll move."

By this point I was sure his first wife had become a Woman in White.

Lou the Knife, contract killer of fifteen men and one wife, second in command to the current Mafia lord of Chicagoland, grabbed a paper napkin and wiped the sweat from his face.

"So we moved here. Classy joint, isn't it? Anita loves it. She started decorating right away. Been hitting the antique shops. Turning the place into a life-size dollhouse, she says." He made the Italian open-hand gesture. "It makes her happy. She's got a good eye for finding classy stuff. But I got to thinking about antiques and the way things can get, you know, attached to them. Like you see on the reality TV shows."

I stood. "It's one possibility. Is Mrs. Pascale home?"

Suspicion bled into the black haze around his head. "Maybe."

"I need to go through every room in the house and I don't want to startle her."

The air cleared. "Oh. Got it. Would you like us to go out to dinner?"

If he didn't see me work, he wouldn't be willing to pay. "No, please. I may need to ask you questions, so it would be best if you stayed."

"Makes sense. I watch the rug cleaners when they're here. Not like you're another cleaning service, I mean, Father."

I gave him a smile to indicate I wasn't offended. "If you'd be so good as to bring Mrs. Pascale down here, I'll start in the kitchen."

The creature haunting this house wasn't in the kitchen; I knew it as soon as I'd walked in. But I also knew never to take a sneaky ghost for granted, so I closed my eyes and searched. Empty.

When I opened them, Mr. and Mrs. Mobster stood in the doorway.

"Father, is it okay?" Lou said. "Can we come in?"

I waved them toward the chairs. "I'll comb the house. It's going to take a while."

"No problem, Father. Me and Anita are going to say a couple Rosaries."

The master bedroom was on the way to my usual starting place, the attic, so I detoured there. The half-antique, all-Catholic room was awash in residual crap. A murder victim lay trapped between the head and footboards of a sleigh bed. I took care of him first.

A teenager in nineteenth-century clothes sat at the dressing table weeping over an ivory brush and comb set. Unhappy women ghosts were the worst. Once she realized I could see her, she cranked the volume on the lovelorn wailing.

Two minutes later, she trudged the path I created for her and slouched through the glowing doorway to the afterlife.

As I dissolved the path and doorway, muffled barks from another room filled the vacuum her silence created. Good God, the Knife's new wife was a ghost magnet.

I listened for a moment. The barks came from a happy ghost dog. No threat. When I returned to the hallway, the combined voices of the Pascales droned from the kitchen. I made it upstairs without encountering anything else.

The attic looked more like a furniture store with its inventory swathed in dust covers. I sat on the dust-free floor and blocked out everything, starting with the dog. From this pocket of silence, I cast my awareness through the house.

Seething hate slammed into me. My eyes opened but all I saw was fog. Whatever this whitish-grayish thing might be doing to the new Mrs. Pascale, it didn't know about me. I pushed back, grasping handfuls of cloth-like mist. Didn't waste time reciting spells either; when they were this pissed-off only superior strength made them retreat and regroup.

It didn't like my cold blue fire. Its screech made my teeth

ache, but the mist flowed through the floorboards and I sat up again.

"Lou," I said under my breath, "didn't they teach you in Hit-Man 101 never to kill an angry wife?"

I heard a cackle.

"Pack your bags. Mrs. Pascale the First. You're moving."

I opted for an upright search this time, feet apart, hands loose at my sides. Deep breaths. In. Out. Slower. In. Out.

Silence.

Downstairs. Not the bedrooms. Not the office. Not the den. Not the dining room. Not the family room.

There. The living room. Sneaky broad had used the little ghost dog as camouflage.

I hefted my messenger bag and hauled ass downstairs. At a dignified pace, of course.

The Pascales were still working through their first Rosary. Interesting how the Knife's faith burned clear and steady despite everything he'd done—and I sensed a shitload of mortal sins in him.

Lou, it's gonna take more than Rosaries to save your soul.

Anita's faith was all tangled up in greed, social climbing, and vanity, but a clear nugget lay at its heart. The nuns had done right by her.

I didn't draw on their faith for this job. I never did. Xav and I had always done our work solo. Except for the long-ago chain-smoking ghost "possession and banish" day.

No distractions. I swept everything from my head and stepped into the living room.

A cast-iron doorstop shaped like a Scottish terrier sprouted a tongue and licked my ankle. I poured an ounce of powdered angelica root into my right hand and held it under the panting tongue. A drop of pearlized saliva splashed into the pale brown powder and I rolled the mixture into a thin cylinder.

"Fetch the stick, boy," I whispered.

A wagging tail burst out of the cast iron. I held my brownish creation under the iron nose and the dog barked.

"One—Two—Three!" I opened a path to the other side and tossed the stick through the doorway. The ghost Scottie leaped from its iron tomb and chased the bit of magic with joyful barks. I closed the door after it.

Pascale hadn't called me here to chase away the God-knew-how-many clinging ghosts his wife had collected. I moved to the center of the room and eliminated objects with the same technique I used on the rooms of the house.

Not the couches, chairs, or tables. Not the antique lamps or chandelier. Not the iron doohickeys in the fireplace or at the doors, now. Not the portraits, despite one old guy looking like an Italian Jeffrey Dahmer.

The mantlepiece. The matching vases. Covered vases. Polished brass with gargoyle head lids and bases shaped into clawed feet. These two pieces clashed with the mostly Edwardian décor.

I wrapped my hands around the belly of the right-hand creature. No anger here, but it wasn't empty, either. The snarling head popped off and revealed a loose roll of handwritten papers.

I unrolled them with care. The inmost one was headed "Great Grandmother's Cheesecake" in small, precise handwriting.

Interesting hiding place if these papers were secret family recipes. They appeared innocent, but they could be code for who the hell knew what. Organized crime might respect priests, but we knew some questions were better not asked. Since I no longer had a death wish, I rerolled the recipes and replaced them in the vase.

I shifted my Sight to the left-hand gargoyle vase. Multicolored slime crawled over its eyes, teeth, claws, and belly like an oil slick on asphalt.

"Mr. and Mrs. Pascale," I called, "could you come into the living room, please?"

They scurried in, their faces paler than before, even Anita's under her skilled makeup.

"May I have permission to move this rug and work on the floor underneath?"

Lou stepped forward. "Yeah, sure, Father. Anything. Lemme get it out of your way." He knelt at the edge of the authentic Persian rug—I spotted the traditional deliberate flaw—and rolled it up against one of the couches. I motioned him back to the doorway.

This floor needed a polish. Perfect. The circle would adhere well. I unbuckled my bag and fanned open the compartments. Odds were fifty-fifty my initial diagnosis would hold: the former Mrs. P. had turned herself into a Woman in White. Angriest one I'd seen, too. She left a mother of six in Fort Worth in the dust. I'd never heard of one who could manifest an oily rainbow effect, though.

I dipped the salt stick in holy water. Because everyone involved in this was—or had been—a traditional Catholic, I used Catholic imagery only for the circle. Through long practice I drew it exactly wide enough to enclose my messenger bag plus myself sitting cross-legged.

The flute. I needed the flute. I slid it out of its pocket. The silver runes for strength and for union with God heated up the moment I touched them. The body of cedar warmed an instant later, its rich aroma filling my head, cleansing it.

My hand reached for the pale blue candles. I placed them in a triangle on the circle and lit them.

Only then did I fetch the vase and place it on the floor three inches outside the circle. I settled my flute in my lap before I slid my hands into the clinging multicolored slime. First I wedged my fingers in the gargoyle's ears and pulled. Nothing happened. I grabbed the legs and tried unscrewing it from the bottom. Then I stopped wasting time and cast my Sight into it.

Oh, really.

I released the thing and picked up my flute. The runes glowed.

Anita whispered, "Jesus, Mary, and Joseph."

I kept my Sight on the coruscating bronze beast and took a breath. I never forced a melody through the flute; the only way was to let the right notes flow through us both. This time, something commanding in the key of E came out. As my fingers played, the melody resolved into an eighteenth-century French "Credo."

The vase shuddered. The oily sheen darkened and smoked. The Credo reached the phrase "*et homo factus est*" and the gargoyle head began to unscrew counterclockwise. The lid rattled when it cleared the threads but stayed on the body.

The song ended. I set the flute in my lap again. Lou's shaky voice muttered the child's guardian angel prayer in Italian.

I removed the lid.

Ashes. On top of the gray dust, a chunk of orange clay from the kind of pot sold by the thousands in plant stores. Latin words covered the pot shard, written with—I leaned closer—a black Sharpie.

Marry again, I translated, *and I will drive you both insane and screaming down to Hell with me forever.*

"Mr. Pascale"—I kept ninety-nine percent of my attention on the vase's contents—"who had access to your deceased wife's ashes in the crematorium?"

Silence. Then a string of curses, also in Italian. "Her sister, that piece of offal. What did she do?"

Wisps of smoke curled around the pottery.

"A second question: Did you tell anyone you planned to keep her ashes on the mantelpiece?"

At the edge of my vision, the second Mrs. Pascale moved away from her husband.

Lou dragged her back. "My brothers. We own the funeral parlor. My sister-in-law's husband runs the crematorium."

The pottery crumbled. The earthly remains of the late Mrs. Pascale sucked it in.

I stood, flute already at my lips. Every light in the room exploded. Sparks flew at me from all sides but died at the perimeter of my circle. I played the melody the candles usually responded to. The three flames shot up seven feet, their light as steady and clear as icicles. The ashes burst out of the vase and loomed over my flaming shield.

I didn't look up. The flute reversed in my hand, mouthpiece balanced like a pencil point.

"*Exorcizámos te, ómnis immúnde spíritus.*" The thing spread over me, above my candle flame pillars. The room vanished. A mouth-sized hole in the ash screeched but no facial features appeared.

I spat out the penultimate words of the exorcism rite and aimed the flute. The runes' light ripped bigger openings in the gray pall. Through them I saw the Pascales clinging to each other. Anita's mouth opened like a Greek tragedy mask, but her screams didn't penetrate the late Mrs. P.'s current form.

"*Ímperat tíbi majéstas Chrísti, aetérnum Dei Vérbum cáro factum.*" I stabbed the flute's silver mouthpiece into the vase.

The apparition collapsed, flame columns shredding it, ash coating my eyes, ears, nose, and mouth. I reversed the flute and clamped my lips around the mouthpiece and blew. The shroud exploded like a Fourth of July firework, the force sucking the ash back into the gargoyle. My ears rang from the pressure. I swallowed, ignoring the lingering taste of incinerated human, and my ears popped.

The candle flames sank to their correct size. Still on one knee, I dipped the salt stick in the hot wax three times and drew three crosses on the vase's inner wall, crossbars touching. Then I screwed the gargoyle head back on.

I sent my Sight through the house. Another half dozen ghosts clung to their various antiques, but they cowered deep in their shelters after the late Mrs. Pascal's tantrum.

Only then did I pull all my power back inside myself. Fatigue hit like a rock, but I couldn't indulge it yet.

I pinched out the three candle flames and allowed my eyes to see the living room again.

Two paintings lay on the floor, frames buckled. Shattered crystal dangly things from the chandelier covered one of the couches. The wallpaper around the fireplace hung in shreds. An end table had smashed sideways against the far wall, the knickknacks it once held now piles of ceramic debris. I hoped the Knife had some furniture and art restorers on the payroll.

I wiped the circle from the floor with a chamois from my bag. It and the candles went in the bottom of my bag and I locked the flap. Too many of my joints cracked when I stood.

Burn holes pockmarked my blacks. My eyes itched. Clumps of sweat-soaked hair plastered my neck.

Anita clung trembling and whimpering to the Knife. He kept his arms around her, but his gaze was locked on the vase. I picked it up and held it out to him.

"She made a contingency plan. She'd written a curse on a piece of pottery and had someone place it on the ashes. The curse gave her power to rise from the grave—in this case, the covered vase—and carry it out. It's a nasty little trick dating back to ancient Rome."

Lou unwound his right arm from his wife and took the

bronze gargoyle. He swallowed, but no words came out when he opened his mouth.

Anita released her death grip on Lou's shirt. Her manicured fingernails had ripped ten narrow strips from the expensive material. Whatever she'd thought about Lou secreting her predecessor's remains on the mantelpiece had obviously been forgiven after said predecessor's performance tonight.

"Is she really gone, Father?" Anita's voice was hoarse.

"To Hell?" Lou said.

"Judgment is for God, not me."

The Knife set the vase between his feet and pulled a wad of cash from his pants pocket. First time I'd seen a chunk of money so thick. He flicked twenty bills from the center, folded them in half, and handed them to me.

"We owe you our lives, Father. Anytime you need a favor, call me."

"Oh, Father, your clothes!" Anita pointed to my raddled blacks.

"It's a hazard of the profession. Don't think any more about it." I turned to the Knife. "The ashes are no longer possessed. Don't remove the crosses I put inside the vase. You don't want a wandering spirit moving into it. Your former wife or her friend at the crematorium altered the original design to work backward. I suggest keeping it closed for good."

Lou's face darkened. "Anything you say, Father."

Anita held out her hand. When I shook it, she said, "Would you bless our marriage?"

Lou squeezed her close. "Yes, please, Father."

I dredged up the marriage blessing from my mind's storage bin.

Chapter Seventeen

The sound of typing greeted me when I opened my door. I almost called out, "I'm home."

Holy God, this had to stop.

"You are here at last," she called.

If I didn't know better, I'd swear she sounded perky.

"Come see the improvements I have given to the website."

I set my messenger bag on the counter and straightened out the contents. Always the first task after a job. The journal should come next, but I wanted peace and quiet for writing, which I couldn't get until I admired Emma's handiwork. Besides, lamb stew simmered on the stove. Never anger the cook.

"I thought you wanted a simple website," I said as I crossed into the living room.

"There is simple and there is effective. I have been toying with different ways to be more effective." She appraised me. "Your appearance suggests you have either performed a difficult exorcism or you have been attacked by feral cats."

"The former."

A triumphant smile touched her lips. "Some women possess no strength."

I came closer. "What?"

The smile deepened. "Weakness offends me. The ghost of the murderer's wife wet herself in terror when I showed her the extent of my powers."

I braced my arms on the side of the couch. "Explain."

"The wife did not know how to make use of her anger. I snapped my fingers and she scurried like a cockroach to her proper Catholic Judgment." She leaned against the back of the couch, preening. "I created an excellent show for the man and his new wife. You did not even know it was me, I disguised myself so well. Now do you see how easy this is?"

Neon-red fury flooded me. "I told you to stop fucking with my life! You wrecked my clothes and trashed a mob boss's house so you could prove a point?"

Her serenity didn't waver. "Certainly not. I performed the part of an angry spirit—and performed it well, thank you—to fatten your bank account."

"You fraud." Blood pulsed behind my eyes.

"You will stop insulting me." Her pale skin flushed for the first time. "I am a chameleon, not a cheap carnival act."

"Semantics."

She settled back into the cushions. "You are not one who should throw about words such as fraud. Have you chosen to forget your performance in the rich man's house the day I arrived here?"

"I told you it wasn't—" I clenched my teeth.

She sprang up. "I win. Come now and eat my lamb stew. The bread is from the store and not as good as mine, but I did not have time to bake. Organizing a business is difficult work."

After a minute, I followed her into the kitchen. I might as well have had a leash around my neck.

While we ate, I banked my anger so it'd burn long and slow. Trying to find a quick-and-dirty banish with a creature this old and powerful had been my mistake. Kicking her ass into eternity required a long game.

She beelined for the Mac after supper. I went to my room to change. Everything in my dresser had been rearranged to fit in the top two drawers. The bottom drawer now held feminine shirts and socks and some bits of lace whose purpose I couldn't divine. I changed into jeans and opened the closet to get Xav's Gretzky jersey. Skirts and jackets and high-heeled shoes crowded my few clothes against the wall.

She'd given me more fodder for the long game. I put on the jersey, tuned the mandolin, and de-stressed with folk songs from France and Italy. After half an hour, I went to the kitchen to make coffee.

When I returned, a Woman in White stood in the living room, her long dress trailing on the floor, her empty eyes staring through me. I almost dropped the coffee. Where the hell had she come from? I hadn't sensed anything. I backed toward the kitchen and my bag.

The Woman in White transformed into a selkie. Mother-of-pearl skin caught the light from the kitchen.

Between one breath and the next, the selkie became a nalusa chito, green skin turning into jagged spines all along its back.

I had only a moment to register its species when it shifted into a jorōgumo. The spider creature snatched my mandolin and played... I recognized it... Opera. The overture to Dvořák's *Rusalka.*

Its multifaceted eyes saw the moment I realized all these

creatures were Emma indulging in performance art, and the spider-woman returned to being Emma.

She set down the mandolin. "Now do you see how easily we can accomplish this?"

I found my voice. "Who are you, really?"

"I have told you." She fluffed her flowered dress.

"You change shapes so easily, you can't know who you really are."

My ancient houseguest rolled her eyes. "Do not speak of what you do not understand. I have survived many centuries because I am both strong and adaptable. You possess the same qualities, yes?"

She had me there. Xav and I have always survived because we're bullheaded and can adapt on the fly.

Had survived.

"Now stop this foolish argument and explore my alterations to the website. If you are pleased, I shall make a cake. Then you will be doubly pleased."

Chapter Eighteen

I woke Friday morning because she was bouncing on my bed.

"Get out." My morning voice didn't carry the authority I needed.

"Your alarm will sound in fifteen minutes, so this is no hardship for you. Listen to all the work I have been doing for the past three days."

I hauled myself upright. "You have five minutes."

She stopped bouncing. "You are not what is called a 'morning person.' This is a weakness you must overcome."

"I don't need lectures from someone who apparently doesn't need a normal amount of sleep." My home had been my own again for much too short a period. So much for regaining my solitude and peace.

"How would you know whether I sleep? You should not spy on me simply because I make my bed in your living room. This is disappointing behavior in a priest." She tried her coquettish expression on me. "I must also say I am disappointed to see you removed my bedding after such a brief interval. If you think I am inconstant you are in error."

"What. Do. You. Want?"

"*Tch.* Now you are radiating mud and spilled blood. It is not good for your aura to cling to such dark shades."

Her playful act had one benefit: it distracted me from her body sitting six inches away. In my bed.

"If I want my aura read, I'll look in the mirror." Thank God my fly was buttoned. "You're wasting my time. Go away."

She pushed me back against the headboard. Snow. Deep water. A surge of power. Her long fingers caught in my chest hair. Her eyes dilated. My heartbeat stuttered. An image flashed across my eyes: Me. Her. In this bed.

I pushed her off. "Personal space, Emma. Ever heard of it?"

Her flowered dress clung to her, revealing her lack of under-wear. I stared at a bare spot on the wall over her right shoulder.

She pinched her lips. "Fine. I have discovered a house of people obsessed with séances and have appeared as a hideous male demon to them, screaming in a mixture of languages and dripping blood-red ectoplasm. I have also frightened seven people in a historic library by appearing as a hungry ghost. You are aware of this creature?"

"Do you take me for an amateur? And what the hell are you thinking, playing with demon lore? Don't mess with demons, even as a joke." Had to get her out of my bed. I had to get me out of my bed without revealing the bulge in my sleep pants. I bunched up the covers and climbed out on the right side, opposite from her.

"You have a distressing tendency to lecture. It is not interesting. In answer to your first question, I take you for a man unused to women." The laughter in her voice had a breathy edge.

"For obvious reasons." I slammed the bathroom door behind me.

More laughter. "Despite your foul attitude, I will make breakfast for us."

I stood under near-scalding water for a good five minutes. Not cold water. I did not need a cold shower.

This woman had me by the short hairs.

"Bad image, Kaine." My laugh pinged back at me from the tiled walls.

If I ignored requests for help from her false hauntings, my reputation would suffer. If I joined in her scheme, my integrity would go down the crapper. Along with my celibacy.

My eyes in the mirror looked only tired while I shaved. Not angry or worried. Certainly not like eyes thinking of the shock between us when our skin touched.

The razor nicked my chin. *Shaving requires attention, Kaine.* The styptic pencil stung me out of my funk.

She'd trapped me. First order of business: escape. If it meant an all-night session finding the exact combination of runes and spells to turn her into sea-foam like Andersen's *Little Mermaid*, good.

The image didn't satisfy me as much as I expected.

Martin closed for the weekend at five o'clock. Good Friday marked his and his partner's annual Easter pilgrimage to Martin's mother's house in Watseka.

"I'll be back Tuesday morning bearing pierogi. Mom says you need fattening up."

I gave Coco and Scout farewell belly rubs without replying. Martin jingled their leashes and the dogs slurped my hands before jumping up and dancing around his legs.

"And don't tell me I shouldn't discuss you with Mom." He snapped the leashes on the dogs' collars. "She says you're fascinating but too skinny."

"Thank your mother for me." I didn't know what a pierogi

was, but I'd have to eat it even if it tasted like liver-stuffed haggis.

———

I walked to Oak Woods Cemetery.

Crowds thronged Hyde Park in this gorgeous weather. No one glanced at me, thanks to the striped button-down shirt I'd used to camouflage the upper half of my blacks.

I kept a steady pace block after block, the rhythm shutting out the world around me. The car was a hindrance on these days. I used the walk to give myself the time and space to prepare.

By the second mile, my breathing was louder in my ears than the traffic on the streets. The everyday part of my brain took over all the outer needs: stopping at lights, waiting for cars, turning in the correct direction at corners.

When I reached the cemetery gates, I was a hollow vessel for bridging this world and the next. I hopped the fence, set a barrier between the soles of my shoes and the earth, and surveyed the territory.

Good Friday never failed me, especially when it fell during Passover, like this year. Not a human to be seen for a dozen acres, despite the multitudinous obstacles of grave markers, trees, statues, and family mausoleums.

Spring covered everything. Pale green needles tipped the ends of the pine branches. A haze of leaf buds covered the willows. The scent of damp earth rose from the grass. Whip-poor-wills called to each other, but the nightingales weren't active yet.

I inhaled all of it—whoa, plus a skunk out looking for love. Skunks will ruin anyone's ode to spring. All right, interlude over. Time to work. I climbed over bushes and through headstone mazes to one of the sections with graves at least a hundred years old.

Cemeteries this size necessitated an alteration to the ritual. I found a square memorial stone tall enough to set my messenger bag on and short enough for my hand to reach the bottom with ease. I'd been blindsided by old, powerful entities before. Broken bones are not the goal of an exorcism.

When I'd arranged the bag to my satisfaction, I reached inside myself, grasped my power, and crop-dusted a two-hundred-fifty-yard semicircle in front of me.

First I called the kids I'd sensed the other day. They raised themselves through the grass at my feet and I caught the essentials of their souls. Two victims of the 1918 flu epidemic. Brother and sister, eight and nine years old.

"Good zombie act, Matthew. Was it your idea or Helen's?"

They stared at me, wide-eyed. Guess they'd expected me to scream and run.

"Helen's," the boy said.

"I thought it was neat." His sister sounded like him.

"It was. It's time to go home now."

Helen shook her ringleted head. "We can't."

A tear shimmered down Matthew's translucent cheek. "We left Mama alone. She didn't have anybody but us. We tried to stay with her, but we were too sick."

I smiled. "Someone said you only had one chance, didn't they? And you missed it so now you're stuck here forever?"

Helen dug the toe of her shoe into the grass. "We tried to get back to Mama. We really did. But we can't go past the iron fence."

"They didn't know about me. Watch." I drew the Yellow Brick Road for them.

Their eyes got even bigger. "Are you the Wizard?" Matthew said.

"Mama used to read from Mr. Baum's book to us every night," Helen said.

I opened a doorway at the end of the shimmering golden path. "She's waiting to read it to you again."

"She is?" Matthew hesitated.

Helen stepped onto the path. She gasped and pointed. "There she is! Mama! Mama, it's us! We're coming!" She grabbed her brother's hand and they winked out a moment later.

Chapter Nineteen

A dozen ghosts crowded in behind them. Two dozen. Unlike the kids, some of these adults flinched when they neared me, but I waved them through the doorway I'd created. A blubbery old ghost glided past me eating a phantom Twinkie and I nearly lost my composure.

The wind whistled behind me, which it shouldn't be able to do on a calm night. I spun around and blocked a baseball bat. A spectral one, or so much for my recently healed arm.

The bat-wielder cursed me in Spanish. Called me a pedophile and shouted about how he was going to make me pay for what I did to his son.

I clamped my hands on either side of his head and forced him to understand that I wasn't the priest who abused his kid. He walked the path dragging his son's baseball bat. He would be okay.

When everyone had passed through the doorway, I closed it and blinked several times to adjust to the twilight. Three pairs of hands burst through the dirt over three neglected graves. Their bodies followed, too fast for zombies. These weren't kids playing Hallowe'en pranks. Besides, no true zombies lurked in Chicago.

I dissolved the path and drew in my net. Concentrated it in the fifty-yard area before me. Reached into my bag, chose mandrake and holy water, and blew some of the powdered mandrake root at them first. They dissolved into bubbling green slime.

Huh. Not the usual reaction.

Two more attacked from my left. I flung enough mandrake to slime them and put my back against a willow trunk.

Nothing to my left or right now. Nothing in front of me. Should've brought a flashlight. The dead have their own luminescence, but the city doesn't install streetlights in cemeteries.

"All right, who's sending camouflaged dead guys to piss me off?" I altered my net to perceive more than the standard cemetery denizens.

A calico cat rubbed against my legs. Shit, I'd forgotten about the qarinah from my scouting trip the other day. I didn't need an ancient Arabic succubus in its cat form attaching itself to me. The woman in my apartment was already too much.

"Furry seductress, leave me alone or tonight you'll be in Hell eating demon-head fruit and swimming in fire."

The cat hissed and vanished. The threat of demon-head fruit might have worked. I didn't want to imagine what it must taste like. I'd have to take care of her soon, though. Succubi are deadly parasites.

Where was the big, unusual thing I'd sensed here last time? My net wasn't giving me anything. Could it be hiding from whatever created those insta-dissolve fake zombies? I pushed my awareness west, north, and east.

Found it. Lurking to the northeast.

I shut out green-goo stink, grass, damp earth, nightingales, crickets.

Big and nasty. A demon. I cracked my figurative knuckles. Maybe this was Xav's murderer, following the tasty trail of my hate and rage all the way from Rome.

"Come get some, motherfucker."

Twenty yards ahead I spotted two points of light about ten feet off the ground. Purplish, like white cloth under a black light.

No red-ass I knew of had black-light eyes. The regular bastards I'd already thrown downstairs must be sending minions.

A crack. Like a sledgehammer on stone. Another.

This was no minion. It was a major player. Oh, yes, come to Papa Denis.

A slow fusillade of cracks. The eyes came closer.

"What's the matter?" I added extra ridicule to my voice. "Red ass too fat to move?"

A rumble. No, a growl, if stone could growl. *Pound—pound —pound.* The ground shook.

I drew kenaz—the torch, the controlled fire—above my head. The sideways *V* burst into sunlit gold, illuminating everything around me.

And I saw it. The demon had slithered inside a ten-foot stone angel. The cracks were the animated stone lumbering toward me. Its eyes flamed dark purple. Its wings flapped in slow motion. Pieces of granite flaked off with each movement.

Archangel Michael, get your sword and shield down here now. Please.

I rerouted the power into a barrier, creating a seven-by-four-foot sphere around myself by the time the angel got within wing length. The demon inside swung the statue's right arm in a backhand that cracked against my shield. Icy blue sparks sizzled up the stone.

The carved mouth didn't alter its sad expression, but the

demon inside bellowed and stepped back. More stone chipped off. The other arm came up. Chunks from the shoulder joint showered the grass. I splayed my fingers to concentrate the power at eye level, holy water still gripped in the last two fingers of my right hand.

Its left arm smashed into my barrier with another shower of blue sparks. Bastard would've decapitated me without the protection.

Michael, haul it.

"We're waiting for you, Kaine." The stone voice rippled the ground. Tiny leaves fluttered around me.

"I'm right here, asswipe." I palmed the holy water. My flute remained quiet in my bag.

Another earth-pounding step.

"Die, Kaine." Its right wing flipped forward ten times faster than before. I stood my ground. The shield held.

It tried the backhand swipe again with the same wing. "I'll roast your balls in Hell." The carved stone wing fell off its back and shattered. Shrapnel sliced my face.

"Shit." The fucker had recalibrated the granite's molecular structure to my shield's energy. My eyes slid back into my head. I pictured the structure of my energy's physical components, and like a scientist experimenting with chemicals I amplified the tight crystalline structure of snow and buffered it with extra shadows.

Smash. Sizzle.

I saw the world again. "You're outmatched, red-ass."

"I'll rip off your cock and ream you with it, Kaine!"

"Always said you big boys were dickless. Have to cut it off to get the promotion?"

I dropped the shield and doused him with holy water.

He screamed like a girl. The stone hands clawed the carved

face and chest. Two fingers snapped off. "I will have vengeance!"

"*Adjurámus te per Déum vívum, per Déum vérum, per Déum sanctum*," I shouted, the words coming faster and faster. He cursed me and screamed and cursed again. Inventive curses. I reached the crucial words.

"Your brother's going to pay for this, Kaine!"

What did he say? The ritual faltered on my tongue. My concentration on the shield stuttered. His remaining wing whipped around and clipped me on the side of my head.

I staggered. The wing fell in a heap next to me. I put his words out of my mind and finished the last sentence. The cemetery spun. I couldn't get my back against the willow trunk. I grabbed two fistfuls of my fire from the perpetual flame of rage in my heart and smashed them directly in his face.

Silence. The angel statue rocked back on its heels and crashed to the ground. The arms broke into seven feet of rubble on either side of the torso. The legs split into a dozen sections, toes pinging off nearby gravestones.

The head rolled to my feet, stone eyes empty. The fractured mouth sneered up at me. The ground twisted. I fell sideways and cracked the side of my head against its granite cheek. White light blinded me.

Woke a few minutes later—five? Ten? Knew I hadn't been out long because the twilight color had barely changed. Drums and hammers beat in my head. My eyes wouldn't focus, but sensation returned: shards of ex-angel statue bit into my hands and knees.

In measured intervals I sat up. Something dripped onto my left hand. I raised my hand—slowly, slowly—and sniffed. Blood. Slowly, slowly, I kept my hand moving until it touched the side of my head.

More light stabbed my skull. My fingers crept along,

measuring the gash. Three inches, as far as I could tell. My blood was soaking my collar and hair.

The ground still swayed. I stayed on my heels listening to the percussion in my head until the world settled enough for me to try getting to my feet.

I groped for the willow trunk. Remembered my messenger bag. Swallowed hard, bent my knees, waved my hand—slowly, slowly—until I banged my knuckles on the leather. Closed and buckled the flap. Inched the strap over my shoulder. Slid upright against the trunk.

Closed my eyes. The percussion cranked up the volume two hundred percent. Opened them. Had to get out of here. If anyone living heard the statue crash they'd be coming to investigate.

I pushed away—slowly, slowly—from the trunk. Didn't know if I was swaying or the ground was tilting or both. Took one step. Jarred my whole body. Took a smaller step. Better.

"Put—one—foot—in—front—of—the—other..."

I sounded drunk. Off-key. Wasn't Christmas anyway.

Another step. Slow and easy. A third. A fourth.

"Put—one—foot—in—front..."

I clutched gravestones, monuments, trees to keep moving. No lights from outside yet. Nobody and nothing else in here but me. The drummers eased up a bit.

Take five, guys. Gotta get home.

It would take me an hour or more to walk home like this. Couldn't take a bus or the L. At least I didn't have to leave my car here.

I reached the first corner. A taxi passed. Taxi. Yes. I leaned against the crosswalk pole and stuck out my hand. Closed my eyes. This time the hammers slunk away. Drums stayed. Bastards.

God-awful loud horn. I opened my eyes. A taxi waited at the curb.

I fell in and closed the door. Voice slurred when I gave my address. Driver gave me a knowing look in the rearview mirror.

"Good idea, buddy. Never drive home drunk."

Yeah, yeah. Thanks for the lecture. Good thing the night was overcast. He wouldn't be so friendly if he saw all this blood.

I sat forward so I wouldn't stain the seat. Didn't need him giving the bloody drunk's address to the cops. Had enough trouble.

As soon as I didn't have to work to keep upright everything crashed in on me.

Xav, you can't be in Hell. You can't be in the demons' power. You were God's perfect student. You offed two hundred seventy-six demons. You have to be in Heaven. You have to be.

"Hey, buddy, wake up. You're home. Twelve and a quarter."

I counted out thirteen bucks—slowly—and paid him.

He tucked the bills into a lockbox under the meter. "Sleep it off."

"Yeah. Thanks."

The five steps to my apartment house door were Mt. Everest. Took me four tries to fit my key into my lock, only because I used both hands on the fourth try.

Inside at last. I leaned against the closed door. Emma stood at the stove. She said something. The drums masked it.

Bed. Needed sleep. I pushed off from the kitchen table. She squawked at me. I kept moving. Made it through the doorway without falling. There. Bed.

Messenger bag.

I clamped my left hand on the brass headboard. Slid the strap off—slowly—until the bag rested on the floor against the wall.

And fell across the bed.

Chapter Twenty

"Wake up. Wake up! What have you been doing?"

Fingers pried open my eyes. I batted at the arms attached to them. "Light hurts. Go away." Pushy woman.

"Your eyes are dilated. You are bleeding. What has happened?"

"Helping ghosts move on. The Plan. One was strong, 's all."

The bed sprang down and up and her footsteps ran away. I concentrated on not falling onto the floor because she'd turned my bed into a seesaw.

The footsteps returned. This time she didn't make the bed bounce.

"I have turned off the oven so the food will not burn. Open your eyes."

Her voice was different. Still deep but sharper.

"'S matter?"

Her hands came around my ribs and heaved. The world flipped over. I pushed at her. "Stop."

"No. You must stay awake." She heaved again. "*Merda.* There is much blood on you. What have you fought?"

"Angel."

"What?" Her voice jumped an octave.

"Like your voice the other way. Low. Rich. Cream in coffee. Go back to before."

"Stop this foolishness." She heaved again and I put both my hands against the mattress to keep from falling off. My head banged against the wall. A ragged groan came out of my mouth.

"There. You are sitting up. Do not fall over. I will be right back."

I didn't want to fall over. Vertical was nice.

Something wet and stinging attacked my head.

"Hey!" My eyes focused for a second. "Go away."

"Silence. Sit still." She tilted rubbing alcohol against a washcloth and wiped my injury again.

"Ow."

She inspected my head. "The bleeding has stopped. This is good. I have removed tiny pieces of stone from your wound. Bah. I missed one."

She prodded my temple. I jerked away but she held up a gray fleck pinched between her fingernails. "This is the last."

The drummers took their places again when the alcohol sting faded. I closed my eyes.

"No." She tapped me on both cheeks. "Do you not understand it is essential for you to stay awake?"

"Quit ordering me around."

"Good. Your words are not as slurred. I hope you are not thirsty because I will not give you water. I do not like to be vomited upon."

I tried to laugh but it turned my head into a Shake 'N Bake bag. "The world doesn't revolve around you."

"Several hundred thousand people would disagree. They are all dead now, but death does not change the facts."

"...Huh?" Her voice had gone furry at the edges.

"Do not try to lie down." She hauled me up by the armpits. "Tell me what you did to cause this injury."

"Bossy."

"You will thank me tomorrow. Speak."

"Told you. It's The Plan."

She smacked the mattress with her left hand. "You have said this twice, but you have not explained its meaning."

"None of your business." I must've frowned because one of the drummers moved his jam session into my forehead.

"Stop closing your eyes." She flicked my ear. Not the one beneath the gash. "I am not above using guilt to achieve my goals. I saved you from drowning yourself in whisky and pills. Thus you will tell me what you mean by this plan."

Her voice faded. I tried to blink. Dark. Fucking demon's hands were holding down my eyelids. Exorcism hadn't worked. Gotta kick his stone ass back to Hell. "*Váde sátana, invéntor et magíster ómnis falláciae.*"

A hand covered my mouth. "What are you doing? You cannot exorcise me."

I recognized the voice. This time my eyelids stayed up when I opened my eyes. "Emma."

A pinched look faded from her face. "It is about time."

"I kicked the red-ass back downstairs."

She huffed. "This conversation is like listening to a radio through static. Do not become distracted again. Tell me of this banishing and this plan you speak of with capital letters." She took my hands in hers.

I stared at our hands on her lap. "We're touching. Where's the shock I always feel?"

She raised her eyebrows. "I do not know why it did not occur tonight. We will discuss this later. What is this plan, you stubborn priest?"

"If I tell you, will you let me sleep?"

"Yes."

I wanted sleep. "Xavier and I exorcise demons. We help ghosts into the next world. We have the gift. Born with it." I yawned. The drummers changed their rhythm.

She raised an eyebrow. "It is no wonder you became a priest."

I touched the side of my head. "Damn, this hurts. What did you clean it with?"

"This foul-smelling liquid." She held up the rubbing alcohol bottle. "Do you see now why I am keeping you awake? You have damaged your brain."

"Whisky would've been better."

She glared at me with those deep gray eyes. "It is your fault you have chosen to keep no liquor in this apartment." She tapped my cheeks again. "Do not close your eyes."

"Get off my bed. I'm a priest."

"You will be a dead priest if I allow you to sleep so soon after a concussion."

A couple of the drummers had packed up and moved on. "Feeling better."

"Better is all well and good, but your aura disagrees. I am not leaving this bed."

I tried to push her off. Mistake. The bed bucked and tried to throw me.

"Do not contradict me, you obstinate man. Breathe." She put her right hand on my chest. "Now."

I breathed in. Out. In. Out. The world settled.

"Good. Now tell me what you have been doing tonight."

I was too tired to argue. "Went to Oak Woods. Been working my way through all the cemeteries in Chicago."

"You are like a different species of human. Do not spend your life among the dead. You are alive."

I held up my index finger. My arm shook as I lowered the

finger until it touched her collarbone. Forgot the point I wanted to make in the muted burst of snow and deep water that coursed through me.

"Felt the shock."

"As did I. You are returning to your senses, which is perhaps why, but you are also distracted. Do you ever concentrate on the task at hand?"

"God, woman, you're worse than my Novice Master."

"He did a poor job if you are still like this so many years later. Tell me of the cemetery."

It was less effort to tell her than to keep fighting. She interrupted once to ask what "pedophile" meant, then made her spitting noise. She didn't interrupt again until the stone angel was a pile of lifeless rocks around me.

"I am impressed. Not many holy men could best such a demon. If I had favors to bestow, I would make you a *pomeshchik*."

I wasn't sure I heard her through the last few drummers. "Did you give me a compliment?"

"Do not let it go to your head." She put her right hand against my forehead and opened my left eye with the other. "You are still dilated. We must keep you awake. Tell me the parts of your story you have omitted."

"Miss Marple would be able to sleuth her way to an answer. You disappoint me."

"What do you mean?" She touched the back of her hand to my forehead. "You are not feverish, so it is not delirium."

My mouth smiled but the rest of my face was too wiped to join it. "You need to brush up on modern literature. Famous fictional detectives, in this case."

She frowned. "Do not confuse me when I am concerned for you. Tell me what you are still hiding from me. Now."

I wished I could unhear the bastard's words. "None of your business."

She put her hands on her hips. The flowered dress showed off those hips well.

"I tell you it is my business because we are partners and I am concerned about you. Also I may be able to help. I have much knowledge of spirits which may be of use to you."

"Because you're not human."

"And what is your point? I was human once. I have an excellent memory of what it is like to be human."

I laughed. "Ow. Shit. Don't make me laugh. At least you admit it. You're a freaky tentacle thing able to change into whatever suits you."

My sight—no, my Sight—must've been improving because furious red exploded through the concerned-healer green in her aura. I hadn't seen her aura since I came home. I think.

Her right hand gripped my shirt so hard two buttons popped off. "I am a freak? I am a thing? You ungrateful, narrow-minded, egotistical priest." Spittle from the *P* hit my cheek. "You are wrapped so tightly in your condescension and celibacy you have cut off the blood to your reasoning. *Idi na hui.*" She flicked my shirt off her fingers but a second later grabbed it again. "No. You will not be fucking yourself. I will be fucking you."

I backed away—to nowhere. I was already sitting against the headboard. Her smile grew hard. Shit, so did my dick. The woman's power was an aphrodisiac. I drew on every shred of control still in my possession... and she let me go.

"There. All men rise to a challenge. You are indeed a man under the clothing of a priest." She pried my eyelids open. "Your pupils are almost back to their correct size."

"You manipulative bitch."

She touched her finger to my lips. "When you are angry

your hair sparks like golden fireworks. I enjoy the sight but I do not like to be called names."

God, my head hurt. But it was more like a migraine now than drums and hammers. An improvement.

"Back off. My self-control is shot to hell already. Are you trying to seduce me?" I replayed what I'd just said. "Where the hell is my internal censor?"

"It has run away from you because you make too much work for it." She studied me. "Your aura is returning to its normal colors. My idea succeeded. This is one more reason you need me as your partner."

She kissed me. Snow again, and river water, and a flood of bright pink. The anal-retentive part of me brought up the aura file but it shouldn't have bothered. The rest of me knew exactly what this shade of pink meant. I shut away the headache and matched her kiss.

Her tongue pushed against my lips. I opened them and her tongue touched mine. She leaned into me. I put my arms around her. She straddled my hips, our mouths locking tighter. She still wasn't wearing anything beneath her flowered dress.

I pulled back. "Stop." My voice had no strength. "Stop."

Multicolored haze surrounded us, filled her eyes. Her lips, always the color of port wine, were darker and slightly swollen. I reached up to pull her against my waiting mouth—and stopped myself.

She caught her breath. "It is cruel of you to obstruct this. You want me, do you not?"

I recited the formula for cataloguing inventory in the computer at Dog-Eared. The pheromones dissipated.

Emma slid off me. "*Pah.* I am sick of sexless priests. It was not always so. As recompense you will tell me the words the demon said of you to make you lose your irritating self-control."

"Not me. Xavier. He said Xavier would pay for me kicking his red ass back to Hell."

Chapter Twenty-One

The headache jackhammered. I shoved my fists into my temples. "Emma, what the hell are you? Nobody but Lisa should be able to worm information out of me so fast."

She wriggled behind me and massaged my shoulders. "The pain in your head will ease sooner if these muscles are not so tight." Her thumbs pressed the area above my shoulder blade. "Who is this Lisa with skills like mine?"

Ripples of tension eased off my back and out of my body. The jackhammer downshifted. "Lisa is a sixty-year-old nun who taught us ancient languages and the unvarnished version of Church history."

"You become human when you speak of her."

I flinched away from her knuckles. "What am I supposed to be when I'm not talking about her?"

She trapped me by the collarbone and worked the same muscle harder. "You are a block of marble with a perpetual frown. Do not move even if this hurts." She moved her knuckles around my other shoulder blade. "Why do you not assume this demon lied to you?" The knuckles pressed deeper. "Do not become tighter. You will undo my work."

My headache was fading. Made it easier to think, not knee-jerk react. "Because... yeah, there. Ow. Keep it there. Because of the way he said it."

"Explain."

"He said he'd take out his anger on Xav the same way he promised to torture me when he got me in Hell. Like it was fact, not an empty threat."

"I have not yet encountered a demon, which is surprising now I turn my mind to it. They appear to be obsessed with torture. They also appear to be angrier than you, which is a distinction not to be overlooked."

"Stop laughing at me."

"I am not." She worked my shoulders with both hands. "Let us discuss this demon's words. Did your brother commit sins which the Catholic Church would deem worthy of its Hell?" Her hands clamped down. "I said do not make your muscles tighter. Are you not capable of dispassion?"

"Not about Xav."

A dramatic sigh blew my hair into my face. "Then I will be rational for us both. Tell me how your brother died."

"No. Not tonight."

"But—"

"I said no."

She drummed her fingers on my shoulders. "Fine."

I turned my head enough to see her face. "You said 'fine' like you were really saying 'you pig-headed bastard.'"

"Now the priest is an expert on women?" She leaned against my back. "I am tired. You have caused me to worry."

Hearing the word "tired" made me yawn. "Can I sleep now, arbiter of my health?"

She yawned into my shoulder. "Your aura has regained its normal shade. You may thank me in the morning."

"Get out of my bed then." My eyes closed. My chin hit my chest.

"You cannot sleep sitting up in this fashion." She tugged me flatter on the bed.

"Stop manhandling me."

"Be silent."

The headache decreased to the annoyance level of a kid kicking the back of my seat at the movies. My legs flopped over. My knees banged into Emma's.

"Mm. Sorry."

"If my skin is bruised, you will be required to make amends." She dragged my legs back onto the mattress.

The bed embraced me. I sank deeper. She lay next to me, one arm across my chest. I tried to tell her to get off. I managed "Get."

———

Ringing. Knocking. I stuffed the corners of my pillow into my ears, but the repeating noises seeped through.

I yelled, "Just a minute."

No headache. The bed didn't try to buck me off. I grabbed for the sheet. I got a handful of flowered dress.

"Mmgrrh." Emma burrowed into the bedspread.

Holy shit, we both must've dropped like rocks last night. I pushed her legs off mine and slid out of bed.

The knocking started again. "I said I'm coming!" The mirror over my dresser was not complimentary: I looked like the end of an all-night drinking binge. Blood stiffened my hair and collar. Random gouges decorated my shirt—the second ruined shirt in a week. I unfastened the plastic collar—also blood-stained—and tossed it on the dresser. My wrinkled pants certainly looked like I'd slept in them. My slow fingers were still unbuttoning the remains of the shirt when I unlocked the door.

Monsignor Powell stood on my threshold. His jaw dropped, as far as I could tell. I'd feel sorry for the chinless bastard if he wasn't such a douchenozzle.

"What the hell did you wake me up for?" The last button gave way and I yanked off the shredded shirt.

"You were in bed at nine o'clock in the morning?" he squeaked.

"It's Saturday. Isn't it?" I bunched up the shirt. "What business is it of yours how late I sleep?"

"If I had my way, you would be defrocked before tonight's Mass."

"Life's full of disappointments. Tell me why you're violating my privacy before I slam this door in your face."

His neck above its pristine collar turned red, the color climbing up to his Adam's apple between one breath and the next. The progression reminded me of those grade-school science experiments with a stick of celery and food coloring in a glass of water.

"His Excellency sent me to drag you, if necessary, to his office to discuss your recent actions and their impact on the Church local and Church global, as we have already told you in several phone calls."

He took a breath. His gaze shifted from my face to something over my left shoulder. Until this moment, I'd always thought someone's eyes bugging out only happened in cartoons.

"You require more rest." Emma's voice, sleepy but commanding. "Return to bed."

"You—she—how—"

"None of your business. Remind your boss that I don't report to him. If he has a problem he can take it up with my Vicar General in Rome."

I closed the door firmly but didn't slam it.

When I turned around, I understood Powell's uncharacteristic speechlessness. Emma stood in the doorway between the kitchen and living room with my blanket wrapped around herself from neck to knees.

"You look like you're naked underneath the blanket."

She opened it wide. "You know I am not."

I choked on laughter. "I wish you would've flashed Powell. His head would've exploded."

"He has never before seen a woman in a wrinkled dress?"

"Not since his mother got up in the middle of the night to nurse him, I expect. You don't see the illusion?"

She rewrapped herself and stood in the spot between the living room and bedroom where the dresser mirror was visible.

"I suppose it is possible this creates an image of nakedness," she said, "if one has the mind of a fifteen-year-old boy."

I shuffled past her into the bathroom. The light was less painful than I expected. The gash on my head wasn't.

"I'm taking a shower." I closed the door.

"Manners of a goat," I heard through the keyhole.

Hot water and soap returned me to humanity. I squashed all thoughts of the highly flavored report Powell was no doubt giving his master. Nothing I could do about it. Nothing I cared to do about it.

The shampoo stung my head injury, but at least no more blood poured out. My clothes had deflected the other attacks and shrapnel enough to leave only scrapes and small gashes on the rest of me. Eh. I'd had worse.

Shaving without a single nick completed my return to the living. I covered myself with the bath towel before I opened the door, but Emma was making noises in the kitchen. Safe. I threw on jeans and a T-shirt and headed toward the noises.

"Good morning." Emma kept stirring whatever was in the

pot on the stove. "I have discarded last night's food. I dislike poor management, but it could not be helped. Please incur your next head injury before I begin cooking a meal."

"I'll post my schedule on the fridge."

She eyeballed me over her left shoulder. "What is the strange expression, priest?"

My cheeks felt stiff but it could've been fight aftermath.

Emma laughed. "You are smiling. You cannot tell?"

My face fell back into its usual scowl as soon as she said it. "I'm going to work."

"You are not. You will drink this coffee and eat this omelet."

"We're not having this discussion." I reached for my car keys on their hook by the door and grabbed air.

Emma was paying way too much attention to the process of adding milk to the coffee.

"Give me my car keys."

"No." She turned off the gas. "You will not leave until you eat."

"Give. Me. My. Keys."

"I said no. If you refuse to take care of yourself I will take on the responsibility." She turned and faced me. "Your eyes have the look of one deprived of too much sleep. Your skin is the wrong color."

"Have I turned green or purple overnight?"

"You are pale and... What is the word in English which means ugly old woman?"

This was a question out of left field. "Crone? Hag?"

"The last one. You are haggard." She moved my hair aside. "The injury, however, is not infected. You are welcome."

I took hold of her wrist. "Personal space."

She huffed. "A ridiculous idea invented by people afraid to touch one another. This injury needs protection. Do you possess those thin strips of bandages which doctors use?"

"What? No. I'm fine. I've had worse. Where did you hide my keys?"

She looked down on me from her two-inch height advantage. "I will tell you after breakfast."

Part of me was pissed, but the deep winter snow in me was sinking in her dark blue river.

Her fingers stroked my hair. "Mountaintop snow. It brings to mind many things long past."

Shivers coursed through me at her touch. At her voice. I realized I still held her wrist. Her skin was smooth under my fingers. I pulled myself partway out of the river.

"You're not going to take over my life."

"Then run it properly."

"I was running it fine until you barged in. Stop messing with my hair."

"More of this personal space?" Her voice had a different edge to it.

"You're pushy. You're high maintenance. You act like you're a queen, and I'm your vassal. You—"

She closed the gap between us. Her closeness raised goose bumps on my arm. She shivered.

"Can you not resist the touch of one woman, priest?"

"I'm a demon-killer, not a boy toy."

She didn't answer.

"That's not enough? What else do you want?"

She opened those dark red lips. "I want—"

I kissed her.

Chapter Twenty-Two

Her lips moved under mine. *I shouldn't be doing this.* She tasted of snow and something else, a spice I couldn't place. Her fingers tangled in my hair and she pulled our bodies together.

And dug her thumbnail into my unhealed demon-gash.

"Shit!" I broke away from her, small bursts of white light dancing across my vision.

"*Merda.*" She dragged me into the bathroom. "Stand still. *Tch.*" She pressed a towel to my head.

"Not so hard." I forced myself not to flinch. The pressure sent more stabs of white through my head. "There's a tube of Neosporin on the middle shelf." I pointed to the mirror above the sink.

"Hold this." She pressed my hand on the towel where hers had been. I kept my eyes on the opposite wall. The room tilted, but nowhere near as bad as last night's seesaw.

She pulled my hand away. The towel fell. Cold goop slathered along my scalp.

"It's a good thing I have a high pain tolerance. Did the bleeding stop?"

"I would not have smeared this ointment on you if blood was seeping from your head." She inspected her work. "Why do you stare at the wall?"

"The floor was moving."

She looked at her feet. "I am having no trouble."

It was even more disorienting to talk to her using only peripheral vision. I slid my eyes over to her face. The floor stayed still.

"It's better."

She washed her hands. "Now will you eat without argument?"

"Yeah."

After the second bite of the omelet—I tasted Gruyère and bacon and fresh mushrooms—I said, "How did you learn to cook so well after being imprisoned for seven hundred years? Eight months shouldn't be long enough to acquire skills like this."

She gave me an arch look over her coffee cup. "You have much to learn about compliments."

"And you're high maintenance. Look, I admit it: the omelet and the coffee are both better than I could make, and Xav and I are pretty decent cooks. Grandmère did her best to pass her skills down to us. She used a wooden spoon across our knuckles or to the backs of our heads to make us remember important steps."

Emma giggled. "It is difficult to imagine you as a small boy under the tutelage of your grandmother. It will complete the picture if you tell me she was less than five feet tall and thin as a sapling."

"Nope. She was six foot one and could split and stack wood faster than either of us. We only bested her at wood-chopping after we turned seventeen."

Emma cut another fluffy piece of omelet. "There. You are smiling again. Do you now remember how it feels?"

"Maybe."

She gave me a look like she was counting to ten. "It is not only me who should accept the label of high maintenance."

I swallowed before I choked.

She didn't bring up the cemetery again until we were cleaning the dishes.

"It is weighing on you, what this *súka* demon said last night."

I set the plate I'd been drying on the counter. "Looks like it'll be sunny today, don't you think?"

Her lips pinched and we finished the dishes in silence.

Neither of us mentioned the kiss.

———

I didn't need to go into work. Martin always had plenty of back-end tasks for me to earn my keep, but any Dog-Eared project could wait until after the holiday. It was me who needed the bookstore today.

Martin had created a reading corner several months back separating the romance section from the rest of the store. When a few of his regulars complained he was segregating their favorite books, Martin pointed out the many shelves of romances. They took up the entire back half of the store. He hung framed covers on the walls, added an antique dresser with a Keurig (a dollar a cup) and cookies (free), and pitched it as an alcove of dreams.

Thus my never-ending cataloguing and shelving of romances.

But Martin also had a small, glassed-in bookcase of rare religious texts, demonology treatises, obscure cult lore, and illustrated manuscripts. Thanks to me. He sold one every couple of weeks and regularly covered half the rent from the proceeds.

I'd found a dozen volumes at an estate sale a few weeks back and hadn't priced or shelved them yet. Today I locked myself in, turned on the reading lamp, and settled in an armchair with the three oldest books.

The 1735 *Testament of Solomon* would pay Martin's rent for two months, despite its water-damaged back cover.

Mice and worms had done a number on the edition of Michaelis's *Marvelous History*. I could read it only because I knew much of it by heart. It might bring in fifty bucks from a forgiving collector.

The *Dictionnaire Infernal* was the one I wanted to dive into. It was a pre-1863 printing without the demon illustrations, but I didn't need them. I'd seen enough of the bastards in real life. This would bring in a chunk of money. Sorry I couldn't unearth an illustrated copy for you, Martin. It'd fetch double the chunk.

Two hours later I had a short list of male demons with enough power to inhabit a granite angel and try to kill me with it. The real trouble was that powerful demons sired powerful offspring. My short list would only be useful if I could track down how many slimy little gits their females had popped out. Since my "friend" inside the angel statue had definitely been male, I could at least exclude female demons from my search. It cut the number of potentials by a third.

Demon sex. Think about it too long and there isn't enough brain bleach in the world to erase the mental images.

Chapter Twenty-Three

E mma was hunched over the computer when I let myself into the apartment close to two o'clock.

"You are back. Good. I am hungry. There is a Vietnamese restaurant whose food I wish to try."

"No. Eating out is extravagant. Besides, there's a pile of notes in my bag I have to organize."

The laptop closed with a snap. I unpacked the nonexorcist section of my backpack and spread my bookstore research on the kitchen table.

Emma's footsteps stopped at the kitchen doorway. "I am not a domestic."

"Mm."

"Do you hear me? I enjoy cooking, but I have not taken it on as a permanent task."

There. A name two-thirds of the way down the list clicked with the name gnawing at the back of my brain. A demon named Crocell had spawned at least thirteen offspring that I knew of. I tore the last page off the legal pad I'd been using and started a family tree on the fresh page.

"Denis. You are not listening. You need food. I wish to go out."

I stopped at the fifth demon-spawn's name. "I'm trying to figure out who the cemetery demon was and if he was lying about Xav."

I had it. Ethraum. Brother's name... I knew this... Ergraum.

"Does this mean you are going to make lunch for us? You must eat."

"I. Am. Working. You don't want to cook? Fine. No one's making you stay here."

I studied the names again, seeking a connection hovering just out of reach.

The door slammed.

The connection clicked. "Twins."

I tripped over the table leg getting to the laptop. I wasted an hour slogging through a metric ton of nonsense. Too much crap on the Net had nothing to do with actual demons. God save me from adolescents who think RPG-style demonic claptrap is "cool."

Finally I gave up and called Lisa. I paced the apartment, living room, kitchen, bedroom, lather, rinse, repeat while the phone rang and rang. Come on, Lisa, pick up. Don't be teaching a late class.

Click. "Blessed Holy Saturday to you, Father Kaine." She sounded out of breath.

"Oh, yeah, it is. I forgot."

"Saint Teresa help us. Denis, get your scrawny butt into church once in a while. You could even say a Mass for the good of your soul."

"You know nothing will help my soul. Why are you breathing at me like a Level One sex offender?"

A snort. "I'll dedicate tonight's Vigil Mass against your millennia in Purgatory. When I saw it was you on my caller ID,

I had to run to a private place to take the call. Easter weekend is a big event for clergy, remember? Our schedule is pretty full."

"Should I apologize for getting you out of Father Stewart's Special Holy Saturday Life of Christ Meditation? 'And the Lorrrrd spake this worrrrd to the Virrrrgin Marrrry...'"

A stifled choking noise.

"I can keep going. My seminary class voted me the Best Stewart Imitation Award. The prize was a pair of earplugs."

"Stop it, you reprobate." She gasped and coughed. "Why are you calling?"

"I need your help." I gave her a recap of yesterday in the cemetery, pacing all the while.

"Quit being a mother hen," I said after she first made me list my injuries, then my symptoms, then my state of health at this moment. "I'm not dead and nothing's broken."

"Except your head."

"Nah. It's too dense."

"From your lips to God's ear." Her voice switched from super-nanny to all-business. "You didn't call me to make my hair turn even grayer."

"Right. When I trapped this purple-eyed bastard in the exorcism rite, he said—" I stopped in front of the framed photo of Xav and me at Ordination. "He said Xav would pay for what I was doing."

More silence on the other end. Then, "Oh."

"I spent most of the day buried in research. You got a pen?"

"No. I'll remember it."

"You know what fucked-up spelling demon names have. Get a pen and paper." I heard myself. "Sorry, Lisa. I'm stressed."

"Understandably." Air swooshed over her voice. "I'm heading back to my room. Don't talk for a minute until I get inside and close my door."

I turned my back to the photo and sat at the coffee table to scribble demonic attributes next to Crocell's name while I waited. Crossed off a couple. Added a few more.

"All right." Lisa's voice came without the wind. "I'm at my desk in my five-by-nine-foot sanctuary. Go ahead."

"Got these from the *Dictionnaire Infernal*. Crocell. C-r-o-c-e-l-l. There are at least two alternate spellings, P-r-o-c-e-l-l and C-r-o-k-e-l. From what I already knew plus what I got from the *Dictionnaire*, the *Testament of Solomon*, and the *Marvelous History* we have in the bookstore, plus the *Pseudomonarchia daemonum* online, he sired at least thirteen mini-Crocells over the centuries. Including at least one set of twins."

"Why are you sure it was him in the cemetery?"

"He talked about vengeance. I think I might've offed one of the twins back in Rome during my three-week demon-killing spree."

"Oh."

"Yeah, old lady." I stood and paced some more. Damn, what was wrong with me? I never let a demon fuck with my head like this. "All right, here's where you come in."

No reply.

"Lisa." Short and sharp.

"Yes. I'm here."

"Number one: Xav isn't in Hell."

"Denis…"

I grabbed the phone as tight as I grabbed my power when I pulverized demon ass with it. "Xav was the bright side of our coin. I'm a thousand times more likely to be demon food than Xav. Saint Teresa herself is more likely to roast in Hell than Xav."

"Denis…"

"Xav not roasting is our base of operations. It is immutable."

"…All right."

"You've got the key to the university exorcism library and I can't use the cathedral's library here. I don't exactly get along with the archbishop."

Her voice unstiffened. "Why am I not surprised?"

"Yeah, well, he shouldn't have picked a walking dick for his personal secretary. Can you see what the library has about this demon and any of his spawn? I'm pretty sure the twins' names are E-t-h-r-a-u-m and E-r-g-r-a-u-m."

"Charming. Who knew demons and Hollywood celebrities used similar naming strategies?"

The door opened as I paced into the kitchen. Emma blew in, six feet of bright colors and smelling of fresh air.

"I have decided to cook for us after all. I expect many compliments on my forbearance with you and on my potato pancakes."

Silence on the other end of the phone.

Emma took sour cream and applesauce from the bag. "Well? Why have you not ended your call? I require your assistance to grate the potatoes."

"You have a houseguest?" Lisa finally said.

"Yes. Well, sort of. She won't leave."

"You are wrong," Emma said. "I have left here many times because of your goatlike manners. I have said as much, but you do not attempt to change them."

Lisa laughed loud enough for Emma to hear. "Tell your houseguest she sounds like she can keep you in line. I'll get going on the research."

She hung up.

"Why were you embarrassed to tell the person with whom you spoke about us?"

I set down the phone. "Sister Lisa was on the other end."

"I remember this name from last night. She disapproves of my presence because you are a priest? Religion is a useful tool, but it makes people stuffy." She stared at me with a pointed expression.

"Religion is the tool millions of people learn to worship and fear God. If you thought of anyone but yourself, you'd see the ways religion—" She was right. I sounded stuffy.

Emma laughed. "I am glad you listened to the words coming from your mouth. Too many more and the sour cream would curdle."

I picked up the grater and noticed her for the first time. No more flowered dress. Now she wore a crimson skirt with a bunch of flounces and a ruffled slip thing underneath it, plus a kind of silvery blouse with more ruffles. A men's top hat sized for a kid perched cockeyed on her head except it was crimson with a silver buckle and feathers of both colors. Her long black hair was done up in loops and curls.

"You look like a refugee from a Dickens theater company."

She laughed again. "I enjoy Dickens, especially his book of the war in France. There is much drama and blood in it."

"Why are you dressed for a costume party?" I nicked my thumb on the grater and sucked the injury.

"Potato pancakes are not blood puddings. Please do not confuse the two. Do you approve of these clothes, priest who knows nothing of women?"

I continued shredding the potato while I took her in. She looked exotic and confident and hot. Unfortunately. "Yeah," I said at last.

"You are not always as dense as you appear." She tied a voluminous apron over her finery. "I discovered more than one clothing store called 'vintage' lwhile I was walking away my anger at your rudeness. The proprietors told me of the fashion called 'steampunk' of which I approve. Clothes in this century are dull. Where are the furs, the silks, the gilding?"

She scooped my potato shreds into a bowl and added egg and flour.

"Only the rich can afford those kinds of clothes."

"Then you and I should be of the rich. I would like to see you in steampunk attire. The shops had brocade waistcoats and striped trousers." She looked up at me, her hands still mixing the bowl's contents. "Yes, a bronze waistcoat and a top hat with gears and narrow chains would suit you. I will take you there tomorrow."

I took out the cast-iron frying pan and poured oil into it. "You will not. I am not your doll to dress up and play with."

"*Tch.* There is not enough amusement in your life. This is also why you need me. I like to be amused. I do not enjoy your dour expression. It is on your face now. You wear it too often."

"If you're going to cook, then cook. If you want amusement, you barged into the wrong apartment. Try the grad students across the hall."

She washed her hands and flicked drops of water into the oil. "It is not yet hot enough. Lunch will be some minutes longer. Go away and be dour elsewhere. I will call you when all is ready." She gazed at me over her shoulder. "Unless you would care to watch while I practice retaining my clothes as I change shapes. Seeing a naked woman would be good for your temper."

I turned on my heel and stalked into the living room. Thank God I'd moved my demon research to the coffee table. I fired up the laptop and lost myself in scans of ancient texts.

Chapter Twenty-Four

Close to four p.m. the website got an email. A ghostly child's voice had been crying and pleading every night for four months, but no one could understand its words. Untraceable noises were scaring the other kids.

Son of a bitch. Ninety-five percent chance I knew exactly what caused this haunting.

The ghost's family lived in a nondescript house on the West Side: beige vinyl siding, edged lawn the shade of green you can only achieve with chemicals, Easter decorations in the windows, plastic eggs hanging from strings on the maple tree in the yard.

Pulsing fog the color of dried blood clung to everything.

The door opened as soon as I rang the bell. The haze was thicker in the house. It churned around a stick-thin mother, a weight-lifter father, four kids under fourteen. Two girls wore long-sleeved beige dresses, two boys button-down shirts and beige pants. Who the hell dressed their kids to match the vinyl siding on their house?

I didn't bother to make a show for this one. The ghost haunted the closet of the girls' room. The dead older girl: Daisy. She told me about her father stealing into their room night after night starting on her ninth birthday. She told me how she'd died because he made her bleed so much it wouldn't stop. She stayed in the house afterward to scare him away from her younger sisters.

I created a path of wildflowers for her to pass to the other side. I might be the definition of hard and cynical, but she kissed my tears when I promised to keep her sisters safe. Then she ran along the path, picking flowers up to the moment she passed through the glowing doorway.

The father went to get money while I cleansed the kids' rooms with sage and white candles. The mother wouldn't leave the kids alone with me. Didn't matter. I accepted two hundred bucks from them and went straight to the cops.

The sergeant at the front desk had a standing order to call Detective Rubio whenever I showed up.

"Father Kaine. Come into my sanctum." His head only came up to my chin, but height didn't equal power. A path opened for us through a dozen desks and three times the number of people.

Rubio's office was squeezed into a corner with half a window and an antiquated steam radiator. But it boasted a real door and real privacy.

"Computers, Don. They save trees." I shook my head at the stacks of old files and new printouts on the floor, the windowsill, the filing cabinet, the desk. "In your case, several acres of rainforest."

"Yeah, yeah." He cleared a chair for me. "When they hire me my personal Halle Berry look-alike to scan all this history into the database, I'll think about it. What've you got for me?"

I gave him the names and street address. "Father's using the boys as punching bags. Using the girls for worse. Mother's high half the time. The oldest daughter died four months ago from blood loss. At nine." I clamped my mouth shut before I lost control. Breathed deep. "She said the parents told the other kids she ran away. She liked Scooby-Doo, so she used the TV show for haunting ideas. She dialed it up every time the father came after her younger sisters. Finally rattled him enough to contact my website."

Don was already plowing through the stack at his right elbow. "You have a website now? About time." He pulled out a thin manila folder and rescued the pile above it before it crashed to the floor. "Got it. Neighbor reported bruises on the ten-year-old boy last month. Saw him out in the driveway playing basketball. Social services got to it two weeks ago. House spotless, kids busy with homework. Parents homeschool them. Not enough to dig deeper."

"They can't see it the way I can. Don, the bastards buried their daughter under the compost pile."

"Four months. That'd make it early December. Winter was snowy, so the body should be viable enough to identify." He opened a document on the PC and typed with two fingers. "Think the other kids will throw him under the bus when we talk to them?"

"Yes. Daisy told her oldest brother what was happening but their father is a hulk and the kid is a toothpick and couldn't help. If CPS rescues the kids, He'll turn both parents in. Daddy for rape and beatings and Mommy for enabling him."

"Excellent. Give me a valid reason for a search warrant."

Don's clinical attitude couldn't hide the rage boiling in the small office. One of the reasons I liked him.

"I put one together on the drive here. A different neighbor saw me in my official garb land unburdened her soul. She wouldn't give me her name, but she didn't tell me under the Seal of the Confessional so I'm not bound as a priest to keep it to myself." I thought for a moment. "This neighbor said she hadn't seen Daisy since Christmas and when the weather warmed up she smelled something strange coming from the compost." I replayed it in my head. Yes, it would work. "Enough?"

"Good. I can use it with your name." He typed for a minute. When he spoke again, his voice was hushed. "What did you see?"

I told him about the blood-colored fog. About the little ghost. About how she worked the hauntings. I reminded him why she haunted.

The detective fumbled a piece of Nicorette into his mouth. "I miss being able to smoke when you tell me this shit."

"You'll live longer and save more kids this way."

"Good point. Glad I used to hide and watch my mother talk to ghosts when I was too young to know any better. It's twenty to one I wouldn't have believed you otherwise."

"I wouldn't have singled you out if I wasn't sure about you." I stood and began to replace the papers on the chair. "I could tell you had the Sight the minute I walked into the station six months ago."

"Get me into Heaven, then. I'm gonna need a lot of support."

"Nailing these bastards and rescuing their kids will go a long way toward balancing your ledger."

His phone rang. I let myself out and drove to the women and children's shelter Rubio's team worked with. Handed the receptionist the two hundred bucks and scarfed two full pumps from the hand sanitizer on her desk. Then I headed to my favorite coffee shop and drank three espressos in a row. The bitter coffee cleared part of the acid out of me. My usual scent—for lack of a more masculine word—was a mix of snow and mountain air, but the stinks of rape and murder had fouled it.

Part of me wanted to sit in a church. Old habits die hard. But it was Holy Saturday, I remembered. The day before

Easter. All the churches would be packed. I didn't do well in crowds.

It was closing in on seven p.m. I needed my beat-up armchair and Xav's Gretzky jersey. I needed to write down Daisy's name and story in my notebook to conclude this incident.

When I touched my doorknob a short time later, I got no sense of Emma. I relaxed. Things were back to normal.

Chapter Twenty-Five

On the way home, I'd made a side trip to old man Russo's for smoked sausage, canned beans, and French bread. Xav and I had adapted Grandmère's cassoulet recipe in our seminary days. She would've whacked us across the back of the head at the mere idea of canned beans, but this shortcut allowed dinner to cook in less than an hour. Perfect for the packed schedule of two young priests on the exorcist track.

At eight thirty I sliced a couple pieces of bread and ate.

At nine thirty I said the hell with it and packed everything away. Her loss. Reheated cassoulet was never quite as good.

I wandered the blasted apartment for an hour.

Ten thirty. No Emma.

Couldn't concentrate on a book. Couldn't get through a single song on the mandolin. I dusted everything, used the floor sweeper on the area rugs, scrubbed the bathroom—and the apartment wasn't dirty to begin with.

In less than a week I'd done a complete one-eighty from my dedicated loner lifestyle. Emma might as well hang a sign in the window: Males domesticated. Rapid results guaranteed.

At ten fifty-three the door opened. I stayed on the couch in front of the Mac. She'd be in soon enough to boast about some clever haunting she'd played around with all day.

Something heavy stumbled against the table and two small somethings *klunked* on the floor. The atmosphere was off.

I leaped off the couch and ran into the kitchen.

Emma leaned on the table. Her skirt was torn. The hem dangled. Her ripped blouse exposed her right shoulder and a button was missing at the throat. Her high-heeled shoes lay on the floor under the table and her stockings hung in shreds from her feet. The fancy hairstyle was a mass of tangles. Only her hat remained intact, feathers still straight in the band.

"What happened?" My voice sounded just as off.

She slid into the chair. Dark circles shadowed her eyes. When she didn't say anything, I crossed the small space and stood over her. "Are you all right?" Stupid question, but nothing else came to me.

She inhaled like she'd forgotten how breathing worked. "Of course I am all right. I am no weakling."

Her voice shook. I grabbed the red wine out of the pantry and poured her half a glass. "Drink."

She drank without stopping and set the glass on the table with a mostly steady hand.

"Now tell me what happened."

"Sit. I do not wish to stare up at you." The order lacked her usual imperious tone.

I sat. Something primitive threatened to engulf me. I choked it into submission.

"Pour me another glass of wine, please." When she finished half of it her normal deep river flowed partway back into its channel. "I was bored. I also wished to show off my new clothes. I walked far. Where there were no people to see me I continued to practice becoming many different creatures while retaining my clothing." She brushed her sleeve. "It requires much concentration."

She'd applied makeup at some point: a smear of lipstick darkened her right cheek.

"I found a coffee shop which makes a proper latte. Their pie is acceptable as well."

I restrained myself from pounding on the table. "What do pie and coffee have to do with the way you look?"

She stopped fiddling with her damaged skirt. A crooked smile touched her mouth. "You do not sound like a disinterested priest. Are you guilty of a human emotion because of my tale?"

I choked the primitive impulse harder. "Don't play games with me."

She opened her hands. "You are right. Very well: it became dark and I desired a glass of wine and some music. The place I chose was unwise. The patrons were drunk or smoking a cloying drug or riddled with sexual disease. You would have had much to say about their auras, which were visible even against the distracting lights." She looked at me again. "Do not say the words I know are on your tongue. I do not mean to make you impatient." She straightened her spine. "Two men were insistent in their advances, but they smelled of harsh alcohol and the cloying drug. I left the establishment but as I passed the alley behind it the same two men attacked me."

I didn't mean to jump out of the chair, but I was on my feet when I shouted, "What?"

This time she smiled. "I would like to preserve your protective expression. Sit down so I may finish."

I paced the kitchen instead. "My mistake, right? You don't need protecting."

"This is true, but I am pleased you wish to try. When the stupid men attempted to ravish me, I became rusalka. My body chose it for me, of which I approve. Rusalka is how you first saw me in Rome; do you remember? The men screamed and tried to run. I ripped out their throats."

"You killed two people?" My voice cracked.

Emma stared at her fingernails. "It has been hundreds of years, but men have not changed. Most think with their *khui*." She picked at a loose button. "I dislike sewing."

"Screw the sewing. Were there any witnesses? Did someone call the police?" I wondered if Don knew any lawyers who'd take on this kind of defense. I wondered how I'd explain Emma to the cops.

She chuckled. "The bartender opened the door when the *suki* gave their girlish screams. My appearance may have inspired him to go live with the Komi and herd reindeer."

"Talk sense. He's a witness. He'll have called the cops. He'll be able to identify you." I kept pacing. "We'll have to find a lawyer. Martin might have a contact."

"Of what do you speak?" She finished the second glass of wine.

"Jesus, Emma, don't you understand? You're going to get arrested for murder."

Her laugh scraped my nerves.

"You think jail is funny? Seven hundred years in a Roman dungeon wasn't enough?"

She shook her head. "You are the one who does not understand. Look." She pushed out of the chair and stood. One moment she was Emma in her wrecked fancy clothes. The next moment a six-foot withered hag stood in my kitchen, some kind of shapeless rag covering her skeletal body, ragged claws for nails on hands and feet, bleached-bone hair falling to her knees. Cloudy pupilless eyes stared at me.

Another moment and she was Emma again.

"You see? This is a rusalka. The door opened with a screech of metal. I heard the noise and looked up from the throat of one of the *suki*." She raised her eyebrows in a sham of innocence. "He will not describe to the police the woman in the steampunk dress. He will tell them of the rusalka he observed in the alley."

I grabbed the back of the nearest chair. Her transformations got through my panic where her words hadn't.

"The police will accuse him of drunkenness himself and think perhaps an animal killed those men." Emma picked up her hat and inspected it. "It is possible they will search for a rusalka. I would enjoy seeing the reports of their search on the news." She looked at the clock over the sink. "It is after eleven o'clock. We will be able to see the news on the computer, yes?"

"Yes." Maybe the cops wouldn't be banging on my door tonight.

"Good. Let us watch it, even though I am as tired as a peasant who plows fields all day." She stood and stretched.

"What? I was thinking of your shape-shifting and how it might have saved your bacon."

"My what?" She tugged at the next loose button on her silver shirt. "You worry like an old woman. This will not affect us." The button came off in her hand. "*Blyat*."

"Son of a bitch." I snatched the button and slammed it on the table. "Forget the damn clothes. I know how to sew. I can repair your fancy outfit."

Her head snapped up. Her eyes sparked silver. "What kind of man are you?"

"Huh?"

"I tell you of sex and blood and death and you talk of servant's work." Disdain crept into her voice. "You are no man. You are a priest."

The primitive urge broke free. "I was man enough to free you from a centuries-old prison."

"But you still cannot banish me."

I leaned closer to her. "Are you challenging me? You ran away the first time, remember?"

She stood toe-to-toe with me. "Do you say I am a coward?"

"I'm saying—" I tried to throttle it.

"What, priest?"

I grabbed her shoulders and kissed her. Her skin warmed under my hands and I kissed her harder. The hat dropped to the floor.

We pulled each other toward the bedroom. I popped open two more buttons on her blouse. She pried at my belt buckle. My knees hit the bed. She pulled off my T-shirt. I unzipped my jeans and she yanked them down to my ankles. She unzipped her skirt and threw it in the corner. She still wasn't wearing any underwear. I reached for the remains of her silver blouse and she dragged me onto the bedspread. Her lips locked onto mine. Her tongue pushed into my mouth and then she broke the kiss.

"You taste of snow on the high mountains, the snow with blue shadows from the sun." She ran her nails through my chest hair. "It is a good taste." She reached for my boxers.

The spell broke. I backed off until I was on my hands and knees looking down at her.

"Stop. I'm—a priest."

Her eyes opened wide. "You are a virgin?"

"No, but it's been fourteen years."

She gave me a slow smile. "*Dorogoi*, the last time I called a man to my bed was more than seven centuries ago. Surely your memory is as good as mine."

She pushed my boxers down my thighs and I lost it. Her fingers kneaded my skin and she tasted like snow and sweat and I couldn't get enough of her and Christ it was so good...

———

Afterward I put my arm around her. "You're not bad for an old woman."

Her hand whipped out of the covers at my face. I caught it. She tried to tug it free but stopped when she caught my expression.

"It is good to see you smile."

My face fell into its usual muscle pattern as soon as she said it. She scowled.

"Bah. Now you are going to wallow in Catholic guilt."

I shook my head, another smile changing my everyday face. "No. I made my choice. Besides, Lisa could list every step in Church history which resulted in the doctrine of priestly celibacy. Followed by all the arguments against its historical accuracy."

She laughed. "I must meet this woman."

I moved my legs, which stuck to hers with our cooling sweat. "I need to shower. Then I'll show you how to fix your steampunk clothes."

Her hand landed on my hip. "No. I do not wish you to leave. Besides, I am able to sew. I simply dislike it." She stroked my bare skin, raising goose bumps which had nothing to do with the temperature in the room. "Do you wish to leave this bed?"

"No. Hell no."

"Good. I do not wish to turn into rusalka and scare you into living with the Komi and herding reindeer."

Chapter Twenty-Six

"Your stomach is making loud noises."

Emma's voice in my ear. Sleepy and for a change not autocratic.

"Mm." I drew her closer. Her ass fit perfectly into my pelvis. She pulled my arm over her bare stomach.

My eyes opened. Holy Christ, I slept with Emma.

She turned her head but kept her body snugged against mine.

I slept with her... and I didn't regret it.

"Tell me what you are thinking."

"Waiting for the world to shift into place. Hold on a sec."

A second was about all she waited.

"Well?"

"I'm wondering where breakfast is." This time I smiled.

"You are an entitled sloth." But she returned the smile. "It is morning. You may leave this bed to shower."

I raised myself on one elbow to look at the alarm clock. "Technically."

She followed my gaze. "Eleven forty. I am apparently a sloth today as well. No wonder your stomach is making rude sounds."

She unwound my arm. "You will shower first and then begin breakfast. While you cook I will mimic a domestic female and repair my new clothes."

<hr>

We sat at the kitchen table half an hour later eating bacon and eggs and drinking American-style coffee.

Emma sipped it and grimaced.

"If you continue to make breakfast I will teach you the way to make a proper latte."

"What? I make a good cup of coffee." I sipped it. Yes, I did.

"*Pah*. Most American food is edible, but—"

"I'm Canadian. Only lack of availability prevents me from feeding you the goodness of peameal bacon."

She stared at the crisp, fragrant slices on her plate. "I enjoy eating this bacon. Do not alter it."

"We'll see." I set down my cup. "Don't."

A forkful of eggs touched her lips. "Do not do what?"

"Don't act like we're a couple. This is not our normal morning." I pinched the bridge of my nose. "I said 'our.' See what I mean?"

She finished the bite of eggs. "You are threatened by me. This is amusing."

"And you're too complacent."

A shrug. "I am practical. Also I do not deny that which is obvious. We desired each other. It was simple."

"No, it wasn't. It's a damn good thing you're seven hundred... eight hundred... How old are you?"

Her lips thinned. "It is impolite to press a woman for her age. Why is this important?"

"Because we had unprotected sex." My voice rose. I tamped it down.

Her brow furrowed. "And this means?" It cleared. "Oh. You are concerned I might conceive? I do not think you need to worry."

"You don't think?" My voice rose higher.

She laughed. "Do not make such a face. I apologize. Truly, you cannot get me with child. I am much too old and no longer human." She raised her eyebrows. "It is foolish to pretend we are not a couple. We should discuss this after breakfast, as I too am surprised at the way things have developed between us."

"Surprised? Christ on a bike, Emma, you have a talent for understatement." I dug the heels of my hands into my eyes.

Her hands pulled mine free. "What is more important is your obsession with priestly rules. I wish you to reassure yourself. You have not committed an unpardonable sin or some similar nonsense."

The insanity of the past week hit me. I laughed until I hiccupped, and Emma's aura flowed from puzzlement to annoyance to a good color when she shared my laughter.

"No," I said after I swallowed coffee. "I don't think this sin is any more unpardonable than a dozen others I've committed. I'm fucked when I die, so one more sin doesn't matter."

She radiated confusion. I picked up the dishes and dumped them in the sink.

"Do not be so negative," she said from behind me. "You believe in the Catholic afterlife like a proper priest should, but why do you presume your destination is filled with demons?"

"You have no idea what I've done. The list is vast."

She added the coffee cups to the soapy water.

"You are feigning ignorance of your own religion." She handed me a rinsed plate to dry.

"Really." I dried it and took the silverware from her.

"And now you are being sarcastic. I once studied this religion. It is faith and deeds which are weighed upon your death, is it not?" She scrubbed the frying pan with steel wool. "You have great faith. I can tell such things. You have also performed many exorcisms of which your church approves, yes?"

"Yeah." I put the silverware away.

"So." She handed me the dripping frying pan. "Such faith combined with your deeds should ensure your entrance into Catholic Heaven. It is obvious."

I found a dry spot on the towel and rubbed down the pan. "Yeah? Then tell me what the red-assed bastard in the cemetery meant on Friday."

She wrung out the dishcloth. "First, you must tell me the story of your brother's death. Next, you will tell me the complete story of the cemetery." When I hesitated, she took the dishtowel out of my hands and pulled me toward the living room. "It is Sunday and you have no other obligations."

I sat on the couch next to her. "Right. It's Sunday. It's Easter, actually. Should've dyed eggs and bought chocolate rabbits."

She dropped my hands. "You should have done what? Why... Oh. You refer to *pysanky*. They are pleasing to look at. I shall acquire some and we will decorate only a few days late." She sat at attention. "Now. Begin."

I needed to tell it, not so much because she was demanding the story, but to organize it all in my head. Organization was the only way I could attack this new demon information.

"Xav and I were the first exorcists to join the Order in a decade. We got a supercharged course of study in the seminary. Four years to Ordination instead of the usual five. We had to fight for time to eat and sleep. We did everything by the book. I worked with deliberation; Xav's charm caught demons off-guard. Bastards didn't expect charm as an opening move. Once we were ordained I broke out of the mold and began to incorporate rituals from other countries and religions. Xav kept to the rules of the Church."

"This surprised no one, yes?"

I scowled at her. "Yeah. Xav was the Church's Golden Boy. Always followed the rules and always successful. I was as successful as he was, but Holy Mother Church doesn't like her uniformed spokesmen moonlighting."

One dark eyebrow raised. "I do not know this word."

I waved it away. "It's simple: I don't play by their rules." Now for the hard part. "Last July, Xav lost his first exorcism. He kicked out the demon, naturally, but the possessed guy died. Weak heart."

Emma got up and opened the windows. A warm breeze blew in, faintly scented with car exhaust.

"And this was a problem?"

"The family sued Xav and the Church for wrongful death."

Emma snorted. "Lawyers. *Pah.*"

I drew myself up. "I am also a Canon lawyer, thank you."

She scooted to the opposite end of the couch. "I am liking you less now that you have admitted this."

I saw the smile in her eyes. "Liar."

The smile touched her mouth. "This is true. Continue."

"Xav got called to Rome. I followed, but the legal machine at the Vatican wouldn't let me represent him. Said I wouldn't be objective enough." I took a few slow breaths. The only other time I'd told this story, to Lisa, I'd barely kept my shit together. "Lawyers on both sides geared up. It got nasty. Xav had saved these people's son and husband from possession by a demon so foul it had made the guy torch his church's tabernacle and the caretaker who tried to stop him. The cops were a heartbeat away from arresting the possessed guy. He would've gotten life in a nuthouse if he managed to dodge the death penalty. Xav gave him back his soul. He shoehorned the guy into Heaven. For thanks, the guy's family wanted the Vatican's riches and Xav's blood."

I got up and paced the room. "It was five days of hell. I saw Xav maybe ten minutes each day. He was getting coached by his lawyers or suffering through the trial or in the chapel praying. I buried myself in the archives, digging up relevant legal history all the way back to the Middle Ages."

As I leaned out the window for fresh air, the grad students from across the hall came out the front door and waved at me. "Hawks won last night! We made it on the fan cam! Did you see?"

I gave them a thumbs-up between the cast-iron bars. "Wish I had. I missed the game."

When I pulled myself back inside, Emma handed me a glass of red wine. I shook my head. "No. I don't drink anymore."

"Bah. You are underestimating the strength of your character." When I still didn't take it, she flounced into the kitchen. "I will make you a latte."

I didn't want to yell, especially with the window open, so I transferred my pacing to the kitchen.

"I was too busy. Xav and I had been in each other's pockets since the cradle but those five days we were like strangers. We only saw each other at morning Mass. The Vatican is always a hive of politics and ass-kissing and tension and I didn't pick up on what was happening to Xav. I didn't sense it." I punched the doorframe between the kitchen and living room.

"Stop," Emma said from her usual place in front of the stove, wire whisk stirring a pot of milk. "You will injure your hand and be unable to conduct business."

"Since when are you the practical one?" But I stopped attacking the varnished oak.

"I am always practical. You should understand this by now." She turned off the gas. "Bring me a cup, please."

When I sat at the table with the latte, she sat kitty-corner to me with the wine I'd refused.

"The Church was doing its best to throw Xav under the bus. The lawyers dithered and plotted. They cared about winning and saving face for the Church, not about my brother. I told them all what a bunch of spineless bastards they were; like they gave a shit what I thought."

I drank some of the latte. Emma's skills weren't Grand-mère's, but she knew coffee.

"Xav didn't show up at Mass the sixth day of the trial. I headed to his room, which was several floors above my temporary one. His was a decent size with a good view. He spent half the year in Rome. They were grooming him for promotion—he was a step away from being named Monsignor. Would've made a good Red Hat eventually. One of the few good ones."

An image of Xav in Cardinal's robes holding his autographed Gretzky hockey stick appeared in my head. Xav grinning like he did when we shared a prank.

"You have stopped talking." Emma's voice reached me from someplace far away. I knew exactly how far: forty-eight hundred miles. The distance between here and Rome.

"Yeah. Well. Xav's door was locked. I knocked and called and finally shut the hell up and listened. I got no sense of Xav. You know how you're a deep river through snowy mountains? Xav was sunlight on spring snow—brighter and warmer than me. The sixth morning of the trial there was absolutely nothing on the other side of his door. So I kicked it in."

To stall, I drank more of the latte. Over the rim, I caught Emma looking at me with impatience. Before she could pin the stall on me, I plunged into the worst part.

"He was sitting cross-legged against the wall, open Bible on the floor in front of him. He'd propped a sawed-off shotgun in his lap. Blood, brains, and pieces of his skull had splattered the wall behind him and dripped down to the floor."

"Ah," Emma murmured.

"Takes a lot to make me lose my shit. Not even Xav's bloody wreck of a corpse could do it for more than a minute. I looked for his ghost. Nothing. I jumped over the bed and touched his face. He was—He was still warm." I swallowed another sharp-edged rock. "If I'd been five minutes earlier. If Mass had been shorter. If I'd spent any fucking part of those days listening to Xav instead of buried in the Vatican cellars plowing through the secret records. Nope. Denis was going to be the one to yank his brother out from under the legal bus. Denis would make sure the Kaines would walk away from this mess together, Xav all ready to forgive while Denis flipped them off."

Emma touched my hand. "Loosen your grip or you will shatter the cup. I do not wish to mop up cold coffee."

I pushed the cup to my left. "I gave my brother Last Rites. Absolved him of any sins. A standard formality. Xav always played by the rules, so he'd want Last Rites. Then I walked to the open door and bellowed for help. Before anyone showed, I knelt next to him to see what he'd been reading. A red pen had rolled partway under the bed. He'd underlined Matthew 8:16, which says 'That evening they brought to him many who were possessed with demons; and he cast out the spirits with a word and healed all who were sick.'"

Emma studied her wine. "The choice is sensible, since it is the way you make a living."

"Yeah. I think he was reassuring me he'd saved the dead guy from roasting in Hell, the important thing, no matter what those legal bastards said."

"But why then did he kill himself?"

"He was tired. Depressed. They'd been shredding every-thing he'd done and said during the exorcism for five straight days. They were threatening to defrock him and charge him with murder." I looked around for something to break.

Emma clutched my hands. "Do not shatter the cup or hit the table. If you require something physical to release this anger, you will squeeze my hands."

Nobody'd held my hands since senior prom, when Mary-Louise Durand, who was not my date, wept mascara into my rented shirt after her date abandoned her in the parking lot because she wouldn't put out. Pissed off my date when I offered to drive MaryLouise home. Ended up dropping off both girls at their front doors before midnight. A real ladies' man, me.

I smiled at Emma and she pretended to be overcome. The staged humor helped.

"The lawyers argued Xav's suicide was an admission of guilt. The Church got the family to agree to silence for a quarter-mil."

Emma blinked. "For a what?"

"Sorry. For two hundred fifty thousand Euros. Then they tried to bury Xav in unconsecrated ground." The fury rose up in me again. "I cursed them in four languages when I found out. They whined about how the Church said suicide was murder. I refuted every one of their arguments with ancient and modern precedents." My grin was hard. "Never fuck with a pissed-off Canon lawyer. After I finished with them, I told them the Church was obligated to restore Xav's good name."

She shook her head. "Your last argument did not have strength."

I shrugged. "They might have caved to shut me up, since I made it abundantly clear if they didn't agree to my demands, I'd spin the story to the tabloids with the Church as murdering scum and Xav as a bigger and better hero than Indiana Jones, Superman, and Captain America combined. I also reminded them I hadn't agreed to keep quiet about any part of this."

"You weave spells with words."

"Nope. I'm simply a smart Canon lawyer who loved his twin brother more than life itself. The slimebags conferred and decided they mustn't have any more scandals about the priesthood. Conclusion: Xav is buried as he should be, in our Order's cemetery in Rome."

"And then you came here?"

I patted her hands. "Then I went on a three-week drinking and banishing binge. Got hammered eighteen nights out of the twenty-one and scoured cemeteries and archaeological digs around Rome. I hated everything and everyone."

She frowned at me. "You hate yourself."

I shrugged again.

"I am saying you seem to have accepted your hate for yourself during those weeks, and also you still do hate yourself. This is not healthy."

"I should've known Xav was in trouble. I should've thought about him more than about me saving the day like a Mountie riding in on his trusty steed. I should've done something else for him. I should've—"

"Cease these useless recriminations." She let go of my hands. "Your brother is dead but you insist he is in Heaven, so this story has ended well."

I dug my nails into my palms. "You don't get it. Xav was the model exorcist. The one the Church held up as an example for others to follow. I'm the black sheep. The one who breaks the rules. The one they tolerate only because of Xav." Something I'd held inside since last July came out before I could shut my big fat mouth. "I'm no loss to the world. Certainly not to the Church. Xav left a hole no priest or exorcist currently on the planet can fill. God fucking should've offed me instead of Xav."

Emma slapped me hard enough to sting. It shut me up. A

moment later she tapped her long fingers under my chin and my teeth clicked closed.

"This is nonsense. It is the result of living alone and brooding like the hero in a romance." She glared at me. "Do not think to insult romances. They are entertaining, and you would be a character in a bad one."

"I... What?"

A theatrical sigh. "Your brain is swimming in an emotional stew. You must conquer this. I prefer you angry and uselessly trying to banish me." Her eyes focused inward. "Was it during those three weeks after your brother died you found the prison into which I had been sealed by a *figlio di una mignotta* Pope?"

"Yeah." The air in the kitchen cleared. "You have a knack for getting me to say things I mean to keep to myself."

"I am good for you. I dislike your tendency to lurk around these rooms with the facial expression which would sour milk." She held up a finger. "Let us focus. You say your brother is in Heaven, but the demon which tried to break your skull implied he is instead in Hell."

Purple-eyed bastard's voice echoed in my ears again. "Yeah."

"Then if we are to keep you from souring the milk we must learn the truth."

Chapter Twenty-Seven

Half an hour later we entered a small downtown store called Harry's Hat. It was dark as a movie theater. I closed my eyes for my first ten seconds inside so I could see when I opened them. Suspicion and defensiveness fouled the air. Velvet curtains in the windows blocked out all light from the sunny day. Candelabras and wall sconces with flickering LED bulbs gave the only illumination.

The place was a weird combination of Toys R Us and Madame Gagnon's Vodoun storefront in the French Quarter in New Orleans. Bright plastic My First Magic Kits on a shelf near the front clashed with charm bags, herbs, and candles on a shelf toward the back. Wicker baskets with different table magic tricks lined the top of the glass counter. Inside the counter, Andúril replicas and kitschy plastic scrying bowls shared shelf space with genuine athames and bowls.

As a cover, it was brilliant.

A thin woman with pointy shoes, pointy bra, and pointy nose listened with a desperate expression as the young man at the counter went over the steps needed to work the Attract True Love spell. On the other side of the cash register, an older, silver-haired man with a black beard measured out red clover and damiana leaf for a forty-something redhead. Easy to tell which customer knew the proper rules.

Emma walked me around a display of spell books and tarot sets. The redhead and the pointy broad paid for their spells and herbs and walked out.

"*Imperatritsa.*" The silver-haired man nodded at Emma.

"*Mag.*" She mirrored his gesture.

The magician's eyes flicked to the young man, who went to the door and changed the "Open" sign to "Back in 10 Minutes."

"What brings you into my web?" His smile had a sharp edge. "Do you desire love? Money? Empowerment?"

"You amuse me. I desire information."

"There's something you can't find out for yourself? Interesting. Or are you too busy with your new toy to seek answers?"

I stepped in front of Emma. "You want to figure out who you're talking to before you label someone?"

He gave me a "put up or shut up" look. I set my messenger bag on the floor next to Emma and we squared off. The atmosphere changed from defensive to hostile. His black beard took on the appearance of scales and I got the unsettling sensation I stood in rising water with no escape. I spread a strand of power and created a shield between my feet and the floor.

Emma clapped her hands twice. "Stop posturing, both of you. The testosterone is ridiculous. Zakhar, who knows of demons?"

The water receded. His beard looked like hair again. I dissolved the shield.

He said to her while still gauging me, "You're slipping into your dotage if you live in Chicago and haven't heard of the priest in Hyde Park. Kaine, his name is. He's the demon expert for the entire Chicagoland area."

I swallowed laughter.

Emma glared at him. "I did not come here to be insulted. I came because you hear of many things from your clients."

He waved a dismissive hand. "You have received my information. Talk to Kaine. I have a business to run."

The air around Emma shimmered. Her suit lengthened into a white kimono as she grew a foot taller. Her skin turned translucent as a chunk of ice. Her black hair stayed the same, but her lips and eyes changed to a blue indicating lack of blood circulation. Ice crystallized on her fingernails. Snow began to fall through the shimmering air. She locked her fingertips around the proprietor's neck and ten sharp icicles pierced his skin.

"Do you still wish to dismiss us?" Her deep voice became soprano, tinkling like ice chips falling into glass. "Ice freezes water. Is there a reason for me not to freeze your arrogant blood?"

A pen clattered onto the glass counter. The young man took a step toward Zakhar.

"Stop, Dan." Zakhar's tenor jumped an octave. "I apologize, *imperatritsa*. Let us discuss your request."

A beat. Emma's nails released his throat. Five rivulets of blood ran down each side of his neck. Emma stepped back. The snowfall ceased. Her skin returned to its usual paleness. Her eyes faded from blue to gray. Her body shrank to its proper six foot two. The shimmering cocoon around her popped without a sound.

"You are intelligent, *mag*. Violence wastes time. So. I am ready to listen."

Zakhar leaned against his counter. "Solana, the dancer in the theater several streets north. Hayato, the archaeologist at the museum of science."

Emma crossed her arms. "*Pah.* I have spoken with both of them. She is too concerned with her train of adoring men. He has regressed so far as to think he is human. Both barely remember their ancient names. Give me someone else."

He stared through us, eyes narrowed. After a few moments he said, "Siobhan."

Emma raised her eyebrows. "She is in Chicago now? Excellent."

"You're welcome." Zakhar put an electronic cigarette between his lips.

Emma gazed at it, her expression curious.

"Cigarettes are the world's worst sin now. This is only nicotine vapor. It's not as satisfying, but I don't want my velvet curtains reeking of stale smoke. The cleaning bill would be obscene."

"I prefer wine. Denis and I thank you for this information."

I elbowed her. "Good thing I didn't want to stay anonymous."

"What? Oh." She smiled. "I am no longer used to subterfuge."

Zakhar inhaled. "Isn't Denis the first name of the Hyde Park priest?"

"Yeah," I said.

"Well, well, well." He blew vapor at Emma. "So you have a weak spot after all. What are you playing with?"

I braced for impact, but she surprised me.

"Play is for children." With a smile, she walked over to the young man at the counter and touched his cheek. "I am Emma Koroleva. And you?"

In a shy voice, he said, "Daniel Holt."

"Good. You are a sweet young man." She turned to Zakhar. "Good day, *mag*."

We walked to the front door and Emma turned the sign around. A middle schooler burst in, dragging his father behind him.

"Here it is, Dad! Here it is!" The kid gazed up at a red box with black lettering: Harry Houdini's First Magic Tricks.

"Hey," I said as we walked back to my car, "what did you turn into back there?"

"There is a creature with which you are not familiar? I am surprised." She waited for me to unlock the car and open the door.

"Since when are you into chivalry?"

"We are in public. It is expected. Also, having doors opened and being driven in private vehicles brings back pleasant memories."

I settled into the driver's seat and said without bothering to look, "Buckle the seat belt."

She pouted. "I do not like to be strapped in like a babe in swaddling. There are too many rules in this century."

I started the car. "When some idiot texting while steering with his knees tries to run you over a guardrail you'll stop complaining. I hate seat belts too, but I no longer have a death wish."

We navigated the holiday traffic. I said as tactfully as possible, "You didn't answer my question."

She started. "What?"

"What century were you wandering in? I said, you didn't answer my question about the icicle thing you turned into."

"Oh. Yes. I was a yuki-onna." She didn't elaborate.

Now I was intrigued. I turned onto the exit ramp for home and said, "So who was the magic-shop guy? Ex-lover?"

All the arrogance returned to her voice. "Your grandmother, the one who taught you with the wooden spoon, would not approve of such questions."

"My grandmother was a force of nature. I'm just an angry priest. What was up between you and the magic guy?" The light turned green and I sailed through it.

"He is a vodnik, a water creature. We have disagreed with each other in the past." She shook herself from her head to her butt, trapped by the seat belt. "He had forgotten my powers are significantly greater than his. I reminded him. He tried to taunt me with my connection to you. In return I made myself aware of his companion."

"The counter kid? He looked harmless enough. His aura was clean."

She nodded. "He is harmless. He is also the vodnik's lover."

"So? Not our business who he sleeps with."

Her smile was tight and secretive. "Knowledge is power. You have said as such to me, but I am also aware of this truth. I wished to show the vodnik that he cannot use our relationship against us without endangering his own."

I made a left into the alley behind my apartment building where the garages were located. "We don't have a relationship. And you're ruthless."

"You may criticize my methods if they fail. For now, I possess a useful contact whom we will visit." She let herself out of the car when I got out to unlock the garage door. "I dislike small spaces. I will wait here for you."

Chapter Twenty-Eight

Good thing I was deluged by work on Monday or I would've brooded every waking minute on what the demon said. And what Emma and I had done. I'd never been so glad to have the bookstore all to myself.

As it was, I lay in bed—alone—all Monday night, chewing on a stick of an idea I couldn't slot into its assigned place.

When demons were involved, my brother was Xav the Giant Killer. Unbeatable. They'd broken his arms, knocked out three teeth, landed him in the hospital for a week with a ruptured spleen. We'd worked together on the spleen job because the guy's wife called Xav's bishop and the guy's son called my bishop. Two demons were fighting each other for squatter's rights in the moron's body. Tag-teaming was lucky for us, since two fighting red-asses in the same meatsuit made the guy unpredictable. I walked away with a broken nose. Big deal.

But the stick prodded me for six and a half hours: no way Xav should have blown a red-ass eviction, victim with a bad heart or not. Something must have been different. Xav had missed something.

Xav didn't miss things.

No wonder I couldn't sleep.

———

Emma trapped me into another fake haunting Tuesday night. She'd used a planchette to give false demonic promises to a séance-crazed household all the way down in Joliet. Damn good thing I was used to wrestling with actual demons since she decided to pretend to be one. She needed a keeper.

It was dark by the time I found the exit off Route 80, then off Cherry Hill, then over to Mills. The rising crescent moon touched the chimney of the one-story brick house. The place looked small and generic and deceptive, like too many of my house calls.

I knocked and rang the doorbell, then knocked and rang again for three minutes before the handle turned. These people had called me. You'd think they'd jump at the first knock.

The door opened wide enough for a nose to stick out. A high, masculine voice squeaked, "Go away or I'll sic my pit bull on you."

Spare me.

"I'm Father Kaine. Someone from this house called Auxilium group earlier today."

An identical voice spoke from farther behind him, "Arthur, who's at the door?"

The nose disappeared. "Lance, did you call a priest?" Arthur's voice modulated downward when he was angry.

"What? No." Lance called to someone deeper in the house, "Guinevere Morgan Van Meer, get up here now!"

At least the night was clear. Standing out here in the rain would've negated the powerful exorcist image. I still hadn't heard a dog growl, either. Might've been an empty threat for the stranger at their door.

Inside, two high voices berated said Guinevere. An equally high female voice argued back. Finally more footsteps came toward me and the door opened a whole twelve inches.

"I guess you can come inside since our sister called you."

"Thank you." Even skinny priests needed more than a foot-wide opening to squeeze through. Arthur allowed me a few inches more and locked the door behind me.

It was good that I knew how to keep a poker face, because these three people wore homemade versions of seventeenth-century clothes. The hall lights shone on Sydney Carton and Charles Darnay. Behind them stood, of course, Lucie Manette in ruffles and lace. The whole house was a Dickens time warp. With a pit bull. Pretty sure Dickens didn't write about pit bulls.

I was busy being curious why these twenty-somethings weren't dressed like their Arthurian namesakes when the pit bull slipped out of Lance's hand and galloped at me. I held out my fist with fingers down for it to sniff. A few snorts, an interrogative *grumph*, and fifty pounds of gray-and-white guard dog flopped at my feet and rolled onto his back.

I squatted and gave him a two-handed belly rub, from his massive rib cage not quite down to his flapping doggie junk. His tail *thump-thump-thumped* on the linoleum as his body wriggled. If these cosplayers raised a dog this happy, they had to be decent people.

"Father Kaine."

Guinevere's voice. I gave the dog a final pat and stood, adjusting my messenger bag.

"Ms. Van Meer. How may I help you?"

She spoke over her ribbon-decked shoulder first. "You see, Lancelot? Merlin doesn't take to untrustworthy strangers. I told you I did the right thing." She smiled at me. "Father, we think our attempts to contact our deceased parents have gotten out of control."

I shoved all thoughts of black-and-white costume movies out of my head. "Please explain."

Lancelot called the dog and Arthur said, "This is our parents' house. They finally kicked it two months ago but didn't leave a will."

Guinevere interrupted. "Arthur thought he was going to scoop it all because he's the firstborn."

"Gwen, I didn't mean—"

"Spare us, dear brother," Lance cut him off. "My lawyer made a deal with your lawyer."

"After my lawyer called both of your lawyers," Gwen added.

"What?" Arthur took a step toward him. "The sleazy ambulance chaser. I'll fire him right now." He pulled out a cell phone.

I stepped between the three of them. "If you wouldn't mind continuing with why you asked me here?"

Lisa would choke with laughter if she heard me being conciliatory. The Camelot Brothers glared at each other, but Arthur put away his phone.

Gwen smiled much too sweetly at them as she said to me, "Our parents were so cheap they dumpster-dived instead of grocery shopping even though our father worked his way up from bank teller to regional manager and was rolling in it. Our mother's side of the family frowned on women going out to a workplace, so she went the home business route."

Lance groaned. "She sold jewelry, makeup, candles, storage containers, and God knows what else as soon as we were out of diapers. She could've sold central heating to the Devil himself."

In normal circumstances I would've cut off this grievance session, but they were telling me more than they knew. The atmosphere in the house reeked of greed and suspicion. Emma sure cherry-picked this place. I suppose I should thank her for planting a fake haunting on people who deserved it. The only aura of love in the bare hallway came from the pit bull. So much for me thinking these three were good people. They didn't deserve this dog.

"We know they hid the money in this house," Arthur was saying, "but we can't tear out the walls. It'll ruin the resale value. I'm in real estate. I can get a sweet price for this place because our parents kept it well. They planned to sell it themselves."

Lance smiled. "It's a good thing the overworked long-distance truck driver fell asleep at the wheel, brother, or we'd be checking your whereabouts the night they died."

"You leech. It sucks to know you'll never be first in anything, doesn't it?"

"Boys, we're keeping the father waiting." Gwen ushered me toward the cellar stairs. "We scoured the house for two months with no luck. So I brought out the old Ouija board we used at sleepovers when we were kids."

"Not us," Arthur said.

"Only hormonal teenage girls would touch one of those things," Lance said.

Gwen brought out her poison-sweet smile again. "Then how did you know where it was when I suggested trying to contact Mom and Dad with it?"

They protested, but Gwen continued. "You can't lie to me, dear brothers. I listened in on the telephone extension when you unsuccessfully begged girls to go to your senior proms. I know how your minds work."

"Gwen, you emasculating bitch," Lance said as Arthur glared at her.

"Oh, get over yourselves." She flipped on the cellar light switch and preceded me down the stairs. "We had to try and contact Mom or Dad to find out where they hid the money. I mean, they have no use for it anymore and I know they would want all their beautiful capital to stay in the family."

"I found three different bankbooks stashed around the house," Lance said from behind us. "Art and Gwen found two more. The deposits listed in them totaled nearly a million dollars."

"We checked with the five branch banks and they all told us our parents had withdrawn all their money over the past six months. So we knew they'd hidden it because they'd never give it up," Arthur said as we reached the bottom.

"We slit mattresses, knocked on walls looking for hollow spots, emptied storage bins, and checked every wrapped packet in the chest freezer." The air around us soured from Gwen's frustration. "Nothing, nothing, nothing."

Arthur flipped another light switch. A finished basement appeared. Recently poured cement floor painted with the speckled stuff you see in garages. Walls flat and white. A stacking washer and dryer. The chest freezer. A card table with three chairs around it. And nothing else. Apparently the only thing Van Meers hoarded was cash.

Arthur walked over to the table. "We set up the board and tried calling first to Mom. When she didn't answer we tried Dad. Night after night, hour after hour, as boring as staring at these walls."

"Last week it all changed," Lance said. "The planchette started to move. We accused each other of messing with it, but when it moved on its own we had to believe."

Emma and I were going to have a long talk when I got home tonight. I kept on a mask of polite interest for their story while I tried to sense Emma's presence.

Gwen stood behind one of the chairs and stared at the mass-produced Ouija board. "It wasn't Dad who answered us. It was... a thing."

"It was a demon, Gwen, admit it." Lance stared at a spot in

the ceiling directly above the board. "It rose out of the center of the planchette."

Arthur said, " It jabbered in some language we didn't understand and tried to slash my throat with its ragged black claws." He shuddered. "We broke our circle and it disappeared."

Lance grinned his unpleasant grin. "I got up to turn on the light and Gwen screamed. Art was bleeding. You should've seen the look on his face when he felt his throat and came away with a hand full of dripping red goo."

"Eat me," Arthur said. "You would've keeled over if it'd been on your throat."

I'd learned enough. I set my messenger bag on the floor next to the card table. "Please describe the entity for me. I need as many specifics as possible."

"It was covered with red scales," Gwen said.

"It had a long tail with a triangular tip and its feet had the same raggedy black nails," Lance said. "The feet are why I don't think it was a demon. Don't all demons have cloven hooves?"

"Not necessarily," I said.

"See?" Arthur said. "You're not a know-it-all, Lance, so quit pretending. The demon had flaming hair too."

"Real flames," Gwen said. "We all felt the heat. It was naked, but it didn't have any... parts."

"You looked?" Arthur said.

Gwen flipped him off. "If you could get it up you wouldn't have to take your frustrations out on me."

"At least I don't spread my legs for anyone willing to buy me a shot of tequila."

"No, you just stalk the receptionists in your office until they file sexual harassment complaints."

I stepped between them. "Bickering won't remove the entity from your house. Here's what I need you to do."

"Wait, Father," Arthur said. "We should discuss your fee."

Gwen touched the Ouija board. The planchette skittered across it. Lance cursed. Gwen leaped backward and crouched behind Arthur.

I definitely wanted to get an agreement with these vultures up front, but Emma's timing had blown my chance.

"Later." I grabbed the board and planchette. "Collapse the table and chairs and move everything against the wall."

They fumbled and pinched their fingers on the hinges, but they did it. I splashed a circle of holy water on the floor where the table had stood and drew several protection runes with my salt stick. I didn't waste time berating Emma for rushing me into this. We'd be giving these three a show they'd remember.

"Stay back against the wall and don't distract me. Got it?"

A deep laugh came from somewhere above the ceiling.

"Yes," they said in voices without all the snark and bitchiness.

I drew another circle around them with the same runes. "Don't cross this, whatever you see or hear. If the lights go out, if you hear noises when the creature appears, anything. Stay in this circle."

I looked up at three faces which held the beginnings of belief. I got back to my circle and placed the planchette on top of the Ouija board. My bag gave up a box of matches. I drew the rune thurisaz with my finger on the board, channeled my will into the pointy capital *D*, and lit it.

The old, pressed cardboard ignited like flash paper. I stood and called to Emma in Early Latin: "Come here now or you'll be sorry! Let's get this over with or the next entity I banish will be you!"

Over the crackle of the fire, more laughter. Then red ectoplasm, dripping into the flames hiss—hiss—hiss—hiss. The light flickered. I stood my ground.

Pop. The exact creature the greedy idiots had described appeared in the air outside the circle. Its flaming hair almost made me lose my stern exorcist face—it looked as cartoonish as the hair of the Heat Miser from a different old Christmas special.

But I was a professional so I played my part. I started the exorcism ritual at the beginning. These siblings would think they'd been to High Mass by the time I was through.

Emma-the-demon put on quite a show. She cursed and screamed and made several feints across the circle which failed and caused more screams and curses.

When I reached "*Écce Crúcem Dómini, fúgite pártes advérsae,*" she cowered like a vampire in the movies. Such histrionics.

But then she did something unexpected. Her flaming hair went out. Her stagey tail thinned and lengthened into a whip. Her eyes divided and divided until her head was ringed with octagonal black holes. The red scales covering her sexless, naked body divided too, overlapping each other in triple layers of gleaming crimson steel.

I continued to recite the ritual, wondering what the hell she was playing at.

A quick breeze warped the air past me and my mind filled with deep rivers and snow. My voice didn't miss a word, still strong and confident. The air settled.

A real demon crouched outside my circle. A pissed-off, cocky demon out for my blood and the three souls cowering against the left-hand wall.

"*...ab animábus ad imáginem Dei cónditis ac pretióso divíni Ágni sánguine redémptis.*"

At the last word, its power punched me in the gut. I choked and doubled over. I had to keep the ritual moving. I tried to swallow. Another invisible gut punch. I bled power from the circle and created a shield. A quick and dirty job, but it gave me a moment to catch my breath. Now to stand.

Two arms wrapped around my chest and levered me up. I didn't see anything. Must be Emma. My lungs finally got a complete breath and I picked up where I'd left off.

"*Non últra áudeas, sérpens callidíssime, decípere humánum genus.*"

It laughed. Not angry like the purple-eyed bastard in the cemetery. More like it was playing with me. I kept going.

"*Ímperat tíbi Déus Pater; ímperat tíbi Deus Fílius; ímperat tíbi Déus Spíritus Sánctus.*"

It spat red acid at me every time I made the Cross in the air, but the liquid only sizzled against my shield. The shield wouldn't hold long, though. I hadn't prepared for the real thing. I was still not at a hundred percent after last Friday.

Suck it up, Kaine.

"*Ímperat tíbi Déus Pater; ímperat tíbi Deus Fílius; ímperat tíbi Déus Spíritus Sánctus.*"

Its tail curled around the outside of my circle. I didn't stop.

"*Ímperat tíbi Déus Pater; ímperat tíbi Deus Fílius; ímperat tíbi Déus Spíritus Sánctus—*"

The tail snapped up. My barrier shattered. I kept going. The tail whipped around my waist and slashed open my rib cage. I hissed but shouted through it: "*Váde sátana, invéntor et magíster ómnis falláciae.*"

It laughed again and finally spoke. "Who is the deceiver here, Kaine?" He chose ancient Hebrew, possibly because the Camelot Kids wouldn't understand it, like the Latin. "Your whore played my part until I appeared and she ran in terror."

"*Humiliáre sub poténti mánu Dei.*"

"You're going to be mine, Kaine."

Snow and water. The air bent, first next to me, then outside the circle.

"Mine to play with for—"

Every eye ringing his head widened. His hands clawed at the air before, behind, on top of him. Now the air bent away from him, part of his power stretching with it, stretching, snapping free of him.

"*Invocáto a nóbis sáncto et terríbili nominé Jésu, quem ínferi trémunt!*" I dumped the rest of the holy water into my hands and enveloped him in a golden fireball of sanctified power.

The walls shook. Cracks spiderwebbed the floor. The demon howled, his tail thrashing the air as his layers of armor turned to charcoal and rained to the floor around him. Through the flames and smoke and pieces of ceiling, I caught a final glimpse of the real him: a wizened gray thing with sunken black eyes. Then he was a pile of ash on the ruined floor.

I pulled the fireball back to me and dissipated it. Emma became visible for an instant, naked and stunned on the floor next to the ash. I threw an opaque barrier over her to let her gather her strength.

Only then did I dissolve the circle.

"Our money!" The three of them leaped for the center of the shattered floor. I never had a chance to scoop up the demon ash. Their feet stamped it into the bits of cement and what lay beneath it: bundles of cash and stacks of gold coins in those square plastic storage containers most people use for leftovers.

Three pairs of hands ripped up pieces of floor, scattering demon ash over everything. I stepped out of their way.

"It's here! It's here!" They laughed and hugged the dirty containers and built a fort with them and sliced their hands and ripped their nails and laughed some more.

In the meantime, my body reminded me the demon had slashed open the skin under my rib cage and it hurt like a hive's worth of wasp stings. Blood soaked my pants and the remains of yet another shirt.

"Excuse me, Mr. Van Meer."

"We're busy." Arthur unearthed two more plastic containers.

"It's time to discuss my fee." Standing straight made my rib cage hurt worse. All I wanted was to curl up on my bed.

At the trigger word, "fee," they swung around and stared at me. I looked pointedly at the walls, the ceiling, the ash their knees were even now grinding into their clothes, the floor, and their precious money.

Some of their money belonged to me. I didn't want to argue with them for it.

They exchanged glances. Lance fingered a packet of bills. Gwen and Arthur fondled plastic containers. I caught Arthur's eye. Pointed my gaze at his throat. Shifted it toward my dripping wound. Counted the seconds until he got it.

He grabbed the packet of bills from Lance and ripped it open. The man must've handled money for a living, because he fanned the stack of twenties and said, "Five hundred." He picked up two more wrapped stacks. Gwen started to protest.

"Would we have ever found this without him?" Arthur said to them.

"Maybe," Gwen said.

"Bullshit," Lance said. "We were at a dead end and you know it, sweet Guinevere."

Gwen pouted but shut up.

"A finder's fee, Art?" Lance said. "Five hundred from each of us."

"It's only fair," the eldest said. "Gwen, any more arguments?"

"No," she said in a small voice, her eyes on the money.

Arthur got up from his knees, cement dust and demon ash covering his once-black pants. He handed me their fifteen hundred bucks, already damp with the sweat of his money-lust. "Thank you for locating our inheritance, Father."

I took it. I'm not stupid. "Thank you for my exorcism fee, Mr. Van Meer." With the slightest emphasis on "exorcism." "The demon is destroyed. I recommend avoiding Ouija boards in the future."

Over his shoulder, on the edge of the splintered floor, the air warped. A second later the scent of rivers brushed past me. I dissolved the shield I'd made for Emma and turned to go.

Chapter Twenty-Nine

I fell into my car. Made sure my bag was safe on the floor, then rested my head against the seat and wondered if I had the ability to drive home, let alone the energy.

The fresh blood dripping into my boxers presented a more urgent problem. I called Detective Rubio for the name of a doctor who didn't ask embarrassing questions. He sent me to an Immediate Care a ten-minute drive away. I pulled off my collar before I went in. Asked for the doctor. Dropped Rubio's name. Told them I'd lost an argument with a drunk and I had cash but no insurance. I didn't want the report showing up in the Diocese's database.

The doctor was overworked, middle-aged, and rocking hot-pink hair. I liked her on sight. She disinfected the slice without wasting time on bedside manner. I kept my reaction to white-knuckling the vinyl examination table and hissing like a pissed-off cobra. She used wound glue on me. I still wasn't used to the stuff, but it was a helluva lot better than stitches. She didn't lecture me on my perceived behavior, either. I gave her a blessing on the sly when her back was turned.

Somehow I made it to my garage without keeling over. Briefly considered sleeping in the car. Thought better of it. What I needed was several plain old boring days consisting of job, home, demon research, sleep.

An Emma-shock jolted me when I touched my door handle. She jumped me as soon as I entered the room.

"At last! Where have you been?"

I detached her arms from my neck. "Getting my skin glued back together. You want to explain where the thing with a whip for a tail came from?"

She took my messenger bag and set it next to the counter. "I admit my fault in this case. I did not expect the child's toy to conjure an actual demon."

Her hair threw off sparks. I rubbed my eyes. No, it didn't. Did it? Shit, I was running on fumes.

"I told you not to mess with demon lore. You don't know how to handle them and I'm still getting up to speed from the cemetery last week." I walked into the bedroom. "I need to shower the blood off and then I need about twelve hours' sleep. Tomorrow's a workday."

I closed the door. Emma barged in, sparks flickering in her hair, off her fingertips, through her eyes. No doubting this time. I saw it.

"You have not complimented me on my courage and skill."

Whatever the hell was happening to her to make her into a piece of foil inside a microwave, it filled the room until the walls creaked.

"What do you mean?"

"Ingrate. You do not recall when the whip-tailed demon wasted energy by threatening you? I reached inside him and captured part of his powers. Did you not see it?" She halted about six inches away from me.

My skin crawled with energy. "Yes... Now I remember. The air vibrated like heat rising off asphalt in the sun. I felt the balance shift."

She laughed. "We are most excellent partners. You will admit this now."

"Well..."

As though my assent was a signal, she grabbed my face and kissed me. Sparks shot between us. I pushed her back.

"What the hell?"

She ripped my shirt open. "Your injury requires care. I will mount you this time so you do not reopen it."

"What?"

She pushed me back two steps and then onto the bed. Next thing I knew she had my belt unbuckled and my blood-soaked pants and boxers off. Silver lightning sparked through her gray eyes. She fell on top of ten inches of freshly glued demon slash and I cried out.

She sat up. "Your injury is distracting you. I will experiment."

I'd closed my eyes to deal with the rush of pain. Without warning the level of pain dropped by half. When my eyes opened, her hands and my skin were glowing blue-black.

"Emma—stop—That color—You still have the demon's power?" The pain dropped by half again.

"Quiet. I am using it to increase mine." An echo overlaid her voice. Now it was hers and something darker.

"Emma—" The pain was close to nothing now. The glow faded. With the last of it, she pasted herself onto my mouth.

Dark blue light blinded me from the inside. How did she do that? What about the consequences? What about—

"Move farther onto the bed." Her voice was husky with lust.

I walked my elbows and butt back until I hit the pillow. The sensible part of my brain waved its arms and said "Demon power! Don't trust it!" The words meant nothing.

The dark blue light cleared. Emma knelt over me, stark naked. Her eyes sparked, or my eyes sparked, like a camera flash blinding me for an instant. I stuffed my sensible brain into a closet, locked the door, and dragged her on top of me.

Chapter Thirty

I woke up around six thirty, tangled in the covers and Emma's long legs. My shoulder was the only part of me still hurting. I felt the injury. She'd bitten me at some point last night. I touched one end of the slash across my ribs, the only part not covered by Emma's right arm. No swelling. No heat. Only an already flaking line of surgical glue.

We'd have to analyze this. I might have read somewhere about siphoning demonic powers, but never assimilating them into one's own.

She murmured and snuggled closer to me. I stroked her wild hair.

The doorbell rang. At six thirty in the morning.

I wormed my way out of the snarled sheets and pulled on a pair of sweats. The room smelled of sex. I probably smelled of sex. Oh, well.

I opened the door on Archbishop Raymond and Monsignor Dickweed. Of course.

"What?"

"Father Kaine," Raymond said in his best sermon voice,

"since you refuse to keep the appointments my office makes, I am forced to come to you."

"At this hour?" I yawned.

He bristled. "You informed Monsignor Powell that your regular work hours prevent you from keeping appointments which fit our schedule. Thus we are forced to accommodate yours."

"What do you want? If it's about the social media picture, it's on the Web. It can't be taken back." I kept on my side of the door. Maybe any stray breeze would blow toward me instead of them. Although Dickweed wouldn't know what sex smelled like.

"You are a disgrace to the Church." He tried to push me out of my doorway.

Clammy-skinned asshole. I pinched his wrist between two fingers and flung his arm away from me.

"What do you want?" I said to Raymond.

His face swelled. His neck turned red. Spluttering sounds came from his mouth. I was about to grab my phone and call 911 to report a heart attack when I heard Emma's voice behind me.

"Tell these rude people not to arrive so early in the morning."

"See? See? I told you he was fornicating!" Powell bounced in place with each emphasized syllable.

"Oh, go away." I closed the door in their faces.

When I turned around, I had to laugh. Emma stood in the doorway between the kitchen and living room wearing one of my T-shirts. "Long enough to cover her up" could only apply in the loosest of terms.

"Do I look amusing?" Annoyance sharpened her voice.

"My shirt needs to be about six inches longer to be decent on you. Now you've scandalized the archbishop and his flunky."

Comprehension showed in her face. "Because I wear your clothes they think we are lovers? Well, it is true."

"Eh. Now I'm in trouble."

She looked down to where the shirt hit. "Would you rather I appear as a young man?"

A dark-haired college-type stood in Emma's place, fully clothed.

I started. "No, it wouldn't help."

The young man frowned and said in Emma's voice, "You dislike this? Perhaps a nun."

A nun of about the same fictional age as the young man appeared, in full habit: floor-length billowing skirts, wimple, veil, and the white waist-cord with attached rosary.

"Good God, no."

She returned to herself, short T-shirt intact. "You are difficult to please."

"I'm showering. Might as well go to work early. You and I have things to discuss."

She wrinkled her nose. "Tension at meals ruins good food. Discuss with me now or not at all."

I sighed. What a difficult woman. "It's about the power you took from yesterday's demon."

Her smile was enigmatic. "Yes." When I didn't say anything, she huffed. "What do you wish to lecture about this time? Do you think to object to my help of yesterday? Or do you think evil can never be used for one's own purposes?"

"Yes. Exactly. Evil power twists on itself. You can't trust it."

She came close to me and traced the line of my already healed injury. "You are complaining about this?"

"No, but..."

She pressed herself against me. "You have complaints about the lovemaking?" She moved her hips. "You are not yet satisfied."

I swallowed. "I'm not complaining. Stop. I can't concentrate." She didn't move, so I backed up. She hadn't been this aggressive before.

"The *khui* is more articulate than the mouth." She stretched her arms above her head. My T-shirt rode up her abdomen.

I stared at the clock over the sink. Boring clock. Maybe I needed something kitschy like the ones at Martin's.

"Ridiculous man. Do not concern yourself with how I absorbed the demon's power and used it as my own. Be happy at the ways I was able to turn it to our benefit." She walked over to the fridge. "Take a shower. I will make breakfast and we will eat without tension."

During the drive to work I could've sworn I heard a voice whispering to me. Then again, static liked to interfere with the classical station's radio signal on clear mornings. Simple.

I wasn't satisfied with Emma's offhand assumption about her absorption of demon power. Power and confidence weren't enough when dealing with the red-assed crew. Knowledge and strength were essential. She wouldn't listen to a lecture. Can't say I blamed her. I'd have to figure out some other way to get through to her.

Mornings were still darkish even three weeks after the clock change. I liked it. By the time I parked the car, the eastern sky glowed white and blue. Only the early buses messed with the calls of mourning doves and black-capped chickadees.

Normally I liked the silence when I came to work this early, but not today. I turned the radio to NPR. I wanted human voices.

I made a cup of the strongest coffee Martin stocked and texted Lisa. "Any luck on the demon research?"

Within a minute, I had an answer: "A little. Don't do anything stupid."

I could hear her voice say it. I replied with: "Me?"

She didn't bother to answer. I missed the old lady. I walked up and down the aisles, adjusting crooked books, changing the spacing on tight rows, keeping a mental note of empty spaces to be refilled.

"What?"

I looked toward the front of the store. Empty. Could've sworn I heard someone calling me.

Martin arrived an hour late.

"Denis, you're my rock. My antique Corolla issued a Do Not Resuscitate order last night. God, public transportation is a nightmare. Here."

He handed me a divided plastic container filled with bulging lumps of dough.

"Pierogi from Mom. Clockwise fillings from the upper right: potato, sauerkraut, onion and cheese, and blueberry for dessert."

"Thanks." They resembled underdone potstickers.

"Don't nuke them. Reheat them in the oven for a few minutes. You'll love 'em."

"I'm sure I will. Thank your mother for me." I sounded sincere, even to myself.

Martin regaled me with dysfunctional family stories off and on through the day. The aunts who ignored each other's existence because of a snarky letter forty-three years ago. The cousins whose Jack Russell terriers spent the entire weekend trying to attack another cousin's ferret. The five-year-old who got the prize egg in the church Easter Egg Hunt and shouted, "Hot damn!" in front of the priest and three nuns.

He stared at me when he finished his last story. "Denis, you're smiling. What's wrong?"

My face reverted to its usual expression. Felt more comfortable anyway. Martin shook his head and ran to the counter to take care of a customer.

Emma snatched the container from me after work when I went to stash it in the fridge.

"Pierogi! Are they homemade? What kinds?"

I repeated Martin's description and she practically salivated.

"You will share these with me, yes?"

"They're all yours. They look too weird for me. I'll tell Martin they were delicious."

She shook a finger in my face. "Liars go to a bad place when they die. I will heat these and you will eat them and thank me afterward." She stashed them in the fridge and dragged me to the door. "Come. We meet with the selkie this evening."

I pulled in the opposite direction. "Right now? I'm hungry and tired and need to do more demon research."

"Do not be an infant. We will fetch food after the meeting. It will not be long. I have directions to the university at which she is a professor. We will get there quickly if you retrieve your car keys and do not argue."

Chapter Thirty-One

According to Emma, this selkie guarded her privacy and was easily startled. This was Emma-speak for "Shut up or you'll blow this opportunity."

She led the way to the art department, mostly empty since it was after five. On the top floor near the back of the building a nameplate read "Professor Siobhan Neró, Sculpture." We entered a studio decorated in greens and blues. A small, slender woman stood in the northwest corner under one of those full-spectrum lamps, molding a fifteen-inch-long dolphin leaping from a two-foot wave. It was stunning.

"Good evening," Emma said, coming halfway into the room. "I admire your skill."

"Thank you." The professor's voice was soft and she didn't raise her eyes from her work. Her aura belied her outward calm: bright yellow spiked through soft lavender. "May I help you?"

Emma glanced over the sculptures of varying skill on an openwork metal shelf. "It is difficult trying to communicate with humans at times, is it not?"

The sculptor snatched her hands away from the upward curve of the water. Her aura flared with panic. An instant later,

Emma turned into a rusalka. Seeing her up close as this creature brought those desolate three weeks in Rome to the front of my awareness. I locked the memories in a trunk and tossed the trunk in a sub-subbasement room in my head.

The professor relaxed. Emma changed back.

"Yes," she said in the same soft voice, "humans are difficult." She touched the clay again, smoothing the sweep of water.

"I would like to ask for your help," Emma said. "Have you heard anything of demons increasing their activities?"

The professor worked on the dolphin's tail as it flipped free of the carved water. After a minute she said, "Have you heard of the priest who lives in Hyde Park? D-something. He would know about demons."

Emma's smile widened. "This is Denis. He is the priest from Hyde Park."

The sculptor returned her smile. "I see. Let me think a moment."

She still hadn't acknowledged my existence. Could be she was the most introverted person—creature—I'd ever met. Could be the Kaine aura. Whether or not they know about us, Xav's and my presence tend to give supernatural creatures the crawlies.

I had to admit it was a good thing Emma was doing the talking.

The selkie's hands continued to smooth the water, alter the shape of the dolphin's nose, add a curl to the end of the wave. "This is Tuesday," she said as though ordering events in her mind. "Yesterday, the Monday after Easter, two of my students mentioned something about the fancy Saturday night Mass at Holy Name Cathedral. Apparently they turn off the lights and the priest blesses fire and water."

She and Emma exchanged a look which plainly said, "We will never understand humans."

"Something happened," the artist continued, "in the transition from dark to light. The students wouldn't talk about the specifics, but they were spooked. Yes, spooked is the best way to describe it." She looked at me for the first time. "Perhaps you can talk to the priests who were there."

Raymond and Powell would have officiated at the Easter Vigil Mass. If I'd known, I would've dragged them into my apartment this morning no matter what they thought of me.

Emma elbowed me, and I thanked this selkie who appeared human. Selkies weren't in my line of work, but since she looked like a regular human it meant someone had well and truly shafted her.

"Many thanks," Emma said. "When this issue is settled, I will ask my contacts about ways to circumvent the rules for skins which have been destroyed."

The artist's dark eyes opened wide.

Emma's smile warmed. "I too have endured much solitude. It is not good. I have no kindred left, but your kin lives long. There is still hope."

I waited until we were back at my car to speak. "Who are you and what have you done with the imperious, self-serving female who invaded my apartment?"

Emma huffed. "Is there a reason you must be handled with tact and sympathy now?"

"Not me. But since when do you handle anyone with tact and sympathy?"

She flounced into her seat. "Your head is made of rock. She is like I am. Age will not affect her. Soon she will have to move to another city and create another identity. It is not good for anyone to be alone for so long."

I started the car so she wouldn't see the surprise on my face. A profound Emma needed time for me to adjust to.

Chapter Thirty-Two

Emma argued when I said I wasn't going home right away. We compromised on a stop at one of the supersized grocery stores and she came out with a single bag whose contents she refused to reveal.

"You will return in not more than one hour and fifteen minutes," she said when I dropped her off at the apartment.

"Yes, ma'am. I hear and obey, ma'am."

She made the expressive Italian gesture which means "asshole." I laughed and drove away. At the end of the street I realized both door keys hung from my key ring in the ignition. Then I remembered watching a Cthulhu tentacle unlock my door last week and kept driving.

Twenty minutes later, I parked behind Holy Name Cathedral. Gorgeous place. Spectacular architecture. Remarkable history. And possibly fucked-up beyond all recognition.

Several dozen cars filled the spaces nearest the door to the parish center. Right. Bingo on Tuesdays and Saturdays. The cathedral proper should be empty and the inside access doors would be unlocked.

I stood in the main vestibule to conduct my ritual. The

carpets and Easter flowers muffled the bingo caller's amplified voice; easy to shut him out. Negligible traffic noise next. Not much else. I walked up the center aisle with slow, measured steps. The sulfur of a struck match caught me halfway up and I stopped. Burning wood. The clean scent of Church candle wax. Water. Voices singing. A trumpet voluntary.

He failed.

The whisper cut through my practiced silence.

You will fail.

Without moving, I scanned the altar, the statues, the Confessionals, the pews in front of me. The voice hadn't come from a particular angle. It was just there, like the scents and sounds from last Saturday were there.

Show yourself, I projected.

Laughter.

Show yourself, red-ass.

Someone screaming. More laughter, tittering like asylum inmates in old horror movies. Another scream.

The screaming voice sounded like Xav's.

No. It couldn't be. No. No. No.

The scent of hundreds of lilies wormed into my silence. I strained to repair it. Another scream floated in. When I tried to identify Xav's voice, my bubble snapped.

The stained-glass saints leered at me. The lilies rotted in their vases. The resurrected Christ above the altar opened His solemn mouth and laughed more crazy laughter.

I ran.

Didn't stop until I locked myself in the Impala. My hands shook so bad I dropped the keys twice. Got myself out into traffic and missed taking out a mailbox by six inches. Slowed down to the speed limit then. I kept hitting the mute button on the radio but it didn't work. Somewhere on South Lake Shore I realized the voice muttering in Latin wasn't from the radio. It was mine. I clamped my mouth shut for the rest of the drive. Parked the car and got the hell out of the garage before I heard more laughter.

Emma opened the door and yanked me inside while I was fitting the key into the lock.

"What has happened? Your panic breached the walls as though they did not exist." She forced me into one of the kitchen chairs and took my face between her hands. "Speak. Now."

A wild impulse to bark like a dog welled up in me. I squashed it. Didn't trust my voice yet.

"Why do you not speak?" She clutched my head tighter. "Has something attacked you?"

"Stop clawing my scalp." My voice lurched. I put my hands up to hers. They shook too much to get a grip.

"No. Not until you tell me what has happened." She hooked a chair toward us with her left ankle and sat. "Have you fought more demons in the hour we have been apart?"

Fighting demons.

I had the answer. My hands stopped shaking. I stopped muttering. I pushed her away and ran into the living room with my bag. Flipped the area rug over the coffee table and the closed laptop. Brought out my salt stick and started to draw the fifth pentacle of Mars from the *Key of Solomon* on the wooden floor.

Emma stepped over the double circle.

"Stay on the other side. I'm only making it big enough for one." I started on the inscription within the circles.

She backed out. "What are you doing? Tell me this instant."

I erased a misspelled word with the side of my fist. "The fuckers are trying to mess with me. I'm gonna force one of them to tell me what I want to know if I have to fry off his skin one layer at a time."

She yelped. "You are going to call up a demon?"

"You bet their scaly red asses I am." I started on the central scorpion.

"Do not do such a rash thing!" Emma paced around the opposite half of the circle.

"Shut up. I need to remember the incantation." Only the four words around the scorpion left to write. "Go away. I need to concentrate."

The atmosphere in the column above the circle pulsed from floor to ceiling. Red-assed bastards knew I was out for their blood.

"Your smile will cause more fear in your enemies than your frown." Emma's voice. I thought she'd left.

"Get out. I'm working."

"You are stupid and suicidal."

"You're wasting my time. I'm starting now. Leave or stay, I don't care. Just don't interrupt." My eyes slid back into my head. Emma's sharp voice said something in Russian. I attuned myself to the circle and the energy expanded and contracted with my breathing.

And then the energy vanished. My eyes slipped down into their usual place. A wedge from the circle was missing along with half the scorpion. Emma was brushing sage and salt from her forearm.

I grabbed her arm. "What do you think you're doing?"

She twisted in my grip. "You must not act in haste. I have stopped you from leaping headfirst into danger."

The world behind my eyes turned red as a demon's ass. "Get out. I have to find out about Xavier. I have to make them tell me."

I flung her away from the damaged circle and reached for my salt stick.

Five glowing scarlet akkorokamui tentacles clutched me. A

sixth ripped the salt stick from my hand. I yanked and squirmed as two more tentacles squeezed me immobile.

"Let me go, dammit!" I tried to kick free but three of the sucker-laden arms slithered around my legs. I cursed and struggled and tried to bite the ones nearest my mouth, but I got nowhere.

I gave up only when I was too exhausted to move. A few minutes later, the tentacles unwound and slithered away and Emma sat cross-legged on the floor next to my prostrate, panting body.

"Now you will tell me what happened tonight. It is a good thing supper was complete before you flung away all common sense or another meal would be ruined."

I wasn't seeing through a haze of anger anymore. My temples weren't pounding, either. "I must've been out of my head."

She snorted. "You have been practicing the art of understatement. I had not yet seen you furious and afraid all at once." She stretched her back. "I have not become akkorokamui for many years. It takes much energy. Tell me what caused you to become unhinged."

"The church."

A long-suffering sigh. "Your reply is insufficient."

What had enough mojo to make me hallucinate so vividly? Auditory, visual, olfactory—no, the fresh Easter lilies were definitely real.

Emma smacked the side of my head. "Out loud, please."

"Sorry. I went to check out Holy Name Cathedral after what your selkie said. I—heard things."

When I didn't continue, she swatted me again. "Do not seal this up within yourself. What did you hear?"

"A voice talking smack. Whispering smack. It found a way through the barrier I wrapped around myself."

"What is this smack? It does not mean what I have understood it to mean, yes?"

"Right. It's slang. Means goading someone with words, picking a fight."

She made a thoughtful sound. "Continue."

Once the words were out of my head and in the air I wasn't so freaked. "I challenged it. It laughed. Then I heard a scream. It sounded... It sounded like Xav's voice." I forced myself to go on. "I concentrated on it and weakened my shield. When my shield collapsed all hell broke loose."

Emma balanced her elbows on her knees. "Specifics, you irritating man."

"The saints in the windows moved. The lilies died. The giant carved Christ, it, well, its mouth opened, and it laughed like the same demon." Shudders rippled up my entire body.

Emma smacked me a third time.

"Stop!" I rubbed my head.

She nodded, an abrupt movement. "Good. Your voice is yours again. These events are why you were about to conjure a demon here in your home?"

"Yeah. I wanted answers. I want answers. Gotta go to the source."

"Do not make me strike you again." She rubbed out the rest of my circle with the hem of her skirt. "When I awoke as rusalka, I understood one truth quite soon: only the foolhardy poke a nest of hornets. You were about to call up something too powerful to contain."

"Don't underestimate me."

"Arrogant man, you were blind with anger and fear. Remember your rituals. Demons are to be challenged only when you are calm and prepared."

I growled. "I hate it when you're right."

She laughed. "It is good for your ego. Now we will eat. You

have need of much nourishment. I require you to please me in bed this night."

Someone knocked at the door.

"Son of a bitch. I've had more visitors in the past week than in the entire eight months I've lived here."

She got to her feet and her dress scattered salt over me "Your complaints are more vocal than an aggrieved mother-in-law. Do you have energy enough to receive the visitor?"

I pushed myself upright. "At least I don't resort to snide insults as a method of communication."

A multipierced courier stood on my threshold. "Delivery from the, uh, Archdio-cheese-ean Office."

He should've ended with "Dude." Raymond must've sent this stoner because he didn't want the door slammed in his self-important face again. Well, it wasn't the stoner's fault. I took the nine-by-twelve envelope and didn't slam the door.

"Is it permissible for me to enter the kitchen now?" Emma called from the living room.

"Huh? Sure."

"You sound perplexed." She joined me at the table. "My presence upset your last visitors. I do not wish to disrupt all parts of your life."

"Too late." I tossed the envelope in the trash.

Emma picked it up. "Why do you ignore this missive?"

"If it's from Raymond, it can only be another summons to appear at his mansion to be officially censured." I went over to the stove and lifted the lid on a casserole pan. "Stuffed pork chops. Perfect. What's in them?" I pulled at the cheese-and-greens mixture oozing out of the sides.

The envelope came down on my hand. "Do not ruin the coherence of the meal." She ripped off the short edge of the envelope and pulled out a single sheet of paper.

"You are correct," she said, reading. "The head priest wishes to chastise you for not stooping under his yoke. However..." Her eyebrows arched. "He offers you amnesty."

I laughed. "On what conditions?"

"He writes about a historic church which is haunted and you are the only exorcist in the northeast area of this country."

I crossed my arms. "Liar. There's Andrew in Maine and Hal in New York City. What he can't bring himself to say is that I'm the best exorcist in the northeast."

She was still reading. "There is more about your vow of obedience and the time and expense of the church to train you... then about familial duty."

I stopped myself from spitting on the expensive piece of letterhead. "Fuck that rat bastard and all his superiors. Skip to the dollar amount he thinks he can buy me with. I know it's in there."

Her eyebrows disappeared into her hairline. "You are right. He offers you one thousand dollars and his assistance with returning to your former position at a university far from here."

For a second words choked me. "He's a stinking piece of shit. Guess he thinks I look poor enough to come like a dog to heel for the week's wage of a middle manager." I snatched the letter out of her hands, ripped it in half, and shoved it into this morning's coffee grounds. "I'll pour you some wine."

We were finishing the last of the pork chops stuffed with provolone, garlic, and greens when the Mac made its "incoming email" chime.

"Will you answer?"

I shook my head. "These are too delicious to rush. You're almost as good a cook as my grandmother."

She swallowed her wine before she answered. "Were I your wife, such a poor compliment would make me angry. However, I thank you for it." She wrinkled her nose as I took a swig from my can of Coke. "Disgusting concoction. You should overcome your reluctance to drink alcohol. Wine is the correct beverage for this meal."

"Don't push me." I savored the final bite. "I'll make you a cassoulet tomorrow so you can pass judgment on my cooking skills."

"I will enjoy the experience." She picked up her dishes. "It is your turn to wash."

She was drying pans when I checked the email.

"I am sending this message to the Diocese of Chicago, my pastor at Assumption Church and Auxilium group. One of you must help my grandson before he harms anyone else. It is now eight o'clock p.m. on Tuesday, April 7th. Come immediately to Northwestern University." The email ended with the dorm name and room number.

I touched the screen the way some tarot readers have their clients shuffle the cards. The woman's fear and panic bled through the LCD film. Beneath it was something big. Fifth- or sixth-circle big, thank you, Dante Alighieri.

I ran for my room and got into my blacks. Transferred my keys from my jeans, but my cell phone wasn't in the opposite pocket. Not on the dresser or nightstand or out in the living room on the coffee table.

"Emma, have you seen my cell?"

She came to the doorway, dish towel in one hand, phone in the other. "Here it is."

I stuffed it in my pocket. "Thanks. Gotta go. Don't know when I'll be back."

She called something after me, but I was already out the door.

Chapter Thirty-Three

Forty minutes to get there, thanks to a three-car pileup on South Lake Shore. The one time I should've taken the interstate...

My GPS got me to the dorm without a problem. Good thing, since it was one anonymous brick building among a group of anonymous brick buildings. A little old lady with bright brown hair stood guard inside the door. She glared up at me—if she was four foot ten it was a stretch—as I stood under the floodlight. When she saw the Roman collar, she pushed the crash bar and let me in.

"Which one are you?" Her voice was as thin as her body, but I could see she was like my grandmère. I wouldn't want to cross her if she had a wooden spoon in her hand.

"I'm from Auxilium group." I followed her down the hall to an elevator.

"*Tch.* My priest couldn't get himself here before a stranger did. He won't like what I put in his collection plate next Sunday." She pressed the "Up" button. "What's your name, Father?"

"Kaine."

"Are you any good?" The elevator dinged, and the doors slid open.

I put on my best poker face as we entered the poster-covered box. "Yes, ma'am."

She pressed the button for "Two" and looked up at my face again. Her head didn't even reach my shoulder. "You had better be. My grandson has pulled the king of all boneheaded stunts and I want him back alive."

Another ding and the doors opened on a male voice screaming. My escort winced. "Follow me."

The long hall was empty. Neon-red fear pulsed around every closed door, stronger to my Sight than the row of fluorescents on the ceiling. Twenty rooms; two people to a room. Way too many innocent bystanders.

Two-thirds of the way down the hall, a kid who didn't look old enough to buy a beer sat on the floor with his arms wrapped around his knees. Blood trickled down his right cheek from under a rolled-up shirt tied around his head. Every pore on his skin hemorrhaged terror.

"Anthony, tell Father Kaine what you and my grandson did."

The kid didn't move. I crouched in front of him, one hand on my messenger bag. "What's in your room?"

He responded to something: my voice, the formidable old lady next to me, another bellow from behind the door at his right shoulder.

"We thought we could handle it at first, you know?" His voice said he was honestly puzzled they couldn't control whatever they'd called up.

His roommate's grandmother tapped her navy-blue Converse All-Star. "The trouble with the two of you is that you're too smart for your own good."

"Mrs. Meyer, we did the research." He didn't look up at her, though.

"There's research and then there's experience. You can't leap from high school chemistry into the Manhattan Project."

Yep. I wouldn't want to piss her off.

"But, Mrs. Meyer, we're science majors."

She stopped short of whacking his bloody head. "You see, Father? This intelligent young man is all of eighteen years old. My grandson is sixteen. Smartest boy in his high school. He graduated at age fifteen and a half with a full scholarship to this university. And what does he do? Tell Father Kaine, Anthony."

Something crashed against the steel door. The kid clutched his knees tighter.

"Fucking coward!" The young voice on the other side of the door had an old and powerful resonance. "Blubbering asswipe!"

Anthony buried his head in his thighs.

"Tell the interfering old bitch to come in here and I'll ram her precious little grandson's textbooks down her throat!"

The grandmother's lips thinned into invisibility.

"It's not your grandson talking," I said.

"You fucking bet I'm not her pencil-necked grandson!"

"Mother, what are you doing?" An angular man strode down the hall toward us. His khakis were as crisp as though they'd come off the rack five minutes ago. His dry-cleaning bill must be obscene.

"I'm saving my grandson's soul, Joseph."

"Mother, you're talking nonsense. Charlene, talk to her."

A clone of the woman next to me appeared from behind the pressed khakis. The clone wore pointy heels and her hair was platinum blonde, but in every visible way dry-cleaning guy had married his mother. Might explain a few things.

From behind the door: "Shut your fucking mouth, motherfucker!"

The clone shied away from the voice which was and wasn't her son's. Her husband's lips did the same pressed-to-invisibility trick his mother's did.

"You see, Joseph?" his mother said.

Something shattered against the other side of the door.

"It's drugs. It has to be drugs," Pressed-khakis said.

"Stupid fuck!"

"Joseph, do something." The clone's shrill voice hurt my teeth.

"I'll do something, you frigid bitch!"

"Stop saying those things to your mother!" from Pressed-khakis.

"Jeffrey, baby, why are you doing this to us?" from the clone.

"Jeffrey baby, Jeffrey baby, Jeffrey baby!"

"I demand respect, young man!" Several hairs escaped Pressed-khakis's sprayed black coif. What man still used hair spray in this decade?

"Come in here and say it to my face and I'll rip off your head and shit down your neck!"

The clone burst into tears. She added squeaky, gasping screams to the show as well. Her husband shouted at her to control herself. Something large and heavy hit the inside of the door and left a pointed bulge on our side. The kid's grandmother shouted at both of them to pay attention to the real problem.

"Everybody shut up!" Anthony's voice.

Everyone did.

In the silence, the thing in the room giggled.

Anthony got to his knees but swayed so bad I sat him down again. Took a jar of salt from my bag. I'd poured a whole three inches of it when the door opened inward.

Above me, a tall, scrawny teenager with pitch-black hair and swirling white eyes aimed a steak knife at my head. I threw the entire contents of the salt jar into his face. The demon-controlled kid dropped the knife, spluttering and coughing. I shoved him back inside and yanked the door shut.

Pressed-khakis landed a weak hit to my jaw.

His mother cuffed the back of his head hard enough to make him stagger.

A light touch on my shoulder. Emma. Nobody else said anything, so she'd done her chameleon thing and blended into the paint on the walls. *Christ, don't make me have to worry about her, too.*

It might not be traditional, but it was a prayer.

I stayed next to the roommate but said to Pressed-khakis, "Don't touch me again."

His shiny Italian loafers backed away.

"So," I said to the roommate, "what are you two into?"

He shook his head and clapped both hands to the bloody undershirt. "He threw my keyboard at me. We're not doing drugs. They're too expensive and they interfere with our higher cognitive function."

Smart but stupid, this one. "Don't waste my time. What is he into?"

Anthony focused squinting eyes on me for real.

"A couple of months ago, the girls down the hall wanted to go antique hunting. We said we'd be their heavy lifters. They're cute, you know? I wanted to get laid." He waited. Apparently satisfied I wasn't going to lecture him about the evils of premarital sex, he continued. "They found a place with goth-type stuff, books and statues and death art. Jeff bought this old book of witchcraft potions and spells."

I groaned. Stupid, idiot, cocksure kids.

A few feet to my left, Pressed-khakis was talking his wife down from her hysteria. Within my peripheral vision, Grandma's right Converse kept tapping the floor.

Anthony's voice got defensive. "It was cool. We met these two hot girls in a chat room. We sent them screenshots of the spells we couldn't understand. They translated them because they wanted to use the spells too. On Good Friday, we drew the diagram on the floor and said the spell and it worked. We caught a real live, um, well, immortal, I guess, demon."

"Idiots."

"We controlled it."

I gave a pointed look at his bleeding head.

"We did," he said. "It was a minor demon and it was forced to obey our summons and it was our servant. It told us how to curse our enemies."

Snickering came from behind the damaged door. Anthony winced.

"You should've seen Professor Griffiths after the demon gave him ringworm in his junk." Anthony laughed and winced again. "We got the demon to make us a peephole into the girls' shower, but we can't see much through the steam."

Gray-green breath puffed through the keyhole. "Humans are so gullible."

"You two need a keeper." I stood and said to the grandmother, "Mrs. Meyer, is there anything else you know about this?"

Pressed-khakis cut in. "There's nothing to tell. These two are obviously on drugs and lying about it. It's all hallucinations."

Air smelling like beer vomit saturated the hall. Everyone gagged. Anthony sneered at Pressed-khakis.

The kid's grandmother glared at her son and said to me, "Jeffrey called me at seven thirty. He told me about the book and apologized. When he took a breath, I asked him what he meant. There was a noise like he'd dropped the phone and then the sounds of struggling and shouts of 'No!' and then silence. I drove right over here. When Anthony told me the whole story,

I sent the email. These new phones should have bigger screens."

I unslung my messenger bag. "Okay. This is going to get loud and possibly dangerous. The other residents seem to have locked themselves in their rooms."

"I told them to," Anthony said. "Nobody argued when they saw me and heard the thing inside Jeff."

"Good. Can you walk?"

He got vertical in increments but didn't sway anymore. Jeff's grandmother took his arm.

"Can you get him out of here?" I said to her. To Pressed-khakis, "Can you please take your wife out as well?"

He turned on the bluster. Typical.

"Who are you to give me orders? We don't need you. Nobody asked you to interfere in our lives. What my son needs is a shrink and detox, not some priest."

His mother released Anthony's arm and planted herself in front of her son, an angry mouse standing up to a barn owl.

"Joseph, you're my son and I love you, but you're an egotistical fool and Jeffrey is the same. I'm not going to let my oldest grandson die because his father is too stupid to see reality." She turned him around and pushed him toward his wife, who'd started to cry again. "Now take yourselves away and let the professional do his job."

A different scream from behind the door, and then a younger, panicky voice shouted, "He's killing me!"

His mother yipped. His father jumped for the door. I threw him back.

"Get out of here."

He raised his fist again. I smacked it away.

"Do you want your son back? Do you?"

He swallowed something hard and pointy. "Yes."

"Then get out."

Anthony pulled Pressed-khakis by the arm. "Come on, Mr. Meyer. We screwed up. Let the movie dude fix it."

God preserve me from any more references to *The Exorcist* for as long as I lived.

Anthony said to me with an attempt at a conspiratorial smile, "So where's your carpetbag with all the holy stuff?"

I indicated my messenger bag. All of their eyes opened wider. Even the kid's grandmother's, despite her earlier championing of me to her son. Nobody ever took me seriously. I should go out in the garden and eat worms.

The moment passed. The grandmother shoved everyone down the hall and into the stairwell.

I turned my back on them and opened the bag. No salt stick came to my hand this time. No flute. Nothing called to me. Not a good sign. I touched a candle and a vial of angelica, then one of horehound. Kaines did not hesitate. Kaines did not waver. I was wavering. Shit.

"Stop," Emma whispered, and she crouched beside me, visible. Her flowered dress anchored me for a second. A bit of the familiar world to stand against the insanity in the dorm room.

"Do not be distracted by what awaits you. Focus."

I didn't waste time bantering with her. I closed my eyes and shut out everything the correct way, step by step. Family on the stairs. Cowering kids in the other rooms. Creaking sounds from inside the kid's room. Emma.

There we go. I opened my eyes and pulled out juniper and holy water. Poured the water over my right hand and rubbed powdered juniper into my wet fingertips. Said a quick prayer of protection to Michael the Archangel. Stood and drew a four-foot-tall algiz rune on the door. The giant bird footprint shone clear pine green on the gray paint. I inhaled its crisp, resinous scent and my mind filled with its defense and protection.

The thing inhabiting the kid made loud retching sounds. I

hoped with all my soul that those were dry heaves and opened the door.

The room could have been in a dictionary next to the word "chaos." Mounds of mattress foam shreds covered the floor and desks. Papers flew in erratic patterns from the ceiling to the floor and up to the ceiling again. A cube fridge lay open on its side behind the door. Milk, yogurt, Coke, and leftover lo mein had spilled into glutinous blobs all around it. A clock radio impaled a computer monitor. Action figures of Darth Vader, Boba Fett, and the last three Doctor Whos were nailed into the wall above the window in cosplay imitations of Christ.

"Really?" I closed the door, the rune on it trapping him in here with me. The kid sat in a plain wooden chair on top of a standard student desk. He topped me by a couple of feet on his improvised throne.

"It's a classic." His voice was back to a weenie kid's with an undercurrent of age and power. "Give me points for not crucifying them upside down. I don't stoop to cliché."

I stood my ground. The entire narrow room was visible to me from this angle. The night-black window behind him framed his head like a reverse halo. And he claimed to disparage cliché.

"Oh look. You brought your pet." He whistled the same way people called their dog.

I didn't look around. Emma should've stayed in the hall and I didn't have time to argue with her. Right now arrogance was the only weakness I perceived in this red-ass. I had to find more.

"How the mighty have fallen." He turned those swirling white eyes on me. "Really, Denis. You should make her tell you her history. It's a wonderful story for pillow talk after you fuck like rabbits." Another giggle. "Oh Father Denis, OFM, ME in Latin, Hebrew, and Greek, ThD, JCD, you're going to go to a bad place when I kill you." He turned those eyes on Emma. "I wonder if you can be killed. Won't it be fun to try?"

The same primitive impulse which flooded me when she'd come back after the alleyway fight returned. I couldn't give into it. No time. I shoved it in the mental storage room with all the unfinished crap from Xav's death and began.

Except what came out of my mouth wasn't the authentic, Vatican-approved, Demon-Be-Gone exorcism. It was Creole. For a moment I was thrown back to my time studying with Madame Gagnon six years ago. She was filled with knowledge and power and freely shared both.

The demon/kid choked on his next taunt. The language flowed from my mouth in my French-Canadian accent, the eternal despair of Madame G.'s precise Haitian ear. Still speaking, I reached in my bag for the mullein. The demon opened his mouth and the power in me turned my words into gibberish.

I didn't analyze what I was saying. I caught elements of a banishing spell and translations of the exorcism ritual combining into its incantation.

"The language of the laity?" the demon/kid choked out at last. "You've sunk lower than I thought, Kaine." His voice got stronger as he completed the sentence. "Did you lose your mastery of Mother Church's fancy speech when you rutted with this ancient fraud?"

Emma leaned against a cracked chest of drawers and cursed him in colorful Italian.

The kid jumped down from his improvised throne and pushed his face right into mine. "Xavier says hi."

My recitation stumbled but I didn't stop. Xav's not in Hell, my mind screamed from its storage room.

Emma sauntered over from the busted chest of drawers. "It is quite vile for something as old as you to attach itself to a child."

The demon/kid turned on her. "I thought you'd be more open-minded."

Emma made a spitting noise. "Parasite."

The demon slapped at her, but she blocked it and grabbed his wrist. I spoke faster now, the rhythm of the language matching my haste. The demon, caught between Emma's grip and the power building in me, let slip a glimpse of his true face.

Bingo. When the mask slips, it's weakened. Exorcism 201.

Emma smiled at him. "Did you perhaps underestimate us, *dragotsennyy?*"

A fat textbook flew at my head. I deflected it, still reciting. The alarm clock worked its way out of the monitor and flung itself at Emma. Her free arm transformed into a tentacle to catch it and fling it against the wall.

A dozen pens and pencils aimed themselves at my eyes. I raised a quick shield and they impaled it, then fell when I collapsed it. Emma fielded a textbook and the chair from the former throne. An unbroken monitor and keyboard came toward me. I had to use both arms on them and the mullein scattered.

The demon screamed. An upward arc of flaming pinpricks appeared on his face. The kid's skin tore away from the mullein-scented fire geysers and charred fur popped out. It reeked of beer vomit, too. So did his breath as he switched from taunts to curses.

"Your brother damns your soul to Hell every day, Kaine! He's waiting for me to send you to him!"

I caught Emma's gaze. The demon's control slipped more with every taunt. I tuned out his words as my spell ratcheted higher and stronger.

"He's going to pay you back for letting him blow his brains out! He's going to make you eat a shotgun over and over until you crawl to him to beg him to stop!"

Emma grabbed the demon's hands and clapped them to the sides of his head. The kid/demon's body jackhammered.

Emma's jaw went slack. Her eyes glowed. The faster the demon vibrated, the more skin sloughed off his face. Emma's body went rigid and the demon's power level nose-dived.

"Now!" Emma said.

I shouted the last of the Creole and reached into the kid/demon. My hands passed through the kid's body and ripped the demon in half.

The kid and the demon screamed as their bodies and voices split. Charred green power exploded out of the kid. The window shattered. The overhead light sizzled. The papers in the air fell to the floor. So did the kid. I caught him before he gashed open his head on the corner of the desk.

Emma's hair was wild with static electricity. Her unfocused eyes stared through me; she was panting like she'd run a 5K race. So was I, I noticed as the strength drained out of my arms and I crashed onto the debris-covered floor with the kid.

At the outer edge of the chaos, Xavier laughed.

Chapter Thirty-Four

"Xav?"

No voice answered me. I heard only Emma and me catching our breath. The kid sprawling on my lap breathed like he was merely asleep.

"Xavier?"

Papers sifting in between other papers. The *zzzt-zzzt-zzzt* of the light. Voices reaching my ears through the broken window from the sidewalk three stories below us.

Not Xav. I let myself breathe. Only college kids' voices. Shouldn't give panic the reins when I was running on fumes.

I flexed my hands. The knuckles and backs were scorched. Nothing that wouldn't heal in a couple of days. "Could've been worse."

Emma smoothed her hair. "I am more powerful than I thought." She jumped on the desk. "I am adjusting. It will be only a moment." Her aura eclipsed mine and the kid's, pulsing with colors wilder than I'd ever seen in it.

The Emma-on-steroids sitting above me was going to take longer for both of us to adjust to. But not right now.

"Can you disappear so I can wake up the kid?"

She grinned, snapped her fingers, and vanished.

I slapped the kid's undamaged cheeks. The demon's burned and ripped injuries hadn't transferred to the kid's actual body. It's one of the undeserved perks for clueless dabblers in demon-summoning.

The kid moaned.

I slapped his cheeks again. "Wake up, asshole."

His baby blues opened wide, then squinted at the fritzing light. "Who—What—"

I sat him up. "Father Kaine, and I just saved your moronic ass. Thank your grandmother."

He stared at the disaster which had once been a dorm room, his jaw hanging open. When his scrutiny took in the crucified dolls, I watched his gears and wheels snap back into place.

"The demon?"

"What do you think, idiot?"

He transferred the scrutiny to me. "You don't sound like a priest."

"You don't act like Kid Genius. Did you enjoy being mind-fucked by a demon?"

One more piece clicked. His lower lip shook and he started to sob. So much for bravado.

"Get up. Unless I'm dumber than a bag of hammers, and I'm not, your parents are waiting in the hall instead of the stair-well where I sent them for safety."

I pushed to my feet using the desk for support. Got my legs steady, fetched a bundle of dried ginseng impregnated with myrrh from my bag, and lit the bundle. It burned to nothing in thirty seconds, cleansing the air and negating the binding rune on the door. Locked my bag, slung it over my shoulder, and opened the door.

The kid's grandmother jumped away from the threshold. I wondered how much of the demon's circus she'd heard through the steel-core door. Pressed-khakis and the clone had pushed themselves against the opposite wall so hard there should've been body-shaped dents in it. The roommate crouched on the floor next to the kid's parents.

Emma slipped out first, her feral new powers fading from my senses as she moved down the hall and into the stairwell.

The clone peeled herself away first. "Jeffrey, baby?"

The kid stumbled toward her. They clutched each other and stood there, rocking back and forth.

"Is it over?" Pressed-khakis said. His eyes goggled at me, at the room behind me.

"Your son should get checked out by a doctor, but he'll be okay."

Jeffrey-baby raised his head from his mother's bony shoulder. "Dad? Grandma?"

His father cuffed him.

His mother snatched him out of his father's reach. "Pay the exorcist, Joseph."

Pressed-khakis tried to look down at me, but we were the same height. "How much?"

"Fifteen hundred."

"What? Outrageous. What kind of a racket are you running?" He turned to his wife and mother for support. "Maybe Jeff was on drugs after all."

His mother poked him in the ribs. "I didn't raise you to be stupid and cheap. If Father Kaine was a doctor you'd pay his bill without question. He saved your son's life and his soul tonight which is more than any doctor could do. Pay the man what he's worth."

Jeffrey said, his voice rough from sobbing on top of all the screaming he did earlier, "Grandma's right, Dad."

From the floor, Anthony said, "Mrs. Meyer?" The kid's

grandmother squatted next to him while he whispered in her ear.

She patted his shoulder and waded into the debris-filled dorm room. A minute later she came out with two items: a metal-bound leather-covered book the size of a Shakespeare folio and a black speckled composition book, the kind sold by the thousands in school supply aisles. She shoved them both at me. "Here."

"Good. I'll burn them." I tucked them under my left arm.

Pressed-khakis stopped writing my check. "Wait a minute, wait a minute. The leather book is an antique. It's worth good money."

Both kids said, "Burn everything."

Pressed-khakis's lips thinned again, but he finished the check and tore it out of the checkbook.

Anthony looked up at Jeffrey. "Good to see you again."

Jeffrey wrapped his arms around himself. "Sorry about the keyboard."

His roommate smiled. "Chicks dig scars."

Jeffrey smiled back, then turned to me. He waited until I pocketed my fee to say, "Um, thanks, Father."

I glared at him. "Next time you're bored and want power, design a better way to utilize solar energy."

The kids said, "We're molecular bioscience."

God preserve me from smart morons. "Then harness biolu-minescent organisms and figure out how to reduce our depen-dence on fossil fuels. You'll need the patent money to pay for the damages."

Emma wasn't waiting in the car. It was a long drive back, alone and drained and replaying everything red-ass said about Xav.

Especially the latter, over and over like a single song on repeat. An extra-large coffee and Act One of *Don Giovanni* at full volume managed to keep me awake.

I trudged into my apartment and set the bag and the books on the floor next to the counter. Restocking the bag could wait until tomorrow morning, but I had to take care of the books tonight. First, though, I ripped off my collar and headed to the bathroom. No damage to my chest showed in the mirror when I unbuttoned my shirt, but splotches of black and blue were starting to discolor my forearms. As red-ass encounters go, this one definitely could've been worse.

When I looked up, Emma's face on a dryad's body stood next to me. I started.

"Cut it out."

She stuck out the tip of her tongue and changed into a gumiho, all nine tails flicking around to caress me.

"I said stop. It's unsettling."

And she was Emma again. "What do Catholics have against amusement? I thought making pleasure a crime was the job of the Puritans." Her eyes unfocused. "The sect which sailed to America. Yes, Puritans." She wrinkled her nose. "Purity is for nuns and sacrifices."

She kissed the back of my neck. Pleasant shivers ran down my back. She made a purring noise and kissed down to my right shoulder and across to my left. Her long fingers reached around to weave through my chest hair...

I pulled away. "Stop. We have to burn the kid's books."

She pouted. "You are being a nun or a sacrifice. This is not amusing."

"We've got a dangerous object in this apartment and I have to defuse it. Would you start a fire in the fireplace?"

A flash in her eyes promised a fight, but she surprised me and went into the living room without a word.

I grabbed the first T-shirt in the middle drawer of my dresser and pulled it on as I returned to the kitchen for the books.

Emma was blowing on the flames.

"Here. Add some of these." I ripped out a dozen pages from the composition book and crumpled them. Again and again I ripped and she fed them into the fireplace until the flames blazed and we had to move back. The flimsy modern book burned away in five minutes.

The spell book resisted my hands. I wrenched it open to a spread near the middle with faded illustrations and handwritten black-letter columns. Wasn't tempted in the least to read it. I tore out those pages and handed them to Emma. The malevolence soaked into this vellum clung to my palms, tried to stop me from destroying it. I tore out page after page. Flung them at Emma. She tore them in quarters, then in half as I ripped pages out faster, fighting to kill this book.

"What is the matter? Why this haste?"

As she spoke, I grasped the empty cover in both hands and ripped the ancient leather down the center of the spine.

A clutch of tiny bones spilled onto the floor.

Emma picked one out of the pile and held it against the firelight.

"These are infant bones." She spread them out like they were a jigsaw puzzle and matched them to each other. "These are the left foot and right hand of a newborn."

"Or a late miscarriage," I said. "The bones are the reason those two idiots were able to summon a high-level demon. Why the hell was a book like this sitting on the shelf of an antique shop for anyone to buy?"

"The answer is obvious. To tempt the unwary." Emma ran her fingers over the delicate bones. "These are four or five centuries old at the least. Poor child." She scooped them all together and made to toss them into the fire.

I clamped my hands over hers. "Stop."

She gave me a puzzled look. "Why? We are burning everything else."

"This fire isn't hot enough to cremate them properly."

"*Pah.* You are sentimental. These bones are so old even this small fire will turn them to ash. All we need to do is pulverize them beforehand."

She started to close her fist, but I swept the tiny remnants into my left hand.

"I'll bury them." I cupped my right hand over my left and murmured a truncated version of the Last Rites. When I finished, Emma had an odd smile on her face.

"What?"

She touched my cheek. "You are a sentimentalist, but this is not always a bad thing."

I shook my head. A thousand years old or only sixty, women were impossible to figure out. I headed to the laundry room. More like a laundry niche, but I had squeezed one of those stacked washer/dryer combos and a half-sized ironing board into it. I spread a scented dryer sheet on the ironing board and wrapped it around the child's bones.

"What strange act are you performing now?" Emma said from the doorway.

"The perfume in the dryer sheet will confuse predators. I don't want stray dogs or foxes disturbing them. I'll bury these in the nearest cemetery at the new moon."

She tilted her head. "Why? Do you wish to become a sorcerer who seeks to use the child's bones for spells?"

"Don't be ridiculous. A moonless night makes it hard for anyone to see me. It's against the law to bury undocumented human remains."

I emptied the rest of the dryer sheets out of the box and set the wrapped bones inside. We returned to the living room and I gave the two pieces of book cover a thorough inspection. Nothing overt, but the resistance to my touch remained. I broke the pieces over my knee and fed them into the fire.

The flames sparked green and black. Puffs of willow and wormwood made us sneeze. I watched it burn. Emma's hands started to work on my shoulders.

"What is wrong? Your shoulders are as unyielding as those logs of wood."

I struggled against the fear—there, I admitted it—that the taunts of red-ass and purple-eyes might somehow, in some inverted universe, be true.

"Tell me," Emma said.

"It's Xavier."

She pushed her thumbs harder into my trapezius muscles. I flinched.

"Do you speak of the demon's words? *Nelepyy*. Demons lie."

"Ow. Not so hard with your fingernails. It's not only him. The red-ass in the cemetery said it too. I told you."

Her hands left my shoulders. "It is useless to massage your muscles when every word from your mouth undoes my work. Look at me." She slid around on the floor so I could see her face. "Tell me the truth. Do you believe your brother is in Hell because he killed himself?"

The words spoken out loud, not locked in my secret room, turned me into a block of ice.

"Answer me." In her most imperious voice.

The ridiculousness of her "I am queen of all I survey" attitude thawed me a bit.

"My life was a lot simpler before you showed up."

She tossed her head. I would've sworn no woman had used such a piece of body language in the last hundred years.

"It is your fault. Do not vie with entities which are stronger than you."

The ice melted. "You might have helped with tonight's red-ass, but you forget about the one in the cemetery. He was a major player in Hell and I sent him back there." She had a "heard it all before" expression and I'd gotten attitude from one supernatural entity too many this week. "You think I'm not powerful enough to throw you in front of the Judgment Seat?"

I lurched to my knees and clamped my hands on her head. Old French crowded onto my tongue. I spoke the first line of an archaic banishing.

She slapped them off. "You only defeated the last one after I drained half of his power, little man. Without me, you would be facing your precious Judgment Seat yourself."

"Little? Listen, *imperatrix*, you're not in Russia anymore. You're in my territory. Here, I own you."

Her laughter dared me to make good on my statement. "Men begged to come to my bed rather than face me in battle. You do not have the power to own me, priest."

I tackled her to the carpet and shut her up with a kiss.

Chapter Thirty-Five

We lay puzzled and roasting on the floor afterward until we remembered we'd built up a roaring fire to burn demonic books. Too lazy to move, neither of us spoke for a while.

"Despite the disparity between us, it appears we are equals in power," she said at last. She reached up and stroked my chin. "We shall declare a truce, I think."

"I think you're right. I've got other battles to fight." Part of me wanted more sex, but more of me wanted to shower and figure out how much of what those demons said was lies.

"You are tense again." She leaned on one elbow.

"Yeah." I got to my knees to bank the fire. "This isn't normal pillow talk."

She smiled up at me. "Who is to say what is normal? I am going to shower without you. Then I will walk to the all-night Chinese takeout restaurant and purchase Singapore Mei Fun. When I return, you will also have showered and we will talk of what the demons said."

I tossed my clothes into the laundry room and her dress into the trash. Grinning, I headed for the bedroom and the bottom dresser drawer she'd appropriated. Beneath the emo stuff she hadn't worn since the day she came home, I found a periwinkle-printed T-shirt. From a hanger in the closet I took a soft knit brown skirt and laid both pieces of clothing on the bed. Then I waited in the bathroom to jump into the shower when she came out.

She gave me an odd look. A few minutes later over the noise of the water, I heard something in Russian. It didn't sound complimentary. Guess no one had ever told her what to wear before, even in such a laid-back manner. My facial muscles informed me I was still smiling.

Several minutes later, at the table with Emma, I drank Coke with the Mei Fun and she drank sake.

"Let me guess," I said. "You found someone who makes fake IDs."

"Not at all. I merely made myself look like an old woman before entering the store. Clerks do not ask for the identification of someone with white hair and wrinkles." She sucked a rice noodle through her lips. "I have been thinking of what happened to you in the church. Why is it the demons are attacking you about your brother now? This has not happened before, yes?"

When she said it out loud, I wanted sake. I wanted an entire bottle of the damn stuff.

"Right. This is something new."

"Perhaps you have angered a demon with a grudge." She pursed her lips. "This still does not answer the question of your brother's current residence."

"Wait." I set down my fork. "Yes, it does." A sixteen-ton weight fell off my back. "This has nothing to do with Xav. I've pissed off someone powerful—the remaining demon twin, maybe, or their sire. There's a chance I killed one of the twins;

demons usually don't reveal their names, and I don't care. So they're attacking my most vulnerable point with lies."

Emma sipped her sake. "Tell me one thing, since you are more versed in demon lore than I. If your brother was in Hell and not Heaven, would all demons know it?"

The weight crept back. "What do you mean?"

"Do not become angry when I say this. Listen and use your reason. You and your brother are important enemies of the demons. If your brother awoke in Hell after he killed himself, does it not make sense a demon of great power would wish to keep your brother—"she rapped the back of her fork on the table—"I said you must subdue your anger while I speak of this. What if a powerful demon was keeping your brother's fate a secret to increase his dominion over his peers? And only now other demons have discovered it and are using the knowledge to weaken you?"

I went cold as an ice storm in February. Xav in Hell all this time. Xav in the power of creatures starving to get revenge on all We've done to their ranks. I should've been saying a daily Mass for the repose of his soul all this time. To ransom Xav I'd say Mass every day for the rest of my life abased before the tabernacle while Raymond and all his cronies gloated. If I'd killed myself back in Rome I would've at least been down there to take their attention off him.

Oh, God. Oh, Christ. What if Xav was in Hell?

I'd kill them. I'd kill all of them.

"—it. Stop it. Wake up." Emma was shaking me.

My head flopped forward and back. "What? Let go of me."

She did. "Do not change in such a way again. It is frightening."

I rubbed my hands over my face. "I've got to find Xav."

"Do not think of killing yourself in a misguided attempt at heroics. I will destroy all the knives in this kitchen if I must."

"How the hell else—"

She clamped her hands on my shoulders. "This serves no purpose. You are tired and emotional."

"I have to do something. I have to do it now."

"I will hold you in this chair all night if I must. If you require me to do this, we will both be unpleasant when the sun rises. Sit there while I put these containers in the trash." Her eyes lit. "Where is the letter you threw into the coffee grounds?"

She wrinkled her nose at the trash can but reached in and brought out both halves of the now-stained letter from Raymond. "It says there is a haunting at a church. I think perhaps he did not ask the priests in Maine or New York about this because the demon in the church talked specifically of you or your brother."

I took it from her. "Maybe."

"Not maybe. Think. Your head priest would not want an outsider priest to come here and learn secrets which could be used to trouble his reign."

"Sounds like the way his mind works." I threw the letter back into the coffee grounds. "I'm not panicking anymore. Demons are lying sacks of shit and Xav is in Heaven trying to figure out a way to slap some sense into me. It makes perfect sense."

She raised her eyebrows. "Good. Tomorrow morning you will go to the archbishop and discover the secret he wishes to coerce you into keeping."

The thought made me gag. "Going into his territory shows weakness."

"*Vvernut' yego.* Do you care what he thinks of you? An intelligent worker uses the tools at hand. Also, you will deposit the check from the weak man for rescuing his son before he changes his mind."

Chapter Thirty-Six

Early the next morning, I left a message on Dog-Eared's machine and drove to the archbishop's residence without phoning ahead. A newly minted Jesuit answered the door.

"May I help you?"

Tight-ass. "I have an appointment with Archbishop Raymond. Father Denis Kaine, OFM."

His neutral expression changed enough to look down his nose at me. His eyes said "Slacker."

And thus centuries-old stereotypes are maintained.

"It's seven forty-five in the morning. Are you sure the archbishop is expecting you at this hour?"

"If you're so worried, go check. I'll wait five minutes. Any longer, and I barge in on him myself."

He glared at me outright but allowed me to wait in the foyer while he asked about me. A minute and a half later, Monsignor Dickweed came to fetch me.

"Father Kaine. How good to see you."

I followed him without bothering to answer. My silence got his goat like I knew it would.

"I can't wait to see him break you." He knocked at the

polished walnut door on one side of another small reception area, opened it, and preceded me inside.

It wasn't as opulent as the Inquisitor's room in Rome I'd been chastised in, but Raymond wasn't doing so bad for himself. Deep green carpet thick enough to turn my ankle, carved walnut chairs with hand-embroidered cushions. I wondered if he got the retired nuns to embellish those for him. At one end of a walnut credenza, a silver coffeepot on a matching tray flanked by real china cups. On the other, a vase of Easter lilies. The room wasn't quite big enough to diffuse their heavy scent. A gold crucifix on the wall behind his desk and framed photos of the last four Popes on either side of the bow window.

Exactly like the pencil-pusher in Rome, Raymond kept me waiting while he finished typing into his PC. Must be a skill the higher-ups learned along with how to keep the fancy headgear on straight at all times.

"Thank you, Monsignor," Raymond said after a few minutes. "Please leave us."

Dickweed started to say something but swallowed it and settled for a big-eyed pleading face, like a cartoon cat. Raymond merely glanced at the door. Powell couldn't disobey and remain ass-kisser in chief.

Raymond wound up the instant the door closed. "Father Kaine, you are arrogant, insubordinate, and in violation of your vow of obedience. Furthermore—"

I said, "What happened at the Easter Vigil?"

His diatribe rolled right over my interruption. "Furthermore, if you do not in future obey our summons at the exact time and day stated—"

I stalked to his desk and slammed both hands on it. A miniature golf bag penholder rattled. "I don't care about your official censure or your unofficial bribe. I want to know what happened at the Easter Vigil."

"The Easter Vigil is not the reason we are asking your help."

I dialed it back. He needed me, which meant I could get what I wanted if I used a little patience. We both knew if push came to shove, the Vatican would cut me a hell of a lot of slack. One of the perks of having rare and essential—if publicly disavowed—skills.

"Archbishop, you may have heard about the possessed Northwestern University student yesterday."

He looked suspicious. "Yes, our office and the family's parish priest received an email about it."

"So did I. Why did you ignore it?"

"These things require time and study."

"Did you read her email?"

He adjusted the penholder. "No. One of the priests on my staff handles all incoming emails. He summarized it in my morning report."

I crossed my arms. "How long has it been since you talked face to face with any parishioner in your Diocese? If you spent more time with the laity and less with paperwork and syco-phants, you'd know the difference between a request for infor-mation and a cry for help."

Raymond opened his mouth, but I didn't give him a chance.

"Her grandson was possessed. A reckless kid who thought he was smart enough to handle anything. What he got was a Cardinal-level demon using his body as a marionette."

"Did you exorcise it?"

"I wouldn't be here if I hadn't. The demon taunted me before I ripped him out of the kid. He was damned proud of something another demon had done at the Easter Vigil."

Demons may lie, and I could tell half truths to get informa-tion, but the archbishop's face was as easy to read as a picture book. I leaned on his desk again, slowly this time, amping up the menace in my voice.

"Tell me what happened."

He crumbled. "It was a series of small things. The lights went out for the blessing of fire a few moments early. The Paschal candle burned with a strange green flame for the first second after we lit it. The same green transferred to the hundreds of smaller candles the congregation held, but for less than a second." His manicured fingers trembled enough to rustle the papers on his desk. "When the electric lights came back on, the cathedral looked wrong in an indefinable way. It seemed somehow distorted. A few members of the congregation appeared to see or hear something, but the phenomena passed quickly and Mass continued."

Pig-headed idiot. "This is what you tried to blackmail me into fixing?"

He shook his head. "No. We want your help with the seminary. No one can enter the chapel without vomiting, fainting, or crying out in pain."

Several possibilities popped into my head. "How long has this been going on?"

"Two months."

"What?" If my jaw dropped any lower, it'd hit my shoelaces.

He kept talking, looking at the papers on his desk. "We tested the vents, the ducts, and the heating system. We pulled up the carpets to test for mold. We dismantled the microphones. We brought in Father Laurence the psychiatrist for some surreptitious testing. It's been getting steadily worse." He glanced up at me and flinched. "Monsignor Powell argued against contacting you. He and I share the same views on allowing cheap Hollywood tricks to infiltrate the Church. But we could lose all six of our seminarians if we don't fix this." His jaw clenched. "Since we've ruled out mundane causes, we're forced to turn to you."

If the man behind the fancy desk had a scrap of sensitivity, he'd wither under the hate radiating from me. "It's a good thing I'm not trying to win a popularity contest."

"This is the twenty-first century. We rely on science. The answers to these cases are almost always mundane rather than demonic."

I recaptured my neutral face. "But not this time?"

His hands stopped their restless movements. "We don't think so."

"I've already lost a day's wages so I can head over there after breakfast."

He looked like he was about to order me there immediately. "Filling your stomach is more important than the needs of the Church?"

"Strength for the body is as important as strength for the soul. If I go into battle weak and lose the fight, the Diocese will get slammed with a massive hospital bill."

His nose wrinkled like he was smelling something bad. "You scorn the life of a parish priest, but you still rely on the Church for health insurance. What interesting lines you choose to draw, Father."

I opened my hands. "I've never denied I'm a sinner."

His memory kicked in with a visible start. "Yes, you certainly are. The other morning—"

I was not going to listen to this. "I'll be there at eleven. You going to meet me?"

"No. Monsignor Powell teaches Latin and Church history there on alternating days of the week. He'll be able to tell you everything you need to know."

"Great."

"Is there a problem?"

"No. It's fine."

Chapter Thirty-Seven

Emma did something with bacon and cheese and eggs and more bacon which made the apartment smell like a higher level of Elysium when I opened the door.

"You're doing this to lord it over me in the kitchen, aren't you?" I said after the first few mouthfuls.

"You have a suspicious mind." Her smile belied her innocence.

"You are not a good liar."

Several thumps shook the door.

"What the hell? I'm going to retire to Assisi and become a hermit if this keeps up."

Emma laughed. "You would beg for rescue in three weeks."

I unlocked the door. "Unless you've arrived direct from Hawai'i with Kona coffee, go away."

Sister Lisa Mackenzie, SSSF, ME in Latin, Hebrew, and Greek, ThD, stood on my threshold carrying her basic black suitcase. "I need caffeine and sugar. Red-eye flights are the pits. Take this, please, and let me in."

She tossed the suitcase at me and pushed me back into the kitchen. I stood where she left me, clutching the suitcase in my arms. She wore those black travel pants she always complained about and a bright red CUA hooded jacket. Her gray hair was mussed but otherwise she appeared as pulled-together and professional as though she'd merely walked across campus to her first class on a windy day.

Emma snapped, "Close the door, Denis, and introduce us. Where are your manners?"

I managed not to drop the suitcase. "Uh, Lisa, this is Emma. Emma, this is Sister Lisa, one of the foremost authorities in Church history."

Lisa grabbed Emma in a bear hug. An odd embrace, since Lisa's head didn't reach Emma's neck. Emma flailed a moment before patting Lisa's shoulders.

Lisa stepped back and looked up into Emma's face. "You're taller than Denis. Wonderful! He needs someone who won't be intimidated by him."

"It is perhaps the other way around," Emma said.

Lisa guffawed. "I smell bacon. If you didn't make enough for three, Denis, I will share your perfidy on social media with all your former students."

My voice came out of hiding. "Lisa, what are you doing here?"

Emma shook her finger at me. "I say again, you have the manners of a goat. This is not the way you greet an old friend."

"I'm used to him. You"—Lisa beckoned me—"I would like the grand tour starting with the bathroom."

Emma set out another plate and started a fresh latte. My brain shorted out trying to come up with a reason for Lisa to ditch her classes and fly out here. She had neither Sight nor powers.

The bathroom door opened. "Thank God for small mercies. The bathroom is modernized. The outside of this building had me picturing flush chains and no hot water."

When she came out, I pointed to the left. "Claustrophobic laundry room next to the bathroom. Bedroom to the right."

"At least it's neat. Denis, you need decent curtains."

"Yes, Mom. Living room in front of you."

"Such a beautiful fireplace. Oh, you set up your mandolin. I hope it's in tune. May I put in a request for '*J'ai du bon tabac*' later today?"

Emma called from the kitchen, "The latte is ready."

I said to Lisa, "Uh, sure. I haven't played it in a while, though."

"You'll do fine." She led the way back to the kitchen and took the coffee from Emma. Her eyes lit up at the first sip. "Marvelous."

The three of us sat down to breakfast.

Lisa slathered toast with blackberry jam and took a ladylike bite. "I feel my humanity returning. Tackling any airport before sunrise is not on my travel wish list. Especially not O'Hare. It's no wonder this town's sprawling beast has its own zip code. Emma, did you make these bacon quiches? Denis only deserves you because he's my favorite. May I have the recipe?"

I kept eating only because it'd be a sin to waste this food. Lisa and Emma talked about cooking and coffee and debated the superiority of cherry pie versus baked apples.

While I washed the dishes and Emma dried, we tried to have a conversation with eye blinks and lip writhings. After five solid minutes of our scenery chewing, Lisa banged her palms on the table.

"What is the matter?" She looked harder at my face and her skin lost some color. "Denis, did you get this young woman pregnant?"

Emma laughed. "No, I am not with child. We are both thinking Denis should have no secrets from you."

The color returned to Lisa's face. "I thought he didn't."

I felt like I'd kicked my mother in the head. "No, it's not... It's, well, you see..."

Emma set down the dishcloth. "Stop." To Lisa: "I am about to do something you will not expect. Do not leave the chair." She smiled. "You cannot see auras or sense supernatural entities, correct?"

Lisa sighed. "No. I've always been a little jealous of Denis and Xavier because of their talents."

"Do you not speculate why Denis and I became intimate so quickly when you were unaware of my presence here?"

"I did wonder. Denis is such a misanthrope."

Emma smiled back. "This is true. You see he does not argue with your judgment."

They practically batted their eyes at me. I scowled. Under the scowl, I was shaking in my stiff black shoes. What if Lisa freaked? What if her acceptance of us crumbled in the face of what Emma really was? Lisa was my only remaining anchor in this world.

"Denis and I met when he was in Rome last summer, after his brother died. He was seeking ancient ruins. You know of this?"

"Yes," Lisa said.

"It was in one of these ruins where I first met him."

Lisa looked even more confused. "You're an archaeologist?"

I blurted it out. "She's the relic."

Emma made the "asshole" gesture at me. Lisa laughed, a nervous little sound.

"This is what he means," Emma said, and vanished, her apron hovering in the air like bandages on the Invisible Man.

Lisa yipped. Emma reappeared.

"You almost have the clothing technique mastered," I said.

"Necessity is a proficient teacher." She smiled at Lisa. "Do not be frightened."

"I'm, I'm not." Lisa swallowed a couple of times. "Denis loves you and I trust his judgment."

"What?" I said.

"You are not in earnest," Emma said at the same time.

Lisa relaxed. "And I'm the one without special powers? Please, you two. It's as obvious as a jewelry commercial."

Emma studied me. "This is interesting. Does she speak the truth?"

"I didn't... I wasn't thinking about the future." I sat. "Wait a minute. She meant both of us."

A tinge of red touched Emma's ivory-pale skin.

"Could you two sort this out later?" Lisa pulled out the chair opposite me. "Sit, please, Emma, and explain. I'm feeling rather like the floor dropped out from under me."

Emma sat. "You have heard of the rusalka?"

Lisa shook her head.

"Denis," Emma said, "why did you and your brother not share your experiences with your teacher?"

"Because I was too busy pounding Church history into their skulls." Lisa raised her eyebrows. "You've been holding an awful lot back, I think."

"Ah. History." Emma stood again. "You are familiar with Charlemagne?"

"Sure."

"This is how I appeared when I visited his court." She closed her eyes for a moment.

In a fraction of a second a tenth-century noble appeared in my twenty-first-century kitchen. Emma's dress and over-cape thing had enough gold thread in them to pay my rent for God knew how long. Huge swathes of sapphire-blue designs alternated with the gold, the blue embellished with ruby-colored dots and squares. Her sleeves belled all the way to the floor. Pearls, rubies, and sapphires studded a stiff collar around her neck and the headdress on top of her fancy braided hairdo.

She looked incredible. Her ancient self gave off the vibe of someone too important to be in the same zip code with someone like me.

Lisa's mouth hung open enough for me to hear her breathing through it. Her eyes didn't know what to look at first: she stared at the dress, then the jeweled hat, then at Emma's face, which had also changed. It was hard to pin down; the best my stupefied brain could come up with was this outfit matched her at her most imperious.

And then she was Emma again in a spangled skirt and a T-shirt covered with lilies of the valley.

Lisa's jaw shut with a click. "Those were Byzantine. I recognized the style of the collar and headdress."

Emma nodded. "As I said, I wore such clothing when I was human. It is difficult to find clothing in this century which is not drab as peasant garb. When Denis released me from the prison in which I was trapped by a *figlio di una mignotta* Pope, I looked like rusalka." She studied Lisa's face. "I will not become such until you are ready to see it. I spent the months after Denis freed me in recovering myself and my abilities. Then I set myself to discover who was the angry priest who freed me."

"Yeah, and the first thing she did was diss my skills."

Lisa leaned back in her chair like the wood spindles were the only thing holding her upright. "Denis, I need a beer."

"I don't have—"

Emma opened the cupboard. "Will red wine suffice?"

Lisa nodded, and Emma poured her half a glass. Lisa downed it without stopping. Stared at Emma. At me. Squeezed her eyes shut and opened them again.

I touched her hand. "Are you okay?"

She waved me away. "Of course I am." She studied Emma

like she was populating a whole new category of research with her at the center.

Emma smiled like a regular, happy human. "Now you wish to ask me much about Charles the Great, yes?"

Lisa lost her composure again. "Good Heavens, of course. You knew Charlemagne."

"He had an excellent opinion of himself."

I said, "And you would know."

Emma stuck out the tip of her tongue at me. Lisa laughed and the tension bubble burst.

Lisa rubbed her hands together. "Emma, I'm going to pick your brain before I go back home."

Emma's brow furrowed.

"It means she wants to learn about history from someone who experienced it firsthand."

"I see. There is a large gap between when the *súka* Pope imprisoned me and Denis released me. But I will be quite happy to talk of ancient days with someone who appreciates them."

Lisa took her wineglass to the sink. "This makes up for the red-eye flight."

I took the glass from her and washed it. "You're taking this in stride."

She gave me a crooked smile. "You think so? I'm freaked out. I seem to be covering it well."

She turned to Emma. "I don't mean to say that you scare me, but to be sitting in Denis's kitchen with, well, a supernatural, er..."

"I prefer chameleon. It is obvious Denis is still in need of lessons from you."

I said, "I got my last doctorate twelve years ago."

Emma gave me an innocent look. "I did not mean schoolwork."

I didn't rise to her bait, but Lisa's mouth went through several gyrations to hide laughter. .

When she conquered it, she took out her phone and opened a memo app. "All right. Denis, what's happening with this demonic harassment?"

"I—what? How do you know?"

"I telephoned her." Emma's posture screamed "challenge me, I dare you."

"You what?" Christ, I sounded like my own echo.

Lisa said, "It's your fault because you're not used to someone concerned about you who's in a position to act on it." She finished the sentence with the "Look" which cowed her students into trembling submission.

"I can take care of myself." I did not sound petulant. I sounded like a man in control of his life.

"Your competence isn't the issue," Lisa said. "It's high time you let someone knock a hole in the wall you constructed."

"I said I don't need—"

"Stuff it. What's the schedule for today?"

Right. Back on track. Thank you, Lisa. "I'm headed to the Diocesan seminary because the archbishop finally grew a pair. He wants me to check out a two-month haunting in their chapel." I gave them both a summary of what was happening there.

Lisa keyed it all into her phone.

"You bring back memories of Exorcist Cram School."

"Good. It'll keep you humble. When do we leave?"

"We?"

"Do you think those seminarians are going to respond to your charm?" She winked at Emma, who bleated like a goat, which set them both laughing.

"She is correct," Emma said over the last of Lisa's chuckles, "you are not one to whom people readily open up. Come. It is nine thirty. The streets will be less crowded."

I put out both hands to them like an old-fashioned traffic cop. "Stop, you two. Hauntings are unpredictable."

"Are you kidding?" Lisa said. "I know when to get out of the professional's way."

"You will need my assistance," Emma said. "We are a business now. I will show you the website later, Lisa."

Lisa beamed. "You're exactly what he needs."

Emma looked thoughtful. "He has improved me as well. I am thinking you and I might become friends."

"Hey." I waved my hands. "Remember me? I'm still in the room." Did married men get treated like this in a room full of women? I'd have to check with Martin and his husband. They were the only couple I knew.

Lisa said to Emma, "Do you have any sympathy for him?"

"Not at all."

Chapter Thirty-Eight

I parked the Impala in the seminary's parking lot and started to explain my plan to Lisa. I brought my messenger bag but I didn't expect to use it. The situation needed to be studied first.

"Is this guise suitable for our visit?" Emma said.

Lisa gasped. A young priest with Emma's dark hair and gray eyes sat in the back seat.

"Christ on a bike, Emma. Who are you supposed to be?"

Lisa cuffed me. "Watch your mouth. Emma, are you in there?"

"Yes." Her voice in this shape was higher than usual, but masculine at the same time.

Lisa reached out, then pulled back. Emma held out a man's hand with black hairs on the backs of the fingers. Lisa touched it, jerked her hand away, touched it again.

Emma preened, a bizarre-looking action in her current shape. "I am clever, yes? Now Denis has an assistant who will not raise eyebrows."

Lisa was breathless. "You're amazing. You changed in the kitchen, but to yourself in the past, right? I guess I didn't think you could go to such an extreme."

"You haven't seen anything yet," I said to Lisa. "And I prefer working alone."

Priest-Emma said, "Those who do not change, stagnate."

Lisa opened the car door before I said something else she could hit me for.

A haggard seminarian opened the front door to the plain brick two-story building. I swear, I should be suspicious of all nondescript houses on principle.

"Father Kaine, Brother—Mark, Sister Lisa Mackenzie to see Monsignor Powell."

The seminarian let us into the vestibule to wait on Monsignor Dickweed's pleasure. The Church must have an immutable blueprint for seminaries. Every one of them in the States and Canada had the same blue rug, same dentist-office chairs, same off-white paint on the walls, same portraits of the last few Popes, same brass crucifix over the door.

Powell strode toward us, led by the doorkeeper. He couldn't make us wait long when there were witnesses.

"Father Kaine. Thank you for coming." He eyed Lisa and "Brother Mark" but put on an impassive face.

Lisa went over to the doorkeeper. "Young man, may I trouble you for a cup of tea? I need to get off these old feet."

The kid warmed to her like she was his favorite aunt. He took her through the right-hand opening at the end of the hall. I didn't have to guess this led to the kitchen on the first floor north side of the building. In fifteen minutes Lisa would have all six seminarians gathered in the reception parlor telling her stories of their mothers and sisters.

And out of my way for this inspection.

"The chapel, please, Monsignor," I said.

Powell kept sneaking looks at priest-Emma but didn't ask. Worried he'd appear less than omniscient to a nearby student, most likely. I didn't need him to guide us down the left-hand hallway to a double door on the east side of the house. I knew how to get to our destination. Suburban cookie-cutter housing tracts had nothing on seminaries.

He opened the doors, but I held "Brother Mark" back with a gesture. I wanted to get a feel for the space while still on the outside. We faced a row of stained-glass windows set to catch the sunrise: the Annunciation, the Sermon on the Mount, the Crucifixion. Confessional in the back on the right. Twelve-inch-high mass-produced Stations of the Cross in plaster bas-relief around the three walls of the nave. Two rows of six short pews faced a small, raised sanctuary to my left. Full-sized altar. Half-sized tabernacle shoved in the left-hand corner with the standard red glass sanctuary light hanging above it.

One hundred percent ordinary.

I stepped across the threshold, Brother Mark and Powell following. Powell doubled over immediately and clutched his stomach. Brother Mark took the cue, slumping against the wall and sliding to the floor. I noticed he took care to face the chapel, not the wall, but he played the part so well I didn't see an eyelid flutter.

Powell made retching noises behind me. Between them he said, "Do you feel it? The pain? The pressure?"

I did, but the phenomena weren't anywhere near enough to debilitate me. Something powerful inhabited this room. I walked the perimeter, entered the Confessional—nothing in it but two straight-backed chairs with flat red cushions—and headed up the center aisle toward the sanctuary. Once my foot touched the single step, I heard it.

From his knees inside the doorway, Powell called out, "Anything? Do you hear or feel anything?"

"Shut up," I called. Damn right I heard it. Hundreds of voices. Not all of them human. They converged on my head, on my brain, pushing against my eardrums, squeezing the breath from my lungs. The room dimmed, blackness pulsing in the same rhythm as the screams. I braced my arms on the altar for support. Couldn't pass out. Had to know what it was. Stared at the steady flame in its red cylinder. Stared at the steadier white glow emanating from the wooden tabernacle.

The screams took a back seat. The pressure eased.

Wrong. Most of the screams diminished. One stayed at full strength.

Denis, you bastard! You coward! You deserted me!

And then it—he—Xavier—screamed like someone was skinning him alive.

Your fault! You bastard!

I stood there and took it. Stared at the tabernacle's light because I was afraid I'd see Xav if I closed my eyes.

Demons lie, I thought. Demons lie.

After God knows how long, I got myself under control and walked around the altar and into the closet-sized sacristy. No particular spot called out to me. Nothing reeked or spiked an aura or puked etheric slime.

What the fuck?

Brother Mark just happened to be waking up when I returned to the double doors. I helped him to his feet and got an arm around Powell. Walked them into the hallway. The doors closed behind us.

Bam. Powell stood upright. Kneaded his stomach a couple of times but only his usual spiritual smell of cheap plastic emanated from him. Brother Mark detached from my helping arm and blinked several times.

"You okay?" I asked him.

"Yes, thank you, Father." The voice, both like and unlike hers, threw me off. Blast the woman.

"Well?" Powell asked, back to full-strength dickishness.

"I'll give my report to the archbishop. Can you send someone for Sister Lisa? We need to leave."

"What? You aren't allowed to leave. I need to know—"

"You need to know exactly what your boss wants you to know. Learn the rules or you'll never be a first-class ass-kisser." I walked to the spot where the hall divided and headed down the right-hand fork. Powell spluttered and fumed behind me but didn't follow. I caught a distinctly un-Monsignor-like epithet involving my parentage before I turned the corner.

I was a professional, dammit. Which meant making sure anybody in my line of sight saw an exorcist on the job. Not Xav's useless brother screaming inside himself loud enough to shatter those tasteful stained-glass windows in their horror movie chapel. If I stayed in there another minute my control might've snapped.

When Brother Mark and I reached the archway separating the dining room from the parlor, I stayed out of sight behind it to absorb the serenity. Lisa and the seminarians—sounded like a '50s rock group—sat in various armchairs and dining room chairs. The six young men crowded as close to her as possible. She sipped tea and nibbled a Chips Ahoy while they told stories of their older sisters and kid brothers. She'd blanketed them with a sense of home and comfort and I'd bet a week's pay she had no idea of the amazing power she wielded.

Couldn't wait too long, though. Had to get out before I clawed the paint off the walls.

"Sister?" I moved into the doorway, the image of a gentleman. "We should leave."

Lisa finished the cookie and handed the teacup to the geeky kid next to her. They stood as a group and thanked her for coming.

One picked up the cookie plate. "Sister Lisa, will you be in town for a while?"

The teacup cradler said, "Will you visit us again?"

The other four might as well have whimpered like puppies.

"I'm only in Chicago for a short time, but I'll do my best." Her smile diffused warmth. They smiled back, six black-garbed clones with circles under their eyes.

Dickweed wasn't at the door when we let ourselves out. Thank God.

Chapter Thirty-Nine

"I need a bug-free hotel with reasonable rates near your apartment," Lisa said when she'd buckled up.

"No such thing as reasonable near me." I gripped the steering wheel and paid hyperclose attention to the traffic. Xav's screams were louder than the taxi horns. "You can crash on my couch. Um, I mean..."

Lisa turned in her seat to face me. "Don't tell me Emma's been sleeping on your couch."

My ears burned. From the back seat, Emma said in her normal voice, "He is embarrassed to tell you that I am not."

Lisa twisted around to stare at her. She gasped. In the rearview mirror I saw Emma preen yet again. It looked better on the real her.

My face and my ears burned now. "The South Loop isn't too pricey. You can get here on the L or I can pick you up."

"Good. Back to your place first. I have sheaves of information in my head I need to write down."

Emma said, "I will make lunch for us because Denis is upset. A distracted cook does not blend spices well."

I weaved in and out of traffic and tried not to listen to Xav cursing me.

***

Lisa sat me at the kitchen table while Emma did something with tomatoes and chicken.

My foot wouldn't stop tapping the linoleum. "The thing possessing the chapel is malicious and evil. I didn't get an impression of its looks, just its voices."

"Plural?" Lisa said.

"Yeah." I tried to control my spasming muscles.

"It is old." Emma searched one drawer after another. "Denis, your kitchen lacks a meat tenderizer. We will remedy this tomorrow." She settled for my heaviest mug and slammed it repeatedly on the chicken. "The entity in the chapel is older than I am, old like the demon we expelled from the college student."

Lisa wrote everything on one of my legal pads.

Emma stopped smashing the chicken. "I am not as familiar with demons as Denis. Therefore I will pose a question. Why is this assumption being made by us?"

"What do you mean?"

"You have not employed your usual term when describing demons, yet you have acquiesced to the label given it by Church prelates. We have followed your example. Why have you abandoned the precise analysis I have always seen you perform?"

"Because I." My tongue tripped over itself. "Because Xav exorcised demons. It can't be anything else."

Emma's left eyebrow arched, but instead of arming for battle she returned to lunch preparations.

Lisa said, "It's playing games with the seminarians. They're putting up a good front, but all they want to do is run home to their mothers."

My foot hadn't stopped beating quick time on the floor. "What games? The archbishop said the problems were confined to the chapel. Puking, fainting, and phantom pains."

Lisa gave me another of her teacher looks: the one we got when we made a particularly dense comment. "As though they'd tell everything to the man with authority to kick them out." She started a bulleted list. "The majority of incidents have occurred in the chapel, but all of them have personal haunting stories. One's crucifix flew off his bedroom wall and landed face-down on the floor. Three more heard voices. One was making an entry in his spiritual journal and began writing blasphemies instead. The youngest one insists a succubus came to his bed."

Emma said, "The spirit I sensed was masculine." She dredged the mug-pounded chicken pieces in flour and set them in the frying pan.

"You're not up on incubus/succubus lore. Lisa, are you?"

"The first is masculine, the second is feminine. Aren't they?"

I shook my head. "Not always. Depending on which ancient sources you read, some incubi and succubi are the same demon switching between male and female. So if it wants to attack a man, it becomes a succubus and collects his semen. Then if it wants to screw with its victims—no pun intended—it changes into an incubus and seduces its target, getting her pregnant with the first victim's semen."

Lisa had stopped writing at "semen." "You're serious."

"Yeah. I don't have the imagination to make this stuff up." My leg muscles were cramping now but my foot still wouldn't stop.

"So what's the next step?" Her pen started moving again.

"I'll do some research and exorcise it."

She inhaled. "Emma, the chicken smells delicious. Denis, how can you announce such things in a calm voice?"

I shrugged. "It's what we do. Did. It's what I do." In my head I focused on the only important fact: demons lie. Demons lie. Demons lie.

Emma and Lisa shared the kind of look which means "he's doing it again."

"Lisa, you know why I'm doing this."

"Yes, but—"

"Old lady, you're my rock, but don't tell me how to live my life."

Lisa held up her hands in surrender.

Emma set thin pieces of golden fried chicken with blistered tomatoes and sautéed green beans on three plates. "I have no such compunction."

I stabbed my chicken. "In other news, the sun rose in the east this morning. Let's focus on the chapel's unwelcome visitor."

Lisa put her hand on my twitching knee. "What aren't you telling us?"

I jerked away. "Nothing. When this is settled, you two can dissect my life all you want. I'll keep working the cemeteries to help lost spirits move on."

I shoved a bite of chicken into my mouth. I'm sure it was great. All I tasted was dust. But I finished everything on the plate because a weak exorcist gets his skinny ass kicked by the red-assed crew. There. I said it. Red-assed.

"Stop giving me those covert glances, you two."

Emma set down her fork. "Fine. I will say it. I observed you in the chapel when I pretended to be unconscious. You heard something which disturbed you when you climbed upon the altar." She stared me down. "Was it your brother's voice from Hell?"

"No. No, dammit, it was not." I flung the fork onto my empty plate. It bounced sideways. Emma caught it. "Demons lie. This one is fucking with me. It wants me rattled so I can't kick its ass downstairs. It doesn't know I'm not kicking it back. I'm going to kill it." The words came out of my mouth on their own. I hadn't planned this decision, but now I had the answer. The voice in my head shut up the minute the words left my mouth. I pushed my chair away from the table. "Both of you leave me alone. I have to prepare."

Chapter Forty

I holed up in my bedroom. My room, my sanctuary, my space. Grabbed Xav's Gretzky jersey off its hanger and pulled it over my blacks.

Demons lie.

I opened my messenger bag and touched every single object in it. Made mental notes of items running low. I'd have to get more mullein and white candles. Needed to top off the holy water flasks tonight, too.

Demons lie.

The flute settled in my hand. Xav's Ordination gift to me, like mine to him: the hockey stick gathering dust in my closet. I brought the flute to my lips and blew into the silver mouthpiece which never tarnished, thanks to a neat little spell I learned in San Francisco.

The old Gibbons Good Friday hymn played from my fingers through its seasoned wood.

"Drop, drop, slow tears..."

Demons lie.

I got to the end of the second verse, "To cry for vengeance sin doth never cease," and the melody went out of tune.

Demons lie. Demons lie. Demons lie.

I set the flute in its place and opened the door. Emma and Lisa sat on the couch looking at the website on the Mac. I took the four oldest demon treatises from the bottom of my bookshelf —suckers were all large and odd-sized—and returned to the bedroom.

First the *Dictionnaire Infernal*. This one told me nothing I didn't already know. I was still convinced one of those demon twins was hounding me, but had I killed one? Was the other one using the seminary chapel as its playground? If I hadn't killed one, was it both of them tag-teaming?

A couple of hours later, I tried the *Key of Solomon*. I didn't need to drag this demon up from Hell since it was already here, but the *Key* had a boatload of how-to directions. I turned the pages with care since this book was worth a staggering amount of money.

My stomach complained of emptiness. I ignored it and went for my mostly complete copy of the *Grimorium Verum*. I was deep into the fourth section when Emma opened the door.

"Ever hear of knocking?"

"I have been. You have ignored the sound."

"Then I must not want to be disturbed." I didn't look up from the page.

"I am quite happy to leave you alone in your cave, but I am taking Lisa to supper and she wishes to know if you are joining us."

A wave of cold river water swept into my room. A beat, and I countered it with blue-white snow. I don't know what was in my eyes when I looked up from the book, but Emma pulled back.

"Leave. Me. Alone."

"Fine." She slammed the door.

When they left, I headed for the bathroom. Splashed cold

water on my face to wake myself up. Back in my room, the *Grimorium* was finally giving up the information I needed. I didn't bother to write anything down. I needed it in my head, letter-perfect. First I paced, book in hand. Not saying the words out loud. Never, never out loud until I had the red-ass under control. My legs got tired. I sat on the floor so the hard wood would keep me awake. Kept memorizing.

"Wake up, stubborn man."

My eyes unglued. The book lay open in my lap, my hand on the last sentence I remember reading. Had a nasty crick in my neck, apparently caused by the acute angle it made when my head flopped sideways against the bed. My mouth tasted like walnut-bark ink and old paper.

"Let go of me."

Emma closed the book and tossed it on the bed. I reached for it and she grabbed my arm and hauled me upright.

"Listen to me. It is after ten o'clock. I have reheated the souvlaki and spiced potatoes we brought home for you three hours ago. You will come out of this room and eat because you will be no good to anyone if you do not have enough strength to face this demon." She shoved me through my bedroom door, across the living room, and into the kitchen.

Lisa was at the table drinking a Coke. Another can of Coke and a plate of steaming lamb and potatoes were set on the far end. My stomach cramped. I folded in half. Emma shoved me toward the empty chair. I managed to unkink myself before I tripped over a table leg.

"Sit, idiot," Lisa said.

I shoveled food into my mouth as fast as I could without choking. I loved Greek food, but I didn't give my taste buds enough time to register it. Even when the Coke scrubbed my palate I barely tasted anything. Even the belch I let out a few minutes later didn't wake up my taste buds.

"Pig," Emma said.

"Bite me. Thanks for supper. I have to get back to work."

"Saint Jude protect us." Lisa mimed swatting me with a rolled-up newspaper. "You need sleep. You look like you've been on a three-day drinking spree."

"This is more important." I stood and took two steps toward my bedroom.

Emma put one hand on the Oilers logo over my chest. "This demon will not run away while you regain your senses in sleep." She made the most of the two inches she had on my six feet. "You are obsessing. You are afraid."

"Get your hand off me."

"Not until you agree to sleep." She lessened the space between us. Her voice modulated from commanding to soothing. "Do not let this fear conquer you."

Red-spiked anger crammed everything else out of my head. I grabbed her wrist and twisted until she let it fall away from Xav's shirt. "Stop trying to manipulate me. You have no fucking idea what I'm thinking. Go waste your time playing dress-up games. Nothing is more important than Xav. Nothing."

Her eyes glowed the way they had after she'd sucked power from those last two demons. "Do not push me aside like an importunate servant. You do not want to challenge me, priest."

The grin stretching my face felt so damned good. "I don't?"

I knew what I must look like because Emma's face stretched with the same type of grin. "You do not."

For an instant, I thought I'd be useless without my messenger bag. The same thought flashed across her face and her smile deepened. She spread her hands over my chest. The air in the room thickened. My Coke can rattled on the table.

The fluorescent light turned icy blue and I knew my eyes caused the illusion.

Her hands crackled. I smelled ozone. I thought: the jersey! A ball of blue fire flung her into the living room. Her momentum skidded her and the rug all the way to the fireplace. Something cracked.

An entire marching band landed in my head. The fire sucked itself back into my chest. The agony hurled me onto the linoleum, blind and deaf. It felt like my fire was trapped in my rib cage, blazing, crackling, eating me alive. If I screamed I couldn't hear it.

Cold water down my neck. Another splash over my head. A third direct in my face.

Now I heard myself keening like a banshee. The headache faded. Half a minute more and it vanished. I shut up and blinked water out of my eyes. Lisa knelt in front of me, the pot Emma used for heating the latte milk gripped in her wrinkled hand. Her skin was so white only the wrinkles retained their normal olive shade.

"Old lady." My voice rasped in my sandpapery throat.

"Denis?" Real fear in her voice now.

"Yeah." I sat back on my heels. "Sorry. Didn't mean to scare you."

"Jesus, Mary, and Joseph." The pot clattered to the floor. "Is this standard operating procedure?"

"Sometimes. It doesn't usually blow back on me." I wiped my face on my sleeves and saw Emma sprawled on the living room floor. I staggered up, crashed to one knee, got up again, stumbled to her.

"Emma! Emma!" I lifted her head. Blood trickled from a cut at the base of her skull. "Shit. Wake up. Dammit. Wake up!" I felt her neck and couldn't find a pulse. I thought she was immortal. What's the unlife span of a rusalka? Was she really a rusalka?

Lisa knelt on her other side and positioned three fingers over Emma's wrist. "I've got a pulse."

"Wake up, you aggravating female. Wake up." The room turned blue again, blue mixed with gold, like lapis lazuli, like a skewed version of the paths I created for the dead. "No, no, no, no, no."

The lapis glow flowed down through my scorched chest, my arm, my hand. It lit Emma's skull. I cried out at the heat and the smell of singed hair filling my nose.

Emma's eyes opened. Her left arm flailed against my ribs right where they felt weakened enough to crumble to ash. Her body shimmered, became the mushroom-haired, pallid-skinned creature I'd first seen in the Roman ruin. Then she inhaled and the rusalka became Emma again.

Her eyes focused on the object directly above her, which happened to be my face. "Why are you dripping water on me, priest?"

I laughed. So did she.

After a second, so did Lisa. "You two have taken ten years off my life. I'm an old woman. I don't have ten years to spare."

"I need some aloe vera." The skin on my hand under her head had the taut feel of a burn.

"I'll find it." Lisa stood and went to the bathroom.

I helped Emma sit up. "I'm sorry. I lost control."

She raised her eyebrows. "An apology. This is new." She bent her head. "I too will apologize. I should not have provoked you."

Lisa returned with my giant tube of generic aloe vera cream. I grimaced when I tried to grab it with my left hand.

Emma took the tube from Lisa. "You are stupid to do this to

yourself. Do you not know the extent of your powers?" She rubbed the cream into my palm all the way up to my fingertips.

"They never bounced back on me before. Never looked like blue shot with gold, either."

She squeezed out more cream. "Something has changed. You must discover its nature."

"I'll add it to my to-do list."

Lisa put the pot back on the stove. "My plans have been revised. I'm sleeping on the couch. You need someone here who can wield a cast-iron frying pan in case of explosions."

"Emma, turn around. I might have burned you."

She looked skeptical but complied. Her blue-black hair fell past her waist without a blemish.

"Emma, I know I smelled burning hair."

"Foolish man, you forget I was rusalka, a water spirit. Water conquers fire. I have repaired my skin as well. You do not need to be concerned."

Lisa raised her voice. "Denis, did you hear me?"

"Yeah. Are you sure? It's an old couch."

She stood in the doorway, the personification of authority. The image brought me back to our first years in the seminary when she caught Xav and me sneaking out to the local micro-brewery to keep our hand in with the brewing process.

Authority shook its silver head. "Despite our earlier conversation, you're worried I'll turn into the Hammer of God when I see you two go into your bedroom together. Admit it."

Emma looked from Lisa to me and back again. "It is that Denis sees you as his master."

"As well he should. The stories I told you at dinner aren't the only ones I have."

Emma perked up. "I am enjoying this trade of information. Over breakfast I will tell you what I saw of the construction of Notre Dame."

Lisa beamed. "You are my new favorite person. Er... sorry. Friend? Is friend okay?"

Emma got to her feet. "I have had no friends in more than seven hundred years. It is pleasing to hear you say the word."

"I thought a lady didn't reveal her age," I said.

Emma drew herself up. "I will place the blame for your remark on stress and not on your goatlike manners."

Lisa gave an unladylike snort. "Denis, I'll need sheets and a pillow, please."

By the time the bathroom shifts had finished it was close to midnight. I lay next to Emma in my bed, the *Grimorium* on the dresser, staring at the ceiling. In time with her even breathing I went over the steps I'd memorized.

The lapis lazuli power I created when I fought Emma could wait for tomorrow. After I dragged the truth from this demon. After I fried his red ass in nuclear-level flame. After he admitted Xav's presence in Hell was as unlikely as mine in Heaven.

Chapter Forty-One

At eight the next morning, Emma took her turn in the shower while I called in sick to the bookstore for the second day. Martin said the dogs missed me and promised to bury me in work tomorrow.

Lisa's cell rang while my boss pretended to torment me. When I hung up, Emma was standing in the doorway, eyes on Lisa. I followed her gaze. Lisa was scribbling on the grocery list notepad stuck to the side of the fridge. Her face was a combination of horror and fascination.

"We'll be right there. It'll be okay. I promise." She hung up and read what she'd written. "Monsignor Powell and Ben, the youngest seminarian, were cleaning up after morning Mass. The Monsignor went into the sacristy to hang up the vestments and set things up for tomorrow. Ben started screaming. When the Monsignor ran out, Ben was lying across the altar. The young man on the phone wouldn't go into details. The Monsignor ran for help and when they got Ben cleaned up, he refused to speak to anyone."

I was already heading for my room to change. "Two minutes."

Emma changed into Brother Mark while I changed into Father Kaine. Emma's transformation still delighted Lisa.

I didn't break any speed limits on the drive to the seminary, only because getting a ticket would've delayed us further.

Before we rang the doorbell, I said, "Lisa, I need to hear what the kid has to say. Can you talk him into it?"

"I'll try."

"If he will only speak to Lisa, I can mask myself with the walls and listen," Mark/Emma said.

Lisa's eyes got as big as latte mugs. "You can?"

I shook my head. "I know you can, but I need to hear him for myself. There could be nuances you wouldn't pick up on."

Mark/Emma shrugged. "As you wish."

The door opened while my finger was still on the bell.

"Thank God." The blond surfer-dude seminarian looked at us, behind him, at the walls, his eyes never staying in one place. "Can you help us?"

"Yes." I led the way inside. "I'm going to kill it. It won't come after any of you again."

He focused on me for a whole two seconds. "You can? You will?"

Lisa shouldered me out of the way. "Alan, take us to Ben's room, please."

Silence on the stairs, in the halls, and in the rooms we passed. The place might have been uninhabited except for the fear oozing from under the bedroom doors, just like at Northwestern.

Alan knocked on the last door on the second floor. "Ben? It's Sister Lisa."

A shaky voice. "She can come in."

Lisa opened the door wide enough to let herself in and closed it behind her. Three minutes later, it opened again and she beckoned to us. "Come in, you two."

Brother Mark closed the door and stayed by it. Not much room in this ten-by-twelve space: twin bed, freestanding wardrobe. PC on the desk, Bible and theology books on a shelf above it. Crucifix fastened to the wall with brackets. Phone on nightstand playing vapid praise music.

"Father Kaine." The kid's voice was as toneless as the music. The sheet over him was a mere loose covering. I could see the codpiece of bandages on his junk.

"Sister Lisa says if I tell you what happened it'll help you get rid of what's haunting us."

Lisa sat in the only chair, so I stood at the foot of the bed, messenger bag slung over my shoulder.

"Yes. The more information I have, the faster I'll be able to kill it."

He started when I said "kill it" but a twinge of pain cut off any comment he might have made. He cleared his throat.

"It happened after Mass. Monsignor Powell was in the sacristy and I was straightening the altar cloth and trimming the wicks on the candles. Right in front of my face the candles lit themselves again. The flames shot up a foot high. Before I could call for the Monsignor, this shadowy thing picked me up and threw me on top of the altar." His pale face washed out even further. "It climbed on top of me and its face was, its face was this grinning—thing—with dark hair and dark eyes and hardly any chin. Its breath was enough to make me puke." He swallowed. "It was naked under all those shadows. Its breasts sagged and flopped and it sat on my"—he glanced at Lisa—"um, Father, could you come over by me? I don't want to say this in front of the sister."

Lisa became the model of a sheltered, demure nun. She pushed herself and the chair back against the desk to make room for me. I squatted on the floor so I could get next to the kid's mouth.

He whispered, "It ripped open my pants and sat on my crotch, Father. Its, um, privates were cold and slimy and stank like a rotting skunk. I was too scared at first to do anything, but when cold, wet goop oozed all over my skin I tried to shove it off me."

He gulped. I waited.

"It got mad when I pushed it. It made this weird shrieky growling noise and flipped around so its butt was in my face. Its hands had these raggedy claws for nails and it, um, well, it started to shred my privates." He grimaced at the memory or at a real twinge of pain. "I screamed and shoved at its saggy, smelly butt. It lost its balance and fell off on the side near the sacristy. I must have closed my eyes for a second because the next thing I saw was the Monsignor standing there and he said he didn't see the thing, not even in the freaky candlelight."

"It's a succubus." I infused all of my confidence into those three words. "Using shadows for clothes is one of the ways they disguise themselves."

"You've exorcised them before?" The hope in his eyes pained me.

"More than once. I've got this, Ben." I made my face stern. "Who treated your injuries?"

Horror filled his face. "Nobody. I can't let anyone see them."

"Wrong." I stood so I could loom over him. "I'm going to call a doctor who can keep her mouth shut, and you're going to go to her office."

"But, Father, if anyone finds out a priest got his, um"—with another glance at Lisa— "privates damaged, rumors will spread. I might be kicked out of the seminary."

I loomed down into his face. "I told you this doctor is safe. Antibacterial soap is not going to eradicate the thing's secretions. It's a denizen of Hell. Do you understand me?"

The kid passed out cold.

I called Detective Rubio's doctor. The receptionist remembered me. Told her I was sending over a stupid kid who pissed off a psycho girlfriend and she took her nails to his junk. The receptionist made sincere sympathetic noises. She said they'd squeeze him in.

I opened the door. All five seminarians were pacing the hall.

"You. Alan. He passed out because I scared the shit out of him. You're taking him to a doctor who won't see anything she isn't supposed to see." I found a piece of notebook paper and wrote down the name and address. "Don't move him until I've dealt with your chapel demon. Got it?"

"Yes, Father." Another set of eyes full of hope.

The other four surrounded me like fanboys. Christ, I was not their personal savior. Couldn't disillusion them at this juncture, of course.

"Sister Lisa, will you take care of the other four?"

Lisa dropped the demure act. "George, Mario, James, Ernest. Please come with me to the kitchen." She glanced back down the hall. "Where's the Monsignor?"

"We don't know, Sister." The one with movie-star looks—James—appointed himself spokesman. "We were worried about Ben and lost track of him."

Lisa's smile embraced all four of them. "We'll find him. I'm going to teach you my recipe for Forbidden Coffee."

She ushered them before her like a mother hen. Their terror-spiked auras eased in her presence.

I closed the door on Alan and Ben but kept silent until Brother Mark and I were standing outside the chapel.

"You convinced the young man of the succubus," he said in his bizarre masculine version of Emma's voice, "but you do not believe it is so."

"Bingo. It doesn't fit any of the standard patterns, especially the junk-shredding. Whoever this demon is, I think he disguised himself as a succubus to try to strip these kids of their Vocations."

"Is what you memorized all night long instead of sleeping able to banish it?" So weird to hear Emma's attitude out of the mouth of this nondescript priestling.

"I slept."

"You employ a loose interpretation of the word."

"Enough." I indicated the double doors. "I need to prepare."

Brother Mark made the open-handed Italian gesture of acquiescence. It threw me back to my last days in Rome: hopeless, hating myself, my insides hollow from the crater Xav left when he died.

"Make use of the darkness I see in you," Brother Mark said. "Tap its power but do not allow it to overwhelm you."

I closed my eyes. First I shut out the passing traffic. Then the bloodhound baying in a nearby yard. The faint noises from the kitchen. The aroma of coffee starting to brew. The smells of old incense, dust in the carpet, and wood polish on the doors. Emma. My breathing. My heartbeat.

Silence.

With my eyes still closed, I pushed open the chapel doors and cast my net.

Chapter Forty-Two

I opened my eyes right after I cast the net. Didn't want to face-plant into a pew.

The lines of the net shimmered with the exact same snow-shadow blue my power's shone with ever since I was a kid. A lump of fear in me vanished. No dark blue veined with gold. No blast furnace. Just me.

And only me. The net caught nothing.

I pushed more power into it. Dropped all my protective shields to find this thing.

Still nothing... Wait.

There.

At the back of the sanctuary. Tall and clothed with moving shadows like multiple arms and heads. I didn't get an image of the succubus which attacked Ben. Maybe it was challenging me as itself without disguises.

I walked behind the pews and up the center aisle. Unbuckled my bag as I walked, my steps even and steady.

No image of its face or sense of what type of demon came to me. It was almost like I'd lost my Sight. Or this thing could mask itself. Which was certainly not correct. Nothing could ever mask itself against a Kaine twin except the other twin. Xav and I used to sharpen our skills on each other by camouflaging our powers and...

The earth dropped out from under my feet.

I don't know how I stayed upright. The walls warped. The light from the stained glass fractured. For a second I thought there were multiple creatures in here until I heard a broken laugh and tasted salt. It was my laugh echoing off the walls. My tears warping my vision. It all emanated from my useless, arrogant, ignorant, damned self.

"Denis." Its voice was and wasn't Xavier's.

I dissolved my net. Brought all my power back into myself. Took out my flute and dropped the messenger bag to the floor. No herbs or candles or holy water between the Kaine twins. I stepped up into the sanctuary and climbed onto the bare altar. Sat cross-legged at one end and raised the flute to my lips. The runes on it stayed as dark as the speaking shadow against the wall.

At the edge of my peripheral vision, Brother Mark became Emma again, wearing her fancy steampunk outfit. For the briefest instant her pageantry lightened my heart.

The sweet, light melody of "*Il est né, le divin enfant*" floated through the chapel. Xav's favorite Christmas carol. The one he whistled when he was brewing a new beer or studying or chopping wood or shoveling snow or mowing the lawn. The one he sang at Grandmère's funeral in the middle of summer.

I played all five verses. My burned hand stretched and stung reaching for the holes, but it didn't matter. The music was the only sound in the chapel. Even my catch-breaths couldn't be heard over the song.

I never took my eyes off the shadow. It blinked first in this game, moving toward me when I finished the third verse. By the last line of the final verse it faced me across the length of the altar. Its face changed as it moved. I saw an iridescent, fanged face with black-light eyes. I saw Xavier's neat blond hair and brown eyes. I played a couple of wrong notes when he appeared but corrected them. When the thing placed itself opposite me its face changed once more. I stared at chinless, dark-haired Monsignor Dickweed.

I set the flute on the altar, my gaze still locked on Dickweed's.

"Which one are you?" My voice sounded as steady as though I was teaching a class back at Catholic U.

"So you don't know everything." A voice similar to but lighter than the one in the granite angel came out of his mouth. "I am Ergraum."

"Did I off your twin?"

"Off?" Its black-light eyes lit with purple. "What a casual word for cold-blooded murder."

I gave it a one-shoulder shrug. "What goes around comes around."

It jumped onto the altar. I brought up a shield before it took a swing at me. The blue sizzle threw it back and its face changed to Xav's, grimacing in pain.

"Fuck you, Denis," Xav said. "You were always so concerned with being the renegade hero. You never thought about me alone in my room in the Vatican, did you? All you wanted was to be the savior, swooping in to redeem the Kaine honor and sticking it to the Church law machine."

I sat there and took it. The face mostly stayed Xav's while it ranted using language Xav had never used, not even when he slammed a sledgehammer into his knee one autumn. Once it changed to the glowing fanged face, once to a crimson head with fire for hair and eyes. Every time I blinked he grew more arms, lost them, grew them back. Once I saw all the heads together. At the end I was looking at Monsignor Dickweed again.

"Didn't think you had the balls to cut a deal with a demon," I said to his insipid face.

He laughed. Christ, even his evil laugh was second-rate.

"This is your fault, Kaine." His long, ragged fingernails played with the shadows cloaking him. The shadows made some kind of noise. I couldn't place it.

"Demonic signs began to infest the area soon after you moved here," Powell said. "After your first few insubordinate meetings with the archbishop, he refused to call you in. I read everything we had on possession and exorcisms to figure out how they worked." The fanged face leered through for a minute. "I knew it couldn't be hard if someone like you could do it."

"You tried an exorcism?" I struggled to keep my voice steady while I faced the thing that had been torturing Xav for eight months.

Dickweed spoke again. "It's much easier than you specialists make it out to be. You read the book, you splash the holy water, you save the soul."

His face melted into Xav's. "You save the soul, Denis. Like you were supposed to save mine. Didn't you understand the message I left you?"

I opened the locked room in my head and brought out Xav's last morning. His bloody brains splattered on the wall. The shotgun. The Bible on the floor. The verse in Matthew he'd underlined with a red pen.

"Fuck."

Xavier laughed. "Grandpère always thought you were the smart one. What a family of idiots I was born into. Has it been fun living in your fantasy world? You should've figured out I didn't expel the last demon. He slithered from the kid to me when I laid hands on him at the climax of the ritual. I've been his chew toy ever since."

My brother's face twisted and he screamed as flames eclipsed his brown eyes.

Every bone, muscle, and vein in my body writhed in anguish. If I thought God would listen, I'd beg Him to swap me for Xav.

So I did the only thing I could. I stayed on the altar. I kept my poker face, the face which never revealed anything to demons. I opened my mouth—but instead of the words I'd spent all night memorizing, an ancient ritual in Aramaic came out. I hadn't spoken Aramaic since a decrepit priest came from Rome to tutor us in it back in our seminary days.

The demon's face took over and cursed me in some secret demon-tongue. I didn't have to understand it to know what he meant. Dickweed seemed to have disappeared. Not surprising. The useless ass-kisser didn't have anywhere near the strength of my brother or this demon.

As it spoke, it cycled through dozens of faces and voices.

It possessed an awful lot of faces for a single red-ass. Crocell-spawn were Neanderthals in the demonic hierarchy. Grunt, stomp, smash. This one shouldn't possess such skill with illusion.

Demons lie.

The accountant in me opened my master list of entities while my mouth recited Aramaic. Powell's new friend wasn't in my demon database. But it had to be. Xav exorcised demons, period.

As if on cue, multiple voices poured from its mouth. They dug into the happy memories of Xav and me and destroyed them. They detailed the smorgasbord of torments waiting for me in Hell.

I kept reciting the ritual. It was similar to what I'd memorized last night, only this one had a lot more power to it. The demon's word-vomit faltered; then his face became Xav's, spewing hate so powerful it ate through my shield.

Of course Xav could break me.

And of course it meant I wouldn't survive this. Okay by me. I deserved it.

"Do not let his words distract you."

Emma. I'd forgotten she was here.

The demon's fanged, fire-eyed face appeared and turned toward her. In the same instant its face twisted and bent and wrenched back toward me and I almost lost the thread of the ritual.

Xav's face—the real Xav, the one I knew—struggled through the flames and fangs.

Then red-ass took over again. "Be quiet, whore."

Emma yawned. "Can you not use an original insult?"

It took a step toward her. I kept speaking.

"You've created a sexy little body to fuck this priest with. Does he know your real body looks a hundred times worse than this creature?" It changed into the succubus it had been when it attacked Ben, multiple stenches and all.

Emma waved a hand in front of her face. "At least one of us bathes."

More illusions. I checked my demon database as I rose to my knees. The ritual's power continued to build. Red-ass took another step toward her and then whipped around to face me again. Emma laughed a deliberate, belittling laugh.

"So easily sidetracked. Denis speaks of you as though you are a saint." She sashayed toward the altar, playing him with her words. "Yet it seems you are as weak as the sycophant priest whose skin you inhabit."

I interrupted the ritual. "Xav!"

Red-ass shuddered. When he turned toward me again he was Xav: the exact image of myself, complete with the Gretzky jersey over his blacks, hockey stick balanced against one leg. He cupped his hands. Six hands. No, twelve. No, only two. A sphere of shadows appeared between them. When it was the size of a street hockey ball he flung it at me.

I parried it and it burst into a puff of fire veined with the dirty gray of winter street slush. A parody of Xav's color, sunshine on spring snow. Like yesterday when my blue fire became darker and streaked with gold.

Xav watched me figure it out, a smirk on his familiar face.

"So we're the same again," I said with another shrug. "Guess I handled one too many demons."

The smirk stayed on his face. "You're nowhere near my level, brother. You absorbed this new power by force. It's fighting you. I embraced it as it changed me from within."

All the screaming fragments inside me crashed and shattered. Xav wasn't struggling to get away. The familiar face I'd seen a minute ago was nothing more than wishful thinking. Xav was part of this red-ass. I could've saved him from it, back in Rome. And I didn't.

Well then.

The Aramaic rite picked up where it'd left off. The fanged face came out again. He was pissed. Good. When multiarms and I killed each other, Xav would be released from his torment. Worth the price. Worth any price.

My database search pinged. Multiple arms. Flames. Fangs. Multiple heads.

Not a demon.

The rakshasa saw the moment I figured out what it was. The tabernacle burst open and the stored Hosts exploded outward into white confetti. The red glass candle detonated next, my damaged shield blocking most of the shards. The hymnals jumped out of the pews and consumed themselves in black flames.

The rakshasa is a master of illusion. Likes to screw with priests of every religion. Powerful enough to fool even Xavier into thinking it was a demon.

I kept talking. The ritual neared its end. The rakshasa in Xavier's clothes flung blast after blast of its tainted power at me. My shield was at its limit.

It smiled at my perforated shield, because of course the Xavier part of it retained our Sight. He created a smaller, denser ball of black light and raised the hockey stick. Xav couldn't miss at this distance. The ritual wouldn't be finished before he slapped the ball at me. If I died too soon, Xav would be trapped inside it for eternity because there'd be no way I could help him from the depths of Hell.

I spoke faster, the sentences coming with enough speed to sound like one multisyllabic word. I kept my eyes on him. Death wasn't going to make me flinch. I was way too familiar with it.

The Xavier-rakshasa set the ball on the altar. Swung.

Missed.

Impossible. Xav could hit anything puck-like blindfolded. The false red-ass snarled and flung the ball at me. I knocked it aside. With a curse, he broke Xav's prized hockey stick over his knee.

The thing in front of me didn't have complete control of Xavier. I knew it as sure as I knew my name. As sure as I knew every hockey souvenir, every amateur trophy, every stitch of the jersey hanging in my bedroom, every inch of the real stick in the back of my closet.

I leaped to my feet and barreled on to the end of the ritual. The rakshasa abandoned its Xavier Kaine glamour and showed its true self.

It grew four feet taller. Its flaming hair licked the ceiling. It opened its mouth and a tongue as long as a snake rolled out, licking the air. Its multiple arms merged into a new covering: a priest's cassock with human skulls for buttons. It shimmered and rippled as I squinted at it, the ancient language still coming rapid-fire out of my mouth.

Emma made a horrified noise. The button skulls echoed it. I craned my neck to see to the top, and the collar button at the center of its neck was Xavier's head.

Two more sentences to go.

The ceiling cracked. Flurries of plaster coated the pews. The nails holding up the Stations of the Cross *skreeked* as thin fissures split the walls. The Stations came to life: carved apostles howled and blood spurted from the hands and feet of the crucified Christ. The altar tried to buck me off.

I jumped the length of the altar right at the rakshasa. Emma's arms appeared through its cassock and yanked out part of its power, the way she'd sucked part of the power out of the Dickens house demon. I shouted the final words and leaped through its midsection, wrenching out the rest of its power in a comet trail behind me.

The rakshasa exploded. Puke-green and blood-red slime sprayed over the sanctuary and the toppled pews. Gray and black shadows burst into thousands of Fourth of July sparklers and vanished. Powell appeared from inside the mess and fell over in a dead faint. The Stations crashed to the floor. The few remaining fires from the hymnals winked out.

The silence hurt my ears worse than the explosion had. I sat up a few inches at a time, muscles protesting every movement. I swept my arms at the demon gore and it vaporized.

I'd destroyed Xavier. Why the hell wasn't I dead?

"You had your head screwed on backward if you thought I'd willingly bind with a demon."

Xav stood in front of me, Oilers jersey over his blacks and hockey stick in his hand.

All the angels from the busted stained-glass windows were singing.

"Yeah, well, if you'd expanded your repertoire like me, you'd have recognized a rakshasa imitating a demon." I think I was crying. Xav shimmered like a firefly.

"Yeah, yeah, rub my nose in it."

I had to ask. Had to know. "Why'd you do it?"

Xav's grin faltered. "It was growing too strong. I knew if I lost control it would've used me to destroy countless people."

"So you blew your brains out? Idiot. We could've handled it."

The grin came back full-force. "Your ego is the size of Québec. You'd have gone all 'I've gotta save Xavier' and your head would've been way too far up your butt to think straight. Before you realized it wasn't an actual demon it would've used me against you. We probably would've killed each other. I had to save you." He turned his head like he was listening to something I couldn't hear. "Gotta go."

"Xav—"

"Stop crying, Den. You saved me today. We're even."

"My total beats yours now."

"I'll have to deal." He executed the courtly bow we learned when Grandmère forced us to take dance lessons. Then he disappeared.

Chapter Forty-Three

The chapel was a disaster. Paper ash, shards of plaster, and Host confetti covered the floor. A breeze was blowing through the shattered windows, magnifying the ashy mess.

I wiped my face on my sleeve. How the hell was I going to get us out of here without walking on those pieces of Host?

Answer: I wasn't. I said a quick prayer for forgiveness and scooped up Emma. I thought the explosion had knocked her out, but she was wide awake and breathing hard.

"Are you okay?"

"I am much more than okay." Her voice was revved.

"What pumped you up? Wait. Later. Can you change back into Brother Mark so we can get out of here?"

"Such a simple request?" She laughed, a manic sound.

"For now, yes. Okay?" I set her on the floor and picked up my flute and messenger bag. When I turned around, Brother Mark stood in front of me, looking like he'd been in a street fight. Smart woman.

I opened the double doors and breathed in coffee-scented air. I let them close behind us before I bellowed for Lisa.

Chairs crashed to the floor and feet pounded down the hallways. Lisa and the seminarians—don't laugh, Kaine—careened around the corner and skidded to a stop on the thin carpet a few feet from us.

Lisa did a good job hiding her reaction, but not the four seminarians. Going by their faces, I looked like I'd fought Godzilla, Mothra, and Ghidora all at once.

"Guys, Monsignor Di—Powell is out cold in there. I'm not sure how extensive his injuries are. He was possessed by the demon which attacked all of you, but I destroyed it." They started to jabber, but I cut them off. "You'd better call one of those emergency cleanup places. The walls and ceiling are cracked and the floor's heaved up. Tell 'em there must have been an underground gas explosion. I wouldn't mention the fight with a major demon from Hell. Just a suggestion." Maintaining the "demon" story would keep them sane.

"Father—"

"One of you tell Alan it's okay to take Ben to the doctor I told him about."

"But Father—"

"I'll call the archbishop and let him know what happened. He needs to send his people here to handle the reporters."

"Reporters?" they said in unison.

"The neighbors probably called the cops because of the noise. When the cops show, the reporters will be right behind them." I stared into the mustached one's eyes. "James, you're in charge now. Give it back to me."

He straightened his shoulders. "Mario is calling 911 about a possible gas leak and explosion. Ernest is telling Alan to take Ben to your doctor. You're calling the archbishop."

"One more thing. The demon exploded the tabernacle and the Hosts. As soon as you make the phone calls, get in there and pick up every piece you can find." I cut off their horrified exclamations. "Don't freak out. Would you rather the demon ate the Hosts?"

For a second I thought they'd fall in a faint like dominoes.

Lisa came to the rescue. She planted her feet in front of them and reached up to grab James's shirt collar. "Pull yourselves together. Father Kaine saved you. Repay his courage by using your common sense."

They stayed frozen a moment longer; then all four smothered her with hugs. One day I'd clue Lisa in on her power. Offing demons was useful, but she radiated the comfort of home. I was jealous.

I resettled my messenger bag. "You'll be okay now. I'm going home." I handed my car keys to Lisa. "Can you drive?"

<hr>

The archbishop doubted it was me on the phone at first. Probably because I was too drained to give him attitude. He squawked when I told him about Dickweed—the "demon possession" version. I enjoyed the conversation less than I thought I would.

Lisa held it together when I explained what a rakshasa was but started crying when I told her about Xav. I stopped talking to let her concentrate on driving. It'd be stupid to survive a gonzo supernatural attack only to become a highway death statistic.

Emma had changed back into herself in steampunk gear. Her energy squeezed us all much too tight in the Impala until I told her to open the windows and let it spill into the air. Her little hat kept bumping against the roof of the car until she pulled it off and let her hair flow out the window along with her excess power.

I stumbled into my apartment and straight to my bedroom. I

needed to close the door so they wouldn't see me lose it over what had happened to Xav.

Emma sailed in behind me. I crashed onto my bed. It wasn't even noon—was it?

"Thanks," I said to her.

She grinned in her new manic way again. "Power is delicious."

"Huh?"

She climbed on top of me. "You destroy these creatures. You are more powerful than them, but you are not more powerful than me."

What the hell? Her eyes were lit like the rakshasa's. They glowed silver—not with fire—so it was her alone on top of me. I tried to get up on my elbows. She pinned me down.

"I took half its power. Tell me, am I delicious?"

She crushed her lips onto mine. It wasn't a kiss. It was an addict getting another hit. I stiff-armed her off me.

Her eyes sparked. She pinned me down so hard the bed frame went concave. Shit. Her knees dug into my thighs and her hands clamped my biceps. She licked her lips. The nightstand light flickered. The bedspread and sheets swirled around us in a blue-and-brown tornado. Her hair added a black cloud to them. Change after change flashed across her face—rusalka, jorōgumo, nalusa chito, rakshasa.

"No!" My vision turned crimson and black. No gold streaks this time. I flung her off me. She leaped right back on. I flipped her over. She wrapped her legs around my hips and both of us crashed onto the floor.

Too much power. Both of us. Had to trap it.

I ripped open her silky blouse and drew the rune gebo on her bare skin for balance, honor, and dissolving barriers. The giant X burned with blue fire. Pieces of the power we'd absorbed flowed between us. When she tore at the rune I ripped open my shirt. The white plastic collar flew off and bounced into the hall. I grabbed her left hand and used her index finger to scratch the same oversized X onto my chest. This one burned white.

The power stretched, connecting us. Our bodies jerked and twitched like we'd been Tasered. I poured my will into the runes, amping up their balancing strength. Emma clawed at me, at the power flowing in the space between our naked chests.

Balance. Partners.

I kissed her. A cloud of black, then gray, then the white of snow and the deep blue of rivers pulsed between us. She stopped fighting and kissed me back.

The rune burned cold on my skin. With an exclamation, she pulled away and rubbed her breastbone. Her eyes returned to their normal gray.

"Your eyes are burning with the blue of fireworks. Oh. Now they are brown again." She was panting and out of breath, but the lightning in her eyes had subsided. "What have you done?"

I gasped like I'd run a mile uphill. "I've bound us. The power was taking us over. I created a balance."

Emma looked past my shoulder, startled. I twisted to see.

Lisa stood over us holding one of my pans ready to clock my head. Or Emma's. Or both.

"Lisa, were you going to hit us with a frying pan?"

Lisa's eyes hadn't changed color, but fear and determination altered her motherly face. "You didn't see what you looked like. You didn't look human. Either of you." She lowered the frying pan a fraction. "Denis, what did you do?"

Emma laughed. "A frying pan?"

After a second, I laughed too. It felt good.

Emma pushed me off her and stood. "Lisa, you must stay for many days. He needs you to teach him the art of laughter."

I sat up and rubbed my face with my hands. "Emma, close your shirt. Lisa, I agree. You need to stay. This one"—I poked a thumb toward Emma—"did something unprecedented back in the chapel. So did I. I had to balance things, otherwise we might have given you an indoor fireworks show."

"It was well done," Emma said. "I apologize."

"Twice in two days. Someone call the local news."

Lisa didn't relax her stance. "Your eyes changed. Both of yours. You burned like fire, if fire could burn white and blue. I thought I smelled snow and an ice-cold river." She slapped her cheek. "You two have me all discombobulated."

I stood and clasped my hands around hers. "This is my only nonstick pan. I'll find my cast-iron one for you to hit us with if things get weird."

Lisa stared into my eyes like she was trying to see through to my brain. She lowered the pan. "Things are already weird, but you seem to be yourself again. Come into the kitchen. I poured wine before you two turned yourselves into indoor lightning."

"Good," Emma said.

"Is there any Coke left?" I said.

"I'll see." Lisa walked away, her knees wobbling only a little.

Emma grabbed my head and kissed me. I wrapped my arms around her and pulled our naked skin together. Only Lisa's presence in the next room stopped us at the kiss.

"You've completely disrupted my life." I tossed my ripped shirt onto the bed and handed her one of her new shirts from my bottom drawer.

"Change is growth." She shrugged out of her torn shirt and put on the new one.

"We're sharing unknown power, Emma. This isn't a good change." I put on Xav's jersey. It felt better than it ever had.

She scowled. "It is not good only if we choose to make it so. Rusalkas are not good always. Angry exorcists are not good always. We will discuss change. Yes?"

I considered the possibilities. "Maybe."

She shook her head, blue-black hair twirling around her shoulders. "It is time you were no longer a fixer-upper. Come. We will soothe your Lisa. Tonight I will teach you something new in the bed we did not destroy."

"I hate to drink alone," Lisa called from the kitchen. "Come prove you're human enough to drink with me and I'll volunteer to make lunch."

"Only if it's sausage-and-pepper sandwiches," I said.

"Only if you make a trip to the grocery store."

Emma laughed. "We will give him orders. It will be good for him."

"I lodge an official protest at this treatment." I took Emma's hand and led her into the kitchen.

The runes shone through our shirts to my Sight. Emma's glowed gold and deep blue. The one on my chest burned white and gold.

The power sizzled beneath my skin. Controlled.

For now.

Acknowledgments

A book this much fun to write was made more so with help from several fellow authors. Thanks to K.A. Stewart, Amy Bai, Alex Jay Lore, Ellen Thompson, and Natalie Case. I highly recommend you check out their books.

About the Author

A.M. Loweecey lives in New York with their dog Zeus, who will happily tell you he's the more photogenic half of the duo. He also wishes A.M. would learn to dictate their stories to make walks around the neighborhood last longer, rather than spending so much time at their desk. When A.M. isn't on walks with Zeus or finding new ways to scare the pants off readers, they're working in the garden, where A.M. endeavors to grow the perfect tomato.

To stay up to date on A.M. Loweecey's newest releases, visit the Epic Publishing website (www.epic-publishing.com), and subscribe to our Epic News List.

Excerpt from In Blood and Bone
By Elias Anderson

CHAPTER ONE

AJ looked up at the clock, not knowing in one minute he'd fall in love and, in three, he'd see his first dead body. It was 2:42 A.M.

A car pulled into the lot, the driver killing the engine and stepping out. AJ expected a night person: the paranoid, the destitute, or the stoned. Instead, it was a girl. Not a crackhead or a whore but a normal *girl*, and not many came in alone this time of night. This rare girl was not beautiful, or anything so mundane, but drop dead gorgeous, with blonde hair just past her shoulders, eyes the color of clover, and a smile that stopped his pulse.

"Hi," AJ said, feeling like a jackass.

"Hi." She headed to the refrigerated drink section, which glowed in the dingy gas station lighting as would the first star in a midnight sky, and with her, she took his heart. He saw a cockroach scurrying across the dirty tile floor and hoped she wouldn't notice.

She set a bottle of soda on the counter. "And can I get a pack of smokes, please?"

"What's your poison?"

She smiled again. "Marlboro Lights."

AJ rang up her purchases, thinking he would sell his soul for a girl like this. "Six thirty-seven."

She swiped her card in the machine. "So, what's it like working here?" she asked. "Get a lot of weirdos?"

"Oh, yeah. You wouldn't *believe* the freaks that come in this time of night," AJ said.

"Oh, *really?*"

"Well, you know. Other than you, I mean." Red crept across AJ's face.

"How do you know?" she asked.

"How do I know what?"

"What kind of person I am. I mean, I could be Lizzie Borden, Tipper Gore. *Anybody.*"

"I've developed an eye for it working here. Now, if you'd come in twitching and talking to yourself, it'd be a different story."

She laughed and opened her cigarettes. "Do you mind if I smoke in here?"

"Nope," AJ said, flicking his Zippo open for her. "So, what's your name?"

"Clover."

Like her eyes, AJ thought. He felt himself blush and occupied himself by getting out a cigarette of his own to smoke with her. "I'm—"

She pointed to his name tag. "AJ. I know. I saw it when I came in."

"So. Clover. What brings you to Vito's Gas-N-Go at this time of ni..." AJ trailed off when a man walked into the store. He was a younger guy but had the old, wizened face of a drug addict. He wore an old, dirty trench coat, faded jeans, and a black, knitted hat.

He twitched.

"Can I help you?" AJ asked. The man in the doorway shuffled inside, the sound of his movements somehow empty.

"You okay?" AJ asked. "You need an ambulance or something?"

The man shook his head and tried to speak. His mouth moved, producing a gravelly whisper.

"What?" AJ's nose wrinkled as the guy got closer. It smelled like the guy had shit his pants.

"A-a..." The man cleared his throat and took another step forward, the only thing between them now was the counter.

His face was covered in acne, and even from where he stood, AJ could plainly see his teeth were for shit. The ones left in his head were either rotten or on their way. Meth, maybe? Smack? AJ didn't know what particular flavor the guy was killing himself with, only that it was one of them. Like he'd told Clover, he kinda had an eye for it.

"A..." the junkie said again.

"A what?" AJ asked, knowing the guy was high as shit.

"You...mmm...A...AJ?"

How in the... Oh. The name tag. "Yeah, that's me. Who are you?"

The man grinned, and then his hands, cold from the night air he'd been walking through, were around AJ's throat.

"Get off him!" Clover grabbed one of the junkie's arms, trying to pull him away. She got a backhand in the mouth that sent her to the floor.

AJ twisted free, ducking toward the counter, and pulling out a wooden baseball bat. It *whooshed* when he swung it, connecting solidly with the attacker's temple. The psycho blinked twice and shook his head to clear it, eyes narrowing.

"Oh, shit," AJ said, thinking, *PCP, maybe?*

The junkie's lips twisted into an ugly grin, and he punched AJ in the face.

AJ staggered back. He could already feel his eye swelling.

Clover was on her feet again. She grabbed a bottle of wine off the rack near the counter and swung for the fences, the bottle exploding against the back of the junkie's head. Cheap merlot and black glass spilled to the floor.

It was as if the man hadn't felt it. He turned, grabbed her by the face, and shoved her. She staggered back half a dozen steps and slammed into a display rack of pre-packaged pastries, knocking Hostess cakes and mini-donuts to the floor.

AJ adjusted his grip on the bat, flexing his hands, and taking an extra moment to square his feet like his dad taught him.

He took another swing.

He'd only played baseball up until his freshman year of high school and had been on the JV squad even then. Still, one fine spring morning, he'd managed to hit his only home run, and he still remembered it. He would sometimes close his eyes and think of that moment because it had been a good one. A great one, really: the smell of the line chalk and freshly cut grass, the contrast on the deep, lush green of the outfield, and the clear, empty blue of the late April sky.

He remembered the sound the ball made when he connected with it and how he hadn't felt it. There had been a split second where he thought he'd given it the big whiff and struck out, but then the bench and the small crowd in the home-town stands exploded. The perfect white sphere of the ball shrank as it went over the centerfield fence, still on its upward trajectory.

This was like that, but it wasn't.

It was almost three in the morning, and it was cold out. Instead of the perfect, crisp light of the spring sun, there was the flickering of old fluorescent bulbs, the bodies of dozens of dead and ancient flies collected in the fixtures. The smell of dirt was there, but this was not the freshly turned and raked dirt of a baseball diamond. Rather, it was old and sour, with heavy undertones of feces.

The sound was different, too. A sound somehow both hard and wet, of something with a thick outer shell and a hollow center, a sound AJ would hear for the rest of life in the bad times, the dark times, the times he didn't want to be alone. The sound of the bat connecting with the guy's skull made his stomach turn.

Clover flinched at the wet crack, the junkie's eyes rolling back as he dropped to the floor.

AJ helped Clover steady herself as she stood amongst the fallen packages of snack cakes. A small rivulet of blood ran from her perfect lower lip, a smear of black dirt along her cheekbone from the man's hand on her face.

"You all right?" AJ asked, his voice shaking in time with his pulse hammering in his temples and the insides of his wrists.

"I think so. How's your eye?"

Eye, he thought. *What eye?*

The only eyes that mattered were hers. He held her chin and gently thumbed the blood away from her mouth. His face was reflected in those deep green pools and knew he could be happy forever if he could only see himself in them every day. For that glimmer in time, they were the only two people alive.

Then she spoke quietly, "We better call somebody."

AJ nodded and handed her the bat. "If he moves, hit him again."

Clover adjusted her hands for a better grip as AJ went to the phone.

To read more of *In Blood and Bone*, visit the Epic Publishing website (www.epic-publishing.com) to order your copy directly, or visit any of your favorite book retailers.